On the Wings of Destiny

The Ship of Treasure

By: Nader Omidi

Editor: Karl Monger

Illustrator: Jay Del Fierro

Contents

Chapter 1

October 15, 1915, two weeks after the great storm of New York City, at two o'clock in the afternoon, Katherine's mother, Laura, sat Katherine on the buggy and went to visit Mary Wilson. They were close friends, and they would meet each other once a week. Katherine was an only child. She was six and a half years old, with blonde hair and blue eyes. She was a very pretty girl. Her father, Peter Vincent, had a tackle shop that brought them a decent income.

At 2:30pm, they reached her friend's house. Mary Wilson was outside trimming the flowers. As she saw them, she removed her gloves and said, "I was expecting you today."

Katherine jumped from the buggy and ran to her. "Hi, Mrs. Wilson."

"Hello, my dear. How are you?" said Mary. Then they hugged each other.

"Do you need help?" Laura asked.

"I was just finishing up here. Let's go inside," said Mary.

Katherine walked to the car parked in front of the house and said, "Wow, when did you buy this?"

"George's father bought it just two days ago."

"It is a nice car," said Katherine.

"Yeah, it is" said Laura. It was a brand new Ford Model T and it was very red. Katherine was amazed. She walked around the car slowly and touched the body carefully taking in every detail. Occasionally she squinted her eyes against the glare of sunlight reflection from the metal. She was very interested to get a ride. The last time she had ridden in a car was six months ago, when Edward Wilson gave her a ride around the block. Her father had promised he would buy a car and take her for a long drive.

"Let's go inside. George will be back from school in a few minutes," said Mary. She and Laura went in together.

"Thank you, Mrs. Wilson. I will be there in a minute," said Katherine.

As Katherine was tiptoeing around the car and inspecting the interior, somebody called, "Hey, Katherine!" It was George, the son of Edward Wilson. He was ten years old and, like Katherine, was an only child. He ran to her, carrying his bag on his back, and said panting, "You like this car?"

"I love it," Katherine answered.

"My dad bought it two days ago. It drives very smooth."

"Where is your blue car?" asked Katherine.

"My dad is driving it," George said. "Would you like a ride in this car?"

"Of course," answered Katherine.

"I think we are going to the old shipyard to visit my grandma. You can come with us. We are going in this car."

"Are you serious?" asked Katherine.

"Yes, I am" George said.

"Let's go ask my mom," said Katherine. They walked inside and found Mary and Laura in the living room.

"Hi, Mrs. Vincent," George said.

"Hello, my son," said Laura. "How are you?"

"Good."

"How was school today?" asked Mary.

"Fine," said George. "What time are we going to visit Grandma?"

"Mrs. Vincent got here a few minutes ago. We are going to go later," answered Mary.

Laura looked at the clock on the wall. "It is almost three o'clock. You better go."

"Don't worry, you'd better go," said Mary, and she sighed. "She is so sick these days, I am worried about her." She dropped her head down.

"Mrs. Vincent, would you let Katherine come with us to see my grandma?" asked George. "We are going to drive that red car."

"Laura paused, and she looked at Katherine and said with a smile, "I am sure she would love to ride in that car." Katherine smiled in agreement without saying anything.

"Don't worry, we will bring her back home before dark," said Mary. Then she turned to George and Katherine and pointed to the table. "Come on, take the cookies. They are for you."They took the cookies and ran outside. In twenty minutes, Mary drove them to the old shipyard.

The place was small and shaped like a half-circle. It was about fifteen minutes drive from the city center, and all parts of the entire area was inhabited by fishermen. All of the inhabitants had settled along the shore, and they all knew one another. It had taken its name from a British ship that sank in a storm in that area a very long time ago. It was said by two survivors of the storm that the ship was carrying a large treasure, and it came to be known as the Ship of Treasure. However, nobody could locate the sunken ship. Although it was covered by tons of sand, many believed it would be uncovered by another big storm someday.

George's grandmother, Elise Benton, was one of the inhabitants. She lived alone. Her husband was a fisherman who had drowned in a sea mishap thirty years ago. It was about 3:45 p.m. when they reached Elise's house. George got out of the car quickly and ran to the door. Elise opened the door and said with a smile, "Hello, George."

"Hello, Grandma. I've missed you so much."

"I've missed you, too, my dear," Elise replied, and the two hugged each other.

"Grandma, I made a painting in my class today, and I got the best grade."

"Well done."

"Hi, mom." Mary approached them and interrupted. "How are you doing?"

Elise nodded. "Fine." Then she looked at Katherine and said, "Who is this pretty girl?"

"Her name's Katherine, she's the daughter of Laura Vincent," answered Mary.

Katherine was standing next to Mary. She said politely, "Hi."

"Hi,. You have a pretty name. Come on in. I baked cookies today. You are going to like them."

"Thanks, Grandma," said George. Then he turned to Katherine. "My grandma bakes the most delicious cookies in the world." Then they all entered the house.

Elise went to the kitchen and brought a plate of cookies, put it on the table, picked one, handed it to Katherine, and said kindly, "Here you are, my dear."

Katherine took a bite. "It is delicious. I love it."

"I told you she bakes the best cookies ever," George said.

Elise looked down at the plate on the table and said, "You know, George, your grandpa liked these cookies." Then she looked outside through the window thoughtfully, and after a little while she put her hand on her forehead, bent over slightly, and grabbed the edge of the table. Everything went black for her. It was clear to everyone she was not feeling good. Faintness settled into her body. She went down to her knees, and she steadied herself with her hands.

Mary said with worry, "What's wrong?" She quickly put her arms around her, helped her to her feet and supported her to her chair. Elise drew a deep breath and fought off her weakness, and soon she seemed to be feeling fine again.

"Are you all right?" said Mary and she pulled up a chair and sat next to her.

Elise looked at George and Katherine, who froze in position, their expression one of concern. Elise smiled and said meekly, "I am sorry. Sometimes I get like this. But I will be all right in a minute-." She sighed with relief and said, "Don't worry about me. I am fine now."

Mary put her hand on Elise's shoulder. "Mom, are you sure you don't need a doctor?"

Elise got to her feet, and she raised her hands and said, "Don't you believe me?"

"I've told you many times to come and live with us," Mary said. "You're all alone here. You're reaching the age where you need someone to help care for you."

George stepped toward Elise and took her by the hand. "Mom is right. We have a big house with lots of rooms. Please come and stay with us."

Elise smiled at him and said, "I'll let you know. Now, eat your cookies."

George took some cookies, handed a few to Katherine and said, "We are going to play on the beach. Let's go, Katherine."

"Don't go far," Mary urged. "We've got to leave in thirty minutes."

The sky was clear. The sun was low, approaching the horizon, and it radiated mild warmth. The sea was calm and occasionally marked with small, splashing waves. Almost two miles from shore drifted a lone fishing boat, manned by a single person. Hungry seagulls hovered and dipped above the boat, jockeying to get the small fish that the fisherman threw into the sea.

Katherine was the first to spot the boat. "Look at that ship over there."

"That is not a ship," George exclaimed. "It is a fishing boat. A ship is much bigger. I think the person in that boat is Daniel's father."

Katherine wrinkled her brows. "Who is Daniel?"

"A friend. He is the same age as I am. That is his house, where he lives with his father," George said, pointing to a house that was a quarter of a mile away, right next to Elise's house. "He should be at home now. Let me draw something on the sand first, and after that we can call him and see if he wants to play together."They walked down to the water's edge, where George squatted down, grabbed a little stick that was carried in by the waves, and started to draw.

Katherine squatted down next to him and said, "What is that you are drawing?"

"It is a boy and a girl holding hands and running on the seashore toward their home."

Katherine lifted up her head and brushed her hair from her face with her fingers. She saw a black boy walking toward them. He was smiling. He seemed to know them. "Somebody is coming this way."

George turned his head and stood up and said happily, "That is Daniel, the friend that I was talking about." George ran to him, and they hugged each other. Then they walked to Katherine, and George introduced, "This is Katherine. She came with me to visit my grandma."

"Hi, Katherine," said Daniel. Then he noticed the drawing. "What is that?"

"I drew the same thing in my classroom today, and I got the best grade."

Daniel bent over it and took a closer look. "Tell me about it?"

"It is a boy and a girl running on the seashore toward the Statue of Liberty," said George. He paused for a second, sighed and continued. "I wish I could draw it on the sand as well as I drew it on the paper."

Daniel looked at it carelessly and said, "Let me draw something for you." He stepped closer to the water's edge, squatted down and moved his forefinger around in the sand. George and Katherine bent down and observed carefully, and George said, "This is a ship."

"Yeah, a ship." He turned his gaze to the sea and with a faraway look in his eyes said in a thoughtful voice, "When I grow up, I want to buy a ship and travel all over the world."

Suddenly, George cried, "Hey, Danni, your ship is washing away. You drew it too close to the water."

Daniel took a few steps backwards and pointed into the distance. "Let's show that broken boat to Katherine. We can play there."

"All right, let's go," said George.

They walked along the shore for five minutes until they came to place where there was a boat three hundred feet from the water's edge. Twelve feet long, and broken on one side, the boat half-buried in the sand.

Katherine stood near the broken side of the boat and asked, "Who does it belong to?"

"He was an old fisherman. He died about six years ago; this boat has never been used since then. Then he pointed to a small house that stood about one hundred feet away. It looked abandoned. "That was where he lived. Now, nobody lives there." Daniel climbed into the boat. "George and I play here every time he comes to visit his grandma." He pulled a harmonica from the pocket of his pants. "I want to play a song for you."

George said, "Daniel plays the harmonica very well."

Daniel disguised his voice to sound like an old sea captain. "Come on, all aboard! The ship is moving."

George and Katherine got in the boat quickly, and Daniel began to play a happy song. As Daniel was playing and George and Katherine were clapping, Katherine saw something glowing in the sand of the boat. She walked over, picked it up and said excitedly, "I found a coin! I found a coin!" Daniel stopped playing and said with wonder, "A coin?" George and Daniel ran to her, and the three of them looked down at the coin. It had the image of a ship on one side and a picture of two petrels flying over the sea on the other. It was large and took up much of Katherine's palm.

George took it from her hand and said, "Let me see." He touched it, studied it skillfully, like a professional shopkeeper, and judged the weight in his hand. "It is only a brass coin. A gold coin would not be so light. You know, I learned from my father how to recognize gold."

Daniel asked, "Can I touch it?"

"Of course," said George, and he handed the coin to him.

Daniel looked at the picture of the petrels for a moment before turning it over. He stared at the picture of a ship for a long time, as if it reminded him of something. He touched it gently and sighed. "I will buy a big ship when I grow up." Then he turned to George and said, "Can I have it?"

"She found it. You have to ask her. Anyway, it is worthless," said George.

Katherine looked at Daniel. Although she wanted to keep the coin, she said, "You can have it."

Daniel held the coin tightly and said happily, "Thank you so much."

Katherine went to where she found the coin and looked around some more. "I am going to find another."

"Maybe we will find a gold coin this time. Let's search everywhere," said George. Then they started digging in the sand with their hands. As Daniel was digging, he said, "If I find a gold coin, I will give it to my father, so he can sell it and buy a new fishing boat. His boat is too old, and he has to repair it all the time."

After ten minutes, Katherine got tired, sat on the sand, swept the sand from her rubber boots and said disappointedly, "There are no more coins here."

"We've got to find another boat." George stood up and looked around. "My dad told me there is a lot of gold in ships that sunk in old times. I think he is right."

Daniel stopped digging suddenly and stared at his father's boat in the sea and stated, "I remember seeing a ship when my father took me to check out the nets a few days ago."

"You saw a ship? Where? Are you kidding?" asked George.

"I am serious," Daniel insisted. "It was a real ship. A big one."

"Did you find any gold?" Katherine asked.

Daniel laughed a little and said, "The ship was under the water. I saw it from my father's boat."Katherine and George were very interested to hear his story. "It was morning. The sea was calm. The water was so clear I could see the bottom. My father was pulling the nets and moving forward. I had lain in the stern, looking down at the ocean floor. Suddenly, I saw a ship. I think it was the Ship of Treasure. I heard about it before. It sunk many, many years ago."

George interrupted. "Did you tell your dad about it?"

Daniel sighed. "Yeah, I told him, but he didn't pay any attention to me."

"He didn't say anything?" asked George.

"He said I was mistaken. There was no ship there. You know what? My dad often doesn't pay enough attention to me." Then he pointed. "I am sure there was a ship over there. It was right by the second buoy on the net. I mean the red buoy, right where my father is working now."

Katherine stood up and searched for the red float, but she couldn't see it. She said, "I am sure there are lots of coins in that ship."

"What good is it if we can't get them, even if that ship is full of treasure?" said Daniel hopelessly.

George jumped out of the boat and puffed up his chest. "When we grow up, we can go under the water and get all of the treasure." He squinted his eyes and continued. "We better not tell anybody about it. It has to stay our secret."

Daniel looked at Katherine. "Yeah, George is right. Don't tell anybody. When we get the treasure, we will be rich, and we can buy anything we want."

Katherine nodded her head in agreement.

Chapter 2

That night, the old ship was the main topic of conversation for the Vincent family. As they were sitting at the dinner table, Katherine mentioned the coin. Everyone was very interested to see it. Katherine said, "I gave it to Daniel."

Laura wrinkled her brow. "Who is Daniel?"

"He is George's friend. They are the same age. He is the neighbor of George's grandma."

Her father was thinking about how much the coin might be worth. "How big was?"

Katherine opened her hand, and on her palm, she drew a circle with her forefinger. "It was this big. It was gold in color. A picture of a ship was on one side, and on the other was a picture of two birds."

"It was a nice coin, for sure," Laura said. "You said it was gold in color. Do you think it was made of real gold?"

"No, George said it was not gold. He knows how to recognize gold," Katherine said quickly. "You know there is a ship full of treasure under the water in that area." Then she told the story that she had heard from Daniel.

When she finished, Laura laughed and said, "My dear, treasures only exist in stories. There is no ship out there. That boy just imagined it."

Katherine was sure that Daniel was not mistaken, and she was sure that there was a ship out there. Nothing could convince her otherwise. She set down her spoon and fork, grabbed the table and moved herself closer to it, and said seriously, "Daniel is not mistaken. He has seen it with his eyes. When we grow up, we are going to go under the water and get all the treasure."

Laura laughed. "You are going to be rich when you find that treasure."

Katherine turned to her father. "Then I will buy a new car for Daddy. We won't have to ride the buggy anymore. We are going to be rich like Mr. Wilson."

Peter smiled and said, "Yes, my dear." As his mouth was working, he suddenly remembered the story of the Ship of Treasure, the same story that he had heard from his father a long time ago. His mind was searching. He was very interested to hear it from Katherine again. He stroked his handlebar mustache, took a deep breath and asked her to tell the story. He listened very carefully this time, while Laura picked up her plate and took it to the kitchen.

Peter thought about the Ship of Treasure all night. He could not get it out of his mind. He knew he would need the help of somebody else in order to get the treasure, so he decided to tell his best friend, Edward Wilson.

The next day, Katherine's family heard the news of Elise Benton's death. She had died of a heart attack in her home the previous night. Peter decided to wait for a better opportunity to talk to Edward. After two days, he went to Edward's jewelry store with Katherine. He parked the buggy in front of the store next to Edward's car. It was a blue Oldsmobile. Katherine's eyes lit up and she said excitedly, "Daddy, this is Mr. Wilson's car, the same car that I had a ride in a few months ago. I loved it!"

Peter smiled and said, "I am going to talk to Mr. Wilson for a second. You stay here in the buggy till I get back."

"All right Daddy," said Katherine.

Peter got down and entered the store.

Edward was standing by the window, looking outside at them. He was a strong man, standing six feet tall, with gray hair and a handlebar mustache like Peter. He was fifty-six years old. He was very smart and had a good reputation in New York City. As Peter walked in, he said, "Hi."

Peter returned the greeting as his eyes searched the place to make sure they were alone. He pulled a chair next to the desk and said, "I've got to talk to you about something very important."

Edward appeared thoughtful, expecting to hear sad or bad news from his friend. He took a seat at his desk and asked, "What has happened?"

Peter continued to look around nervously. "Nobody is in here?"

"No, what is going on?" Edward asked.

"You remember us talking about the Ship of Treasure, right?"

Edward squinted his eyes and said, "What do you mean?"

"The ship that was sunk years ago in the old shipyard," said Peter.

"Yeah, I remember," answered Edward.

"I think that ship may really exist," said Peter. "I remember my father saying that it would be uncovered one day by another big storm. And now it has."

Edward looked into his eyes for a few seconds and asked with wonder, "How do you know? Have you seen it?"

"No, but somebody else has." Then he told Edward the story that Katherine told him.

Edward listened carefully to everything his friend had to say. When the story was finished, he peered outside through the window and brooded, his eyes contemplative. He was convinced now that everything he had heard about the Ship of Treasure was true. He touched his handlebar mustache, took a deep breath and said delicately, "Yeah, it makes sense to me that the ship was uncovered by the recent storm."

Peter stood up and said restlessly, "There is all sorts of treasure in that ship. Let's go and get it."

"You always think simple and decide in a hurry," said Edward. "It is not that easy. Not only will we need a boat, we will also need somebody who is very familiar with the area, not to mention the equipment, like diving suits."

"Don't worry, I can get that stuff," Peter said with confidence. "I can borrow it from one of my friends."

"Be careful. Don't give away too much," said Edward with concern. He thought for a moment and said, "We might need another person." His mind searched for somebody who had a boat and lived in the old shipyard. Something told him it was crucial to their plan that they find such a person. After a minute he said, "I know somebody. He used to have a fishing boat."

"Who?" Peter said eagerly. "Let's go and talk to him."

Edward exhaled and said, "It's my half-brother, Louis. I haven't seen him for a long time. He is not someone I would normally trust, but he lives in that neighborhood."

"Don't worry, we'll find a way to convince him not to tell anyone about the treasure," said Peter.

"He has been fishing there for years, and he knows that area like the back of his hand. In case residents of the area see us, we need to be with someone who lives there, someone the others would not suspect. I think he is the best person to help us."

Peter was excited and wanted to get to the treasure as soon as possible. He struck the desk with his palms and said, "Why are we waiting for? Let's go and talk to him right now!" He looked outside through the window and said, "Come on."

"Let's not be too hasty. We need to think through. We can talk to him another time," said Edward.

"Why put it off. The ship may be swept away by another storm." Peter said.

Edward gazed into space as Peter was talking. Finally, he agreed. "What are going to do with Katherine? Are you going to take her home now?"

Peter smiled and said, "I already thought about that. We'd better take her with us. She is the one who's going to show us where the Ship of Treasure lay."

Edward stood up and looked around. "All right, we can go in my car." Then they went outside and drove to the old shipyard.

On the way to the old shipyard, the conversation between Katherine and Peter turned to the Ship of Treasure. Edward was quiet the entire way. He listened carefully, searching for the best way to get at the treasure.

After twenty minutes, they reached the old shipyard. Edward continued to the house of his mother-in-law, Elise Benton, and pulled up in front. He turned his face to the sea, his eyes looking for something and failing to find it.

Peter asked Katherine with smile, "Where are the buoys of Daniel's father's fishing nets?"

Katherine got out of the car and searched the horizon. The signs were visible, although their colors were not easily recognizable. She pointed and stated, "There! Daniel said the Ship of Treasure was right by the red sign."

Peter got out of the car and said as he pointed to the signs, "I see them." He approached Edward and put his hand on his shoulder. "Get out of the car and come look at this."

Edward was already looking at the signs. He sighed and said, "Don't be so anxious. We've got to pretend this is not that important to us. We don't want her to suspect that we intend to go after that treasure. Otherwise, she may tell her friends about us."

Peter nodded in agreement. "You're right."

Edward got out of the car and they walked over to Katherine and stood beside her looking at the buoys. Peter put his hand on her shoulder. "You know, Katherine, I think Daniel's father was right."

"What do you mean Daddy?"

"I don't think there is any ship out there," said Peter, trying to sound casual. "If there were, it is certain his dad would have seen it in all years he has been fishing in the area."

"No, Daddy, Daniel saw it," Katherine insisted.

"All right, we'd better forget all about it. Let's go see my friend now," said Peter, They got in the car and drove off.

Soon they arrived at Louis's house. "Is this your friend's house?" asked Katherine.

"Yes, my dear," said Peter. They sat in the car looking at the house.

It was old wooden house; dirty and surrounded by trash. Shouting could be heard coming from inside. Peter turned to Edward waiting for him to say something. Edward knew Louis and his wife wouldn't be happy to see him because Edward had rejected his request for money eight years ago. At the time, Louis already owed him two hundred dollars. Louis and his wife were envious of his wealth and did not like him, and they always thought of him with hate. They were bad people.

As they were looking at the house, the curtain moved slightly, and a few moments later the door opened and two boys, ages ten and twelve, and a girl of eight stood in the doorway and said loudly and fearfully, "Our father is in the backyard." Then Louis's wife, an ugly, fat woman with a long, crooked nose, came to the door, and glared at Edward. Her nose had been broken in a fight with

24

Louis three years earlier. She had an angry face and was always ready to fight. None of their neighbors had ever seen her exhibit good, decent behavior. She kept staring at Edward with a frown and then she pushed the kids into the house and shut the door. This was followed by screaming of children coming from inside the house.

Katherine asked with wonder, "Dad, why is their mother so mad?"

Peter dropped his head, searching for a reasonable excuse. After a few seconds Edward said, "I think the kids must be behind on their homework."

He looked at Peter and continued, "It is better Katherine sit in the car while we talk to Louis."

"Yes, stay here, my dear. We will be back soon," said Peter.

Edward opened the door and got out. "Katherine, you can sit in the driver's seat until we comeback."

Katherine smiled big and scrambled into the front seat and grabbed the steering wheel with both hands "I am going to drive you back home today."

Everybody laughed, then Edward and Peter walked toward the house. Before they got to the backyard, Edward said to Peter, "It is better to tell Louis that you saw the ship when we talk to him about it."Peter nodded, and they moved on.

Louis was sleeping in an old wooden chair held together with pieces of rope. He was over six feet tall, bald, skinny, and had an old burn mark stretching from his left ear to his chin. He was fifty-three and known widely for his dark, brooding expression. Louis opened his heavy eyelids and looked at Edward and Peter morosely and said angrily, "What the hell are you doing here?"

Edward looked at him for a moment without saying anything. He knew he had to be tough with Louis so he would listen to them. He scowled and said, "I want to talk to you."

Louis said angrily, "You want to talk to me about what?"

"Something important."

"Something important." Louis grinned. "Last time when I asked you for twenty bucks, you refused. Now, you come here to talk to me about something important." Then he looked up at Peter sulkily. "Who is this guy?"

"My friend, Peter," said Edward.

Peter reached out his hand and said with a smile, "I am Peter."

Louis's expression grew meaner and he looked at his hand for a second and said sullenly, "I don't care who you are." Then he turned to Edward and said, "Get to the point. I don't have time to talk to you all day. I want to sleep."

"You heard about the Ship of Treasure?" asked Edward.

"What do you mean?" asked Louis.

"The ship that sank in this area and nobody could ever find it," Edward said.

Louis's eyes searched aimlessly as he thought about the treasure. He asked himself, Did they find it? Did these two actually find it?"He tried not to show his excitement as he continued. "That British ship that was cursed by an Indian sorcerer?"

"Cursed by an Indian sorcerer?" Peter said in wonder.

"The treasure that ship was carrying, it actually belonged to some Indians. It was stolen from them, and that's why the sorcerer cursed the ship to sink with everyone on board," said Louis "but..." Then he continued. "But nobody has seen that ship since it sunk."

"The Ship of Treasure has been uncovered. Peter has seen it," said Edward with confidence. He turned to Peter for confirmation. "Right?"

"Oh, yeah, I saw it a few days ago," said Peter hastily.

Louis studied them for a long time, trying to gauge whether or not they were telling the truth and, if so, why they chose to share this information with him of all people. "Why me?"

Edward got to right the point. "We need somebody with a boat who is familiar with this area. I thought I could trust you. You have been fishing on these waters for years."

Louis had his answer. He knew now that they needed him to find the treasure. He sat back and asked, "Are you sure you can trust me?" "That is why we are here," said Edward. "I could find somebody else, but I wanted to talk to you first."

Louis sensed an opportunity to take advantage of Edward, so he stood up and said, "All right, let's go check out my fishing boat." Edward and Peter followed him to the beach.

As they walked, Louis turned to the car, looked at Katherine and asked, "Who is that girl?"

"She is my daughter," Peter answered.

"Don't bring her to the boat while we talk," Louis said.

Katherine was sitting behind the steering wheel, turning it left and right. She saw them and waved happily. Peter returned her wave and said loudly, "We are going to see the boat. You stay in the car, my dear. We will be right back."

Katherine nodded her head with satisfaction as she continued playing.

When they got to the boat, Louis rested his hands on his side and said, "It needs some work."

It was an old wooden fishing boat twenty-five feet in length. All the metal parts of it had rusted, and the bottom was covered with barnacles. Peter put his palms on the boat and said excitedly, "Oh man, this is perfect."

Edward looked at the boat wordlessly. Louis stepped to the front of the boat and saw the two skinny cats eating a dead fish in the shade of the boat. He turned his face to the sea and asked Peter, "Tell me, where did you see that ship?"

Peter looked at the sea thoughtfully and hummed, but before he could indicate the direction of the ship, Edward interjected. "That is for another time."

Louis wrinkled his brow and said, "I see you don't trust me." He kicked the cats hard and then he kicked his boat. "Why did we even come here if you don't trust me?"

Edward walked over, placed a firm hand on his chest and looked into his eyes. "Listen to me. I trust you. That is why I am here. Now I don't want to hear any more stupid talk."

Louis took a deep breath and hung his head without saying anything. He would wait patiently if it meant a chance to take advantage of him in that situation.

Edward turned and pointed out to sea and said, "The ship is near those buoys."

"Which ones? You mean the floats right there?" asked Louis.

"Yes. We will tell you the exact place when we go out in the boat," Edward said.

"Well, I can see one problem right away," Louis said.

"What do you mean?"

Louis sighed. "Those nets belong to a man named Sam. He and I are not friends, and I don't like that bastard. We will have to search for the ship in the dark."

"It is going to be very hard to find that ship in the dark. We need to look in the daylight," Edward exclaimed.

"Look over there," Louis said, pointing. "The house after your mother-in-law's is his house, and that boat on the shore in front of that house is his boat. He will stop us when he sees us getting close to his fishing nets."

Edward and Peter gave the matter some thought. Peter said, "We use underwater lights and search for the ship at night that way."

Edward took a deep breath and said, "Flashlight will not be enough. Plus we've got to think about the oxygen tanks and how best to conserve them."

Everyone looked at him without saying a word. They knew he would find the best way and keep things on safe side. Edward continued. "I didn't mean to say we should search for the treasure in the middle of the day, when we could be seen by everybody, no. We can go there before it gets dark, so we can see the ship easier while it is still light and do some preliminary work. That way we can wait until it is completely dark and have our bearings underwater from the outset."

Peter put his hand on his shoulder and said, "You are right. You are a genius."

"What about the diving equipment?" asked Louis.

"Don't worry, I'll bring what we need," Peter replied.

"When will we do it?" Louis asked.

As Edward looked at the sea thoughtfully, he said, "As soon as possible. I don't want to wait too long and risk the Ship of Treasure getting buried by another storm. We can go tomorrow if everything is ready."

Louis approached him and said, "I need some money to fix the boat."

"How much do you need? How long will it take?" asked Edward.

"With twenty bucks, I can get the parts we need and get it ready today."

Edward took twenty dollars from his pocket, handed it to him and said, "Here is the money. We will come back tomorrow afternoon with the rest of the equipment and tools."

Louis grabbed the money. "Don't worry, it'll be done."

"This is our secret. Don't even tell your wife about it," Edward warned. Then walked to his car alongside Peter and they headed to New York City.

Chapter 3

The next day at three o'clock, Edward and Peter drove to the old shipyard with the equipment they would need loaded into the trunk. Edward was preoccupied with the dangers they would face, and the many ways things could go wrong. As he drove, he warned Peter, "We've got to be very careful about Louis. Don't forget that he is not to be trusted."

"Don't worry. There's no way he can foul this up," Peter assured him with a chuckle.

"One of us will stay in the boat, and the other will dive with him," Edward suggested.

"I know diving much better than you, so you stay in the boat. He and I are going to have fun together down there."

Peter intended to lay his hands on the treasure as soon as possible, and he was overcome by visions of wealth. He smacked the dashboard with his palm and rubbed his hands together, laughing and carrying on. "Imagine all that treasure that'll soon be ours."

"Make sure when we find it we take it all to my mother-in-law's, and then we give him his share."

Peter leaned back, sighed and continued excitedly. "I hope we can find a nice necklace in that ship for Katherine. I promised her a long time ago I would get her one, but I never had enough money to buy it for her." Then he smiled. "The first thing I want to do for my family is buy a nice car and take them for a month-long vacation."

Edward nodded his head gently in agreement. "I hope."

When they reached the old shipyard, they drove directly to Louis's house.

They found him standing by his boat at the water's edge, smoking a cigarette, waiting for them. Edward parked the car next to the boat and they got out and put all the equipment in the boat. Peter stayed with Louis while Edward drove to his mother in-law's house and parked his car in the backyard and returned to the boat.

He looked in the boat to make sure they had everything they needed, and then they all climbed in. The boat broke the glassy water as it chugged away.

They scanned the area. No one was to be seen on the shore. All they saw was a lone fishing boat far off in the distance. Soon seagulls appeared, hovering above them in hopes of getting some fish, and they accompanied them the entire way.

In a few minutes, they got to the buoys. Louis slowed down as they approached the red buoy and said, "Hey, grab it."

Edward quickly moved to the other side of the boat and with his strong hands, grabbed the red buoy and tied it to the boat. Peter lay down on his chest, looked down at the water and said with a smile, "Look how clear the water is. We should see the ship easily from here."

"We should all look in different directions, so we have a better chance of spotting it," suggested Edward.

"Yeah, good idea," said Peter.

Edward turned his face to the shore and sighed. "I hope Sam doesn't show up while we are out here."

Louis chuckled and said, "Don't worry about him. I messed up his boat. It'll take him at least two days to fix it."

Edward looked at him gravely for a second and said, "Come on. We don't have much time. We've got to find the ship before dark." They positioned themselves on three sides of the boat and searched the waters for the ship.

It was about four o'clock in the afternoon. The sun still shone and although the wind was blowing very gently, it sent ripples over the surface of the water that made it difficult to see down to the bottom. So all they could do was scan the surface like seagulls in search of fish, and from time to time they picked up their heads and checked to make sure nobody was coming. After a few minutes, Louis stood up and said angrily, "Where is that damn ship? You said that you saw it here by the red buoy."

Peter picked up his head and said, "Actually, the son of that fisherman, Sam, saw the ship."

Louis walked over to him, wrinkled his brow and asked, "What did you say?"

Peter stood up and continued, "Yeah, Daniel, the son of Sam's son, saw that ship when he came to check the nets with his father a few days ago. Then he told my daughter about it."

Louis grabbed his collar and yelled, "You told me that you saw that ship! Why did you lie to me?"

Edward got up, grabbed his hands off Peter and said angrily, "What difference does it make if he saw the ship or somebody else?"

"If that boy has seen the ship why didn't he tell his father about it? Why didn't they get the treasure themselves?" said Louis loudly.

"When the boy saw the ship and told his father about it, Sam didn't pay attention to him."

"Of course he didn't pay any attention to him. If the ship was there, Sam would have seen it at some point during all these years," Louis said.

"Edward looked at the water and said, "The big storm caused the Ship to appear. I have no doubt that the boy saw it."

Louis chuckled a little. "Edward, you're a very smart man. I am wondering how you can believe such a childish story. That ship was cursed to sink by that Indian sorcerer and it will never come out any more. T hat's what I believe. "

Edward examined the water thoughtfully. "That boy was right. The Ship of Treasure is here."

Louis tossed a stick up to the seagulls and shouted, "Get out of here, damn birds." Then he went to the buoy and tried to untie it from the boat. Edward came to him and asked, "Hey, what are you doing?"

"That ship sank because of a curse. It will never come out of millions of tons of sand, and nobody will see it ever again. I am wasting my time here. I'm going back to the shore," Louis yelled.

Edward grabbed him and said in a deep voice. "You'll leave here when I say you can. Otherwise, I will tie you to your boat like this buoy."

Louis felt the strength of Edward's grip, and he looked up at his angry eyes and dropped his head without saying anything. Edward said to Peter, "We can't see the ship from here. We've got to go under the water."

"I agree. Come on, we've got to hurry," Peter said. Edward helped him into the diving suit and he dived down into the water holding the flashlight in his hand.

Edward searched the shore and saw Sam's boat, but there was nobody near it. He trained his gaze on the place where Peter had dived and kept it there without paying any attention to Louis. Louis was sitting on a wooden box in the middle of the boat, looking at him. He knew that Edward was a serious person and he could not do anything without his permission. On the other hand, he did not believe there was any ship down there. He stood up and took a few steps toward him. "How did you ever come to believe that story, man? I told you, if that ship was here, Sam would have seen it by now. It is buried under a million tons of sand, and it's going to stay that way."

Edward had not budged, and continued staring at the water, waiting for Peter to come up. Louis sat beside him and put his hand on his shoulder. "There is no ship here. Let's go back home."

Edward took a deep breath and said, "I am sure the ship is somewhere around here."

"I'm ready to bet that your friend can't find the ship," said Louis.

As Edward looked at the water, he said, "If he finds the ship, what do have to say?"

"If he finds it, I will help you carry out all the treasure for free. If he doesn't, you have to give me two hundred bucks."

Edward turned to him and looked at him for a long moment. Finally, he said, "All right, deal. But don't forget you are going to help us to take out all of the treasure for free."

Louis chuckled. "If You don't forget to give me my two hundred bucks when you lose."

As the conversation wrapped up, Peter came to the surface and Edward helped him quickly into the boat. Edward and Louis waited impatiently to hear the news from him. As soon as he removed the helmet, he hugged Edward tightly and cried, "I saw it, I saw the Ship of Treasure. We are going to be rich."

Louis grew very angry. He kicked the boat and cried out, "Shit."

"Are you crazy? Didn't you hear what I said?" said Peter.

Louis dropped his head down and said nothing, though in his head he was searching for another plan.

Edward said, "Hey, don't worry; I will take care of you. Now, you wear the diving suit and help Peter to bring the treasure to the boat."

Although it was getting dark, there was still a little light under the water. Forty-five feet separated the sunken ship from the surface of the water. It was a large wooden ship. Peter and Louis searched the various sections of the ship using two flashlights and a long metal lever to pry open some of the doors that were closed. Most of the upper parts of the ship had been destroyed, but the lower levels were still intact. Even these areas were fragile, and some parts were easily broken. They searched about and finally arrived at where the treasure was. There were seven chests that measured 2 feet by 4 feet and were 2 feet in height. Peter quickly opened one of the chests and looked inside. It was filled with jewels, diamonds, and golden coins. Peter blissfully ran his fingertips over them in the light of his flashlight. Then he closed the lid and they returned to the surface of the water.

It was dark now, and Edward sat in the boat waiting for the other two. As soon as he heard the news, he waited anxiously for them to bring the treasure to the boat. There was a constant worry about him that he was going to miss a perfect opportunity. He quickly turned on the winch, released the chain and sent it to the bottom of the sea, and Peter and Louis dived down again.

Louis didn't like helping them get the treasure, but he had no other choice, so his plan was to get whatever he could out of the situation.

In three trips, they hauled the chests of treasure up to the boat busing the winch. As the last two chests were on their way up, Louis gestured to Peter to indicate there was still another chest in the ship, so they went back down to get it. As soon as they were alone there, Louis attacked him from behind and stabbed him with a knife, killing him. He tied him up and left him there, turned off the flashlight, and returned to the boat quickly.

Edward was covering the chests with a large canvas when Louis surfaced, and he stopped what he was doing to help Louis into the boat. As soon as he removed his helmet, Edward asked, "Where is Peter?"

Louis tried to act normal, and as he removed the wetsuit he answered without looking at him, "He gestured for me to go to back to the boat. I think he wants to make sure there is not another chest."

"Why did you leave him?"

"I told you, he sent me up. Don't worry, he'll show up."

After fifteen minutes of waiting, they heard a splash. They turned their heads and listened. The sound seemed to be getting closer. Edward asked with worry, "What is it?"

Louis searched in the dark for a few seconds and said, "Somebody is rowing up to us. I hope it's not Sam. We've got to leave here now." He walked over to the buoy and tried to untie it. Edward jumped up and restrained him.

"What are you doing, man?"

"I told you, if it's Sam he won't let us stay here," said Louis.

As they were arguing, a flashlight came on and somebody said angrily, "What the hell are you doing on my fishing nets?"

It was Daniel's father, Sam.

Louis said, "We were just passing by here when my boat broke down. We had to hold onto this buoy to stay here to fix it."

Sam stood up and looked at Edward, who wore a sport hat, and he tried to recognize him in the flashlight, but he did not know him by his face. Edward dropped his head and covered his eyes with his hands, pretending to avoid the light, and sat on a box in the middle of the boat, so he wouldn't be recognized. All the while, he was worried that Peter would come to the surface of the water, and their deceit would become known.

Sam shone the flashlight for a second on the diving suit that lay on the canvas and continued. "You've been here for hours. I saw you searching my nets. I thought you learned a good lesson with the punch you got in your face from me ten years ago."

"I told you, I was fixing my boat," Louis said, ignoring his comment.

Sam exploded with anger. "I don't care about your boat. You can't stay here any longer. Keep away from my nets."

"I already fixed it, and we are leaving," said Louis. He untied the buoy, switched on the engine and steered toward the shore.

Edward was very worried about leaving Peter. As they were leaving the area, Edward asked Louis to stop, but he ignored him and kept on going toward the shore. Edward switched off the engine and yelled, "We've got go back to where Peter is."

"Are you crazy? Didn't you hear what Sam told us? We are going to be in big trouble if we go back." Then he turned to the chests filled with treasure and said, "Look at all this. That's why we came here, and now they are all ours. Let's just go home. Peter is a good diver. I am sure he will reach the shore in a little while and join us."

"No, we can't leave here without him," said Edward.

Louis switched on the engine and said angrily, "This is my boat and you can't stop me. I am going to go home now."

Edward held his wrist tightly. His eyes were wide with anger, his lips were thin, and his jaw was tight.

He was dangerous as a rising storm. "We can't leave here without him. If you try to leave one more time, I swear to God I will kill you."

Louis had never seen so angry. His legs jerked and his hands shook. He flinched at the sternness of Edward's face, then he dropped his head like a timid dog and sat in the middle of the boat without saying a word. Edward dropped the anchor, stood by the steering wheel and kept looking in the dark.

As Louis sat there, another plan came to mind. He considered that Edward would do anything to find his friend. Eventually, he would go into the water to look for him, giving Louis his big chance. He went over to Edward and said, "All right, I understand that Peter was your best friend and you are worried about him. Why don't you go down and find him when we reach the diving spot."

Edward gave him a cold stare, for he could see through Louis's suggestion. He looked at the diving suit, but he didn't see the flashlights. He remembered Louis didn't carry one with him when he returned to the boat. Knowing it was impossible to go under the water without a flashlight at that time of night, he searched the darkness without saying anything.

After twenty minutes, when he was sure Sam was back on the shore, he asked Louis to return to where they had found the treasure. Louis had no choice but to comply, so he switched on the engine and returned to Sam's fishing nets.

The buoys were still visible in the dark when they got very close. Edward grabbed the same float and looked around. He knew Peter couldn't stay under that long without changing air tanks. A profound sense of worry settled over him, and the images of Peter's wife and daughter, Katherine, passed before his eyes. Edward didn't know what he would do if Peter died. He blamed himself. His eyes searched the darkness with worry and he called, "Peter, Peter…" He waited a minute, listening carefully, but he didn't hear anything. He was beginning to think Peter was gone forever, and he sat in the boat feeling hopeless. He thought he had blundered in trusting a person like Louis, and he suspected he had done something to Peter. He turned to Louis, who was standing by the steering wheel, looking around. The more he looked at him, the angrier he became. He stood up, walked over to him, took him by the arm and turned him around. "Tell me what happened to Peter down there."

Louis shivered and his teeth chattered. What little courage he had abandoned him, and his voice grew shrill with fright. He cried weakly, "I don't know."

Edward grabbed his collar and shook him. "Why did you leave him alone? Tell me the truth!"

Louis could see the disbelief in his eyes even in the dark, and his shoulders sagged in defeat. He looked at him in horror and said in a throaty whisper, "He gestured for me to leave. I don't know what happened to him after that. He may be stuck in the ship somewhere."

Edward cried, "How do you know he is stuck in that damned ship?" Then he pushed his neck against the steering wheel.

Louis began to cry and said somberly, "You think I am not sad about him? I swear to God I didn't do anything wrong. You've got to believe me."

Edward looked into his frightened eyes, exhaled deeply, and removed his heavy hands from his neck. Then he turned around and stared out at the sea. Despite the fact he was worried about his friend, he knew that he couldn't stay at Sam's fishing nets for much longer, so he decided to steer to a spot a few hundred feet away. He peered out at sea, his hope diminishing. Finally, after two hours of waiting, they returned to the shore.

They came ashore in front of Edward's mother-in-law's, waiting in the boat for a few minutes to make sure nobody was around, before moving the chests of treasure to his car. When they had put the last chest in the trunk, Edward said, "Come to my store for your share tomorrow." Then he drove away. Louis walked to his boat, grabbed the diving suit, threw it in the water and steered his way back to his house.

Chapter 4

The next evening at 7:00, Louis went to Edward's jewelry store, expecting that his share would at least amount to one of the treasure chests. He approached the front of the store, looking around for a second, and then he entered.

Edward was sitting behind his desk, contemplating his state of affairs with sadness. Nobody else was in there. Louis walked over to him like a creditor, as always, and put the bag he was holding on the desk and said, "I hope this is big enough to hold my share." Then he turned to the big safe to Edward's right side by the wall.

Edward's eyes rolled up a little and he said, "Sit down."

"I don't have time to sit. I have to go. I want my share."

"Do you? What are you talking about? Did you forget what you said before we found the treasure?"

Louis began to get worried. He wrinkled his brow and asked, "What do you mean?"

Edward touched the magnifying glass that was always on his desk and said, "Did you forget our bet? The bet you lost?"

Louis was enraged. His face grew red and his eyes were wide. His breathing quickened, and for a moment, he bit his tongue, which he did whenever he got this angry, and he cried, "You cheated me."

Edward interrupted him. "Let me finish." He took an envelope out of his desk. "This is for your help. You will be fine if you know how to use this money."

Louis grabbed the envelope and greedily tore it open. "Three hundred bucks! You call that fair?"

Edward remembered that he was talking to a man who did not deserve to be treated fairly, and he stood up and said with anger, "Listen, you deserve nothing. Do you understand?"

Louis thought of the money that he believed was rightfully his, but when faced with Edward's anger, he was convinced that he could not get more than what he held in his hand, which was a large amount of money for a person like him. He put the money in the pocket of his coat and said, "Listen to me, we didn't go anywhere together and nothing happened." Then he left there angrily.

Chapter 5

At nine o'clock Louis went to Donald's Saloon. He took his cousin with him to protect him in case something happened. His cousin was forty-eight years old, and his name was Alex. He was a stout man, but his brain had not kept up with the rest of his body. He had no ability to hold onto anything for very long. When he had money he spent it prodigally, he spent his time without reason. His clothes smelled bad, for he took a shower once a month. His hair was like yellow grass and he had very big eyes. His voice was hoarse and he was a hard-faced man with a bad mouth like Louis. He had a silver tooth between his top front teeth and an abnormally wide chin like a hippo, for which his friends called him, Hippolex.

Louis stood in the doorway and looked around. The place was crowded, as it was most every night. The waiters and waitresses were kept busy. His eyes went to the table in the corner where his friends were, and he walked with pride to them. The owner of the saloon, Donald, a broad, fat, lazy man with a walrus mustache, was standing behind the cash register wearing a Stetson hat. Laying eyes on Louis, he immediately recalled the money that Louis owed him. Donald looked at his book to check the due date, discovering the deadline for paying it off was last night. For this, Donald was mad.

Louis sat at the table and called over a young waiter, named Brandy, a tiny young boy of seventeen. As soon as Louis placed his order for some beer, Donald called Brandy and told him not to fill any orders for Louis until he paid off his debt. After ten minutes, as Brandy was serving the other customers, Louis got mad, stood up, grabbed the boy by the collar and said angrily, "Hey, where is my beer? I ordered it twenty minutes ago."

Brandy held his hand and said, "After you pay off your debt you can order beer."

Donald, who was looking at them, yelled, "Hey, Louis, come on over here."

The saloon was quiet now, as everyone was looking on carefully, not wanting to miss whatever was taking shape between Donald and Louis. Louis got up and touched his breast pocket to make sure the money was there, and he walked sullenly over to Donald and said, "What the hell is going on here?"

Donald looked down at the book. "You have an unpaid balance here."

"How much is it?" asked Louis.

"Did you forget? It is six dollars, and your due date was last night. No more excuses. Either you pay it off now or else you've got to leave right now."

Louis touched his pocket again and dropped his head, trying to figure out if there was any way he could take advantage of Donald, which was what he always did. He came closer and put his hand on the cash register and said, "Tell me, how much is your saloon worth?"

"What do you mean?"

"I said how much for your damn saloon? I may buy it and give everybody in here tonight free drinks."

Donald touched his new flat-brimmed Stetson, chuckled for a while and looked at the customers. "Look at him. He doesn't even have money to pay his debt, and now he wants to buy my saloon." Then he turned to Louis and asked, "Are you sure you are not drunk?" Then he burst out laughing. Wanting to get rid of Louis as a customer once and for all, he said, "I am ready to sell my saloon to you right now for two hundred bucks."

Louis dropped his head without saying anything, feigning defeat. Donald was a little drunk, but he knew what was going on. He downed another shot of Jack Daniels and said, "Come on, loser. Let's see the money right now. Two hundred bucks." He brought out a paper from behind the cash register and a pen and looked around at the customers and cried, "Hey, folks, I am going to write down that I sold my saloon with everything in it to Louis Wilson for two hundred dollars and sign it, but only if he gives me the money right now. Otherwise he has to get out of my place and stay out."

Louis looked at him without saying anything. He knew it was now or never if he wanted to seal the deal before Donald could change his mind. Donald came out from behind the bar and stood in front of him and said, I think you'd better walk out of here on your own before I kick your ass out."

Everyone in the saloon was quiet. Even the waiters and waitresses had stopped serving the customers and were looking on.

"I am not a man to be laughed at," said Louis and turned to the people. "You heard what he said. He is going to sell his saloon to me for two hundred bucks." Then he thrust his hand into his pocket, pulled out the money and slapped it on the counter, snatching up the bill of sale that Donald had already signed.

Donald looked at the money without making any movement. His eyes and mouth were wide, and for a moment, he thought he was dreaming. He closed his eyes, opened them quickly and touched the money. It was like a nightmare for him. He looked at the bill of sale and the people gazing at him. Everybody was in shock, even Louis's friends and his cousin. They approached him to make sure everything they were seeing was real.

Louis took the money, put it in Donald's hand and said, "Take your money and get out of my saloon."

Donald fussed with his hat and studied Louis without saying anything. He seemed none too happy with the turn that events had taken. Louis's cousin, Alex, sauntered over to him and pulled up his sleeves and put his filthy hand on his hat and said, "Didn't you hear what he said? Do I need to kick you out of here?"

Donald looked at Louis and his friends, who stood in a half-circle about him, scowling and waiting for him to leave, then he turned to face the customers. It seemed all of them were against him, and they started chanting, "Leave, leave this place," for they wanted the free beer Louis had promised them.

Donald was sorry that he had never hired a bouncer for his place, but it was too late now. Finally, he put the money in his pocket and left. Soon Louis stationed himself behind the cash register. He grabbed an open bottle of Jack Daniels and smacked his lips and smiled, looked at the customers and said generously, "Have a drink on me, my friends.

Tonight you all are my guests. Drink deep. He imagined himself famous among the people of New York City, like his half-brother, Edward. The news got out to passers-by in the street, so they came in to join the party. The news even reached the homeless who wandered nearby, and they came in for free beer. One of Louis's friends asked him, "Where did you get this money?"

Louis smiled vaingloriously. "I found a treasure."

The word spread quickly among those in the saloon. They gasped, "Treasure…"

Some who knew him well said, "If it is true that he found a treasure, it might be enough to drive a man like him crazy."

When Louis realized everybody was focused on him, he tried to divert their attention. He clicked his tongue, smiled and said simply, "Just kidding. You better drink your beer and enjoy tonight."

Alex was standing beside him drinking beer wryly, he said, "Why do you ask him such a stupid question? It is none of your business. Just drink your free beer."

"Hey you, Hippolex, are you going to keep your cousin's secret?" said the man to a surge of laughter.

Louis cried with pride, "Drink and enjoy, my friends."

The customers were so happy; they applauded and chanted, "Louis, Louis…"

The accordion and violin played by two passers-by who had come in for free beer, and some of the customers began to dance, the shrill notes of excited, happy voices filling the saloon. It was the most business the place had ever seen. Louis did not gamble that night, choosing instead to spend time with the customers.

By two o'clock, all the customers had left the saloon, and before closing up Louis assembled all of the staff members and said, "You can all keep your jobs here, and I look forward to working with all of you." He also promised to raise their salary. Then he looked at the young waiter, Brandy, who had argued with him, and said, "Except for you. I don't ever want to see your face around here again."

Brandy stepped closer to him and spat, "You know what? I wouldn't work in your bar for all the money in the world."

Louis grabbed his collar. "Get the hell out of my place." And he pushed him out.

Alex approached and put his square, well-muscled hand on his face and pushed him out and said, "Get out of here before I kill you."

"Keep your hands off me, jerk," Brandy said and he walked away.

The waiters and waitresses did not say a word, out of fear of losing their job right when business was finally about to pick up. Even after Brandy left Louis continued to fume, enraged at having been insulted in front of his staff. After everyone had left, he took Alex outside and said, "Do something for me."

"What is it?"

"I want you to teach that idiot a lesson, so that he learns he cannot talk to me like that and be careful nobody sees you."

Alex drunkenly stood back against the door in front of the saloon, rubbing his back on the heavy post. He nodded and ground his heel against the floor.

Twenty minutes later, as Louis was waiting for Alex in front of the saloon, Alex stomped up, scuffing his shoes in the process. Louis stepped over to him quickly and asked, "What did you do?"

Alex said jocularly, "Yeah, I really punished him."

"Tell me, how did you punish him?"

Alex stuffed his shirt into his pants, unbuckled his belt and tightened it again and laughed. "I got the job done."

"I don't understand," said Louis. "Damn it, tell me what happened!"

Alex laughed. "He was moving on the ground like a snake when I stabbed him with a broken bottle, and then I think he stopped breathing."

Louis looked at the blood on his shirt and his eyes went wide. "Stupid." He looked around to make sure nobody was looking then he grabbed his collar and said, "You killed him? I told you to punish him, not kill him." He ran his hand through his hair. "Did anybody see you?"

"No, nobody was there."

Louis glanced around nervously. "You can't stay here. Let's go."They quickly made their way to the old shipyard in the buggy.

Chapter 6

Peter's house was quiet that night. The clock on the cupboard showed 9:00 p.m. Laura and Katherine were sitting in the chair by the window, looking outside for Peter. Katherine pictured necklaces of every shape and size and waited restlessly for the moment her father would bring her the one he had promised. In time, she grew tired of waiting and fell asleep in Laura's arms. Laura took her to bed and returned to the window to keep watch. It was the first time Peter had ever been this late, and Laura was worried. She thought about what might have caused him such a delay. As she was looking outside, she noticed one of her neighbors, Dean Charlotte, an old man who had lived in the neighborhood for many years with his wife. Laura walked outside and called, "Mr. Charlotte."

Dean turned and looked at her for a few seconds and said, "Hi, Mrs. Vincent. What are you doing outside at this time of night?"

Laura approached him and said, "Peter went to Boston this morning, and he hasn't come back yet."

"Did he go with Katherine?"

"No, he went by himself. He used to go once a month and buy stuff for his shop, and he was never late getting home."

Charlotte turned back to the road and said calmly, "Maybe the train broke down. I've heard about that happening before. Or maybe he didn't get to the station on time."

Laura looked at him without saying anything.

"Don't worry. He can take care of himself. You better go inside and be with your daughter now."

Laura was calmed a little by his words, and she went back inside and returned to her seat at the window, assuming Peter would come by the last train.

The night passed, but he didn't show up. Laura became very worried.

The next day at 4:00 p.m., Laura and Katherine were in the house when they heard a car pull up in front. They quickly went to the window and looked outside, where they saw Edward's blue Ford Thunderbird. Laura said, "Mr. Wilson is here." Then she ran outside, and Katherine ran after her.

Edward remained sitting in his car, looking like somebody entangled in an enigma. He didn't know how to tell Laura about Peter. When he saw Laura and Katherine he got out, stood by the car, and waited. Laura said, "Hi, Mr. Wilson."

"Hi," said Edward.

"Do you have any news about Peter?" Laura said.

Edward squinted his eyes a little and gave her a questioning look. "Peter?"

"He went to Boston yesterday, but he hasn't come back yet. Something is wrong," said Laura anxiously.

Edward looked down at Katherine, who was looking inside the car. He took a long, slow breath to calm himself. Then he turned to Laura and said, "He is very late, I know. He used to go to a wholesaler in Boston who was called The Samuel." Then he shook his head slowly.

"Do you know where in Boston?"

Edward nodded as he was thinking. "Yeah, I know the owner of that shop."

"Didn't Peter mention anything to you about going to Boston?" asked Laura nervously.

A wave of caution overtook Edward momentarily and then moved on. He paused, drew a careful breath and said, "No, he didn't tell me anything." Then he dropped his head and waited to hear what other questions Laura might have for him.

"I am so worried about him," said Laura. "I will go to Boston tomorrow morning if he doesn't show up by tonight."

Katherine stood by the car, listening to them. She looked up at Edward and asked, "Will you come to Boston with us, Mr. Wilson?"

Edward cleared his throat while searching for something to say. As he was thinking, Laura said to her, "Katherine, you know Mr. Wilson is busy. He can't come to Boston with us."

"No, I can go with you," said Edward. "As a matter of fact, I need to go there for business anyway."

"We don't want to bother you. We can go by train."

"Not a problem. We can all go in my car."

The decision that Edward had made was sudden and unexpected. He was fearful of what had happened to Peter, and he felt guilty about his death. He just wanted to be with his family, and he might have a chance to tell her about what had happened.

The next morning at ten o'clock, they left for Boston. Katherine sat in the back seat looking outside excitedly. It was her first time to go to the city, and every aspect of the trip interested her. She asked her mother about everything she saw along the way. When they were still miles away from the city, she saw many people on the coaches heading somewhere. She asked Laura, "Where are they going?"

Laura looked outside and thought of Peter. She answered doubtfully, "I think New York City." Then she asked Edward to confirm.

He replied, "That's right, New York City. This city is growing tremendously, and people from all over the country are moving here in search of a job, not just people in America, people are migrating to New York City from different parts of the world."

"Mr. Wilson, is New York City bigger than Boston?" asked Katherine.

"Yes, New York City is the biggest city in America," answered Edward.

"But my dad told me Boston has the biggest port and that people travel to other countries from there," said Katherine.

"That's true. It is the biggest port," said Edward. Then he sighed and mused.

Katherine thought of overseas for a moment and asked her mom, "Do you think Daddy traveled to another country?"

"He just went to Boston to buy some things for his shop," said Laura firmly.

"Then why is he so late?"

"Don't worry. We will see him today."

After four hours, they reached the city of Boston. Edward treated them to lunch in a restaurant across from the port, so that Katherine could see it. After that they drove to Samuel's store.

Edward pulled up in front. It was the biggest tackle store in Boston, and the display window was neatly organized with scores of popular items. A sign reading, "The Samuel Wholesale" in big wooden letters was nailed overtop the door. Edward took a deep breath and said, "That is the place."

"Is Daddy here?" Katherine asked happily.

"I don't know, let's go see," said Laura. They got out of the car and walked inside.

There were ten customers, and a man of about sixty was standing by his desk speaking to some of them while two twenty-something footboys were helping the other customers pack their items.

Katherine's eyes searched all around looking for her father. She asked Laura, "Where is Daddy?"

Laura answered, "He should be here." Then she looked at Edward, hoping to hear something from him.

"The man over there is Samuel," said Edward.

Samuel turned around and immediately recognized Edward and said loudly, "Hi, Mr. Wilson. How are you doing?" He walked over and they hugged each other. Then he looked at Laura and Katherine and introduced himself.

"This is Laura and Katherine, Peter Vincent's wife and daughter," said Edward.

Samuel bent down and put his hand on Katherine's shoulder and said with a smile, "How are you, Katherine? Do you like Boston?"

Katherine nodded her head.

Samuel turned to Laura. "Where is Peter? I haven't seen him for a couple of months."

Laura looked at him blankly, her body devoid of movement. She was completely shocked, and for a moment, she thought that Samuel must be kidding her. She smiled with worry and said, "Peter came to Boston two days ago. Didn't you see him?"

"No, he didn't come to me, "Samuel said with a smile. "It's been about two months since I last saw him."

Laura's concern skyrocketed. Her eyes searched around involuntary for a short time. "But he told me that he was coming here to buy some things from you."

"Well, he never contacted me," said Samuel persuasively, and he looked to Edward for some sort of input.

Edward had dropped his head and was looking at the floor. Laura's mind raced with questions. "Is there another Samuel who has a tackle shop in Boston?"

Samuel thought for a few seconds and said, "I know all the tackle shops in this city, and there are no other shops owned by someone named Samuel." Then he sighed and continued. "I just know one Samuel who has a grocery store in Liberty Square, but I am sure Peter doesn't go there."

Laura wanted the address anyway so that she could go check for herself. They got the address, and then they drove to the grocery store.

Fifteen minutes later, they reached Samuel's grocery. Laura asked Katherine to wait in the car and she and Edward got out and entered the shop. It was a midsize shop and very crowded. Samuel was an old man. He was sitting cross-legged behind the counter tapping his fingers gently on his knees, waiting for the first paying customer. He was angry because some customers had not brought their payment on time. Laura and Edward approached him slowly, and Laura said, "Mr. Samuel?"

Samuel eyed them closely. "Yes."

Laura stepped closer and asked anxiously, "Has Peter been here?"

Samuel raised his head slightly, wrinkled his brow and asked, "Who is Peter?"

"Peter Vincent. I am his wife."

"Peter Vincent! I don't know anybody by this name," Samuel answered grumpily.

Laura was devastated and felt as if she had lost her last chance to find her husband. "Don't you know Peter? He came to Boston two days ago. Nobody has seen him. Where can he be?" She burst out crying.

Samuel stood up and said angrily, "What are you talking about?" Then he quickly turned to Edward and said, "Tell me what is going on here! What does she want?"

Edward looked around at the customers holding their items. He put his hands on Laura's shoulders and said, "Calm down." Then he said to Samuel humbly, "I am sorry, sir. We came from New York City to find her husband. He came to Boston two days ago and never returned home."

"Why is she asking me about him?" Samuel interrupted.

"Because he told her that he would be seeing a shopkeeper named Samuel."

"I am not the only Samuel who has a shop in Boston. There are many shopkeepers by this name in the city."

"We also went to a Samuel who has a tackle store, but he couldn't help us."

"I can't help you either."

"I am very sorry," said Edward, and he put his hand on Laura's shoulder and pushed her gently toward the door. As Laura was crying, she said hopelessly, "Where can he be? Where else could we look for him?"

"We better go back to New York City. Maybe he is home by now."

Laura wiped her wet eyes with the back of her hand, and they walked out without saying goodbye.

Katherine was sitting in the car, playing with the steering wheel, turning it right and left. As soon as she saw them, she moved to the rear seat and asked her mother, "Where is Daddy? Wasn't he there?"

Laura sat beside her and looked straight ahead, so that Katherine wouldn't see that her eyelashes were still wet. She replied, "Your dad was here earlier. He is probably back home by now."

"He must have bought my necklace here," Katherine said happily, laying her hands on Laura's knee.

Laura shook her head and said, "I'm sure you're right." Then they headed to New York City.

Edward went over what he had done to his friend and how he was now acting with his friend's family. Everything he was doing was inhumane. He felt guilty, and had enough of himself. A cloud of sadness surrounded him, as if all the joy had gone out of his life. He thought bitterly, "What would the people of New York City think if they knew what I had done? It would be an utter shame for Edward, who was a beacon of honesty, generosity, and humanity. With every moment that passed it became harder for him to tell Laura the truth. He yearned for a quiet place to be alone, like a criminal escaping from the law.

In the car nobody said a word. After a few miles, Katherine fell asleep thinking of the necklace. Laura stared at the road, impatient to get back and find Peter.

It was almost dark when they reached New York City. Edward stopped at his jewelry store. He looked back at Katherine, who was still sleeping. He said slowly to Laura, "I'll be right back." Then he went inside the store. After a few minutes he returned to the car holding a jewelry box. He handed it to Laura and said, "Give it to Katherine when she wakes up."

"What is it?" asked Laura.

"It is a necklace. Please don't tell her it is from me."

Laura turned to look at Katherine for a second and nodded.

When they reached home, Katherine was still asleep. Laura got down, took a few steps and faced the house and said dejectedly, "He is not back yet. I don't know what to tell Katherine when she finds out her father is not here."

Edward was standing beside her. He looked into her eyes with sympathy and dropped his head. His body was shivering, but he tried to control himself and fought to overcome his fear refusing to let it win out over him. He moved his legs slowly and mechanically, picked up his head and touched his chin with his fingers and started to tell her about Peter, but before he could say a word, Mrs. Charlotte, Laura's neighbor, came out of her house and asked Laura about Peter. So Edward changed his mind, deciding to tell her another time. When Laura hugged Katherine outside the car, he said goodbye and left them ruefully.

Laura took Katherine inside the house to her bed, and she went to the dining room, sat down and looked around. All was quiet, and she was a little scared. She thought of what might have happened to her husband. She did not know how to even start looking for him. She lay her forehead on her crossed arms on the table and began to cry. It was then she heard footsteps. She quickly wiped her eyes, turned around, and saw Katherine approaching. Katherine looked into her eyes carefully and asked, "Are you crying, Mom?"

Laura didn't know what to say. The last thing she wanted was to say something that would make her happy. She said happily, "Come on, I want to show you something." Then she picked up the jewelry box on the table and handed it to her, "This is for you. Open it."

Katherine opened the box and took out a necklace with a silver rose pendant. She held it out and looked at it in surprise and said, "Where did it come from?"

Laura answered, "It was on the table when we got home. I think your daddy bought it for you."

"Where is Daddy?"

"I didn't see him. I think he is in the shop."

"I knew Daddy was going to buy me a nice necklace. I knew it." Katherine held the necklace tightly and cried, "This is the best gift ever!" Then Laura helped her put it on. Katherine touched it and said, "It is a nice rose."

She walked over, looked at herself in the mirror, and said, "This is the most beautiful rose in the world." She hopped on her heels and cried. "What time is Daddy going to come home? I miss him so much."

"He will be home soon." Laura answered.

Laura continued to conceal the reality of the situation so that Katherine wouldn't suffer during her father's absence. All the while Laura's mind searched for something to tell her if Peter didn't show up that night.

Chapter 7

The next day Louis rented a house in downtown, and relocated his family there. He was plagued by thoughts that the murder would be traced back to him. That night, he went to the saloon at eight o'clock, preferring to take Alex with him so that nobody would suspect him for his absence. He stood behind the cash register at all times, looking and listening for those whose conversations tended toward what had become of Brandy. He always kept an eye on the door, expecting at any time to see the marshal walk through the door.

It was ten o'clock in the evening when the marshal entered. He stood by the door and touched his handlebar mustache, his eyes scouring the place before finally landing on Louis. The place was so quiet you could hear a pin drop. It seemed he had found his suspect. All eyes were on the marshal. Alex dropped his head down to play cards, but when the marshal walked to a corner table the customers resumed their talking and the saloon was soon back to normal. Louis trembled with fear, so he drank a few glasses of whiskey, hoping to calm his nerves. He flagged down a waitress named Sandy and sent her over to the marshal's table. She approached the table and asked him flirtatiously, "What can I do for you, marshal?"

"I am here to see the owner," said the marshal humorlessly.

"You mean the new owner, Louis?"

The marshal nodded gravely.

"Let me get him for you," said the waitress as she smiled and walked away.

Soon Louis appeared at the marshal's table, holding a bottle of Jack Daniels and an opener and two glasses and said in a friendly voice, "Hi, marshal, how are you? Did you come to congratulate me on my saloon?"

The Marshal rolled his eyes and said somberly, "Sit down. I need to talk to you."

Louis uncorked the bottle and filled the glass.

"Brandy was killed last night," said the marshal without premise, and he gazed at Louis to gauge his reaction.

Louis said coolly, "Who? Brandy?"

"Brandy, the boy who worked here till last night."

"Oh yeah, I heard about it a few hours ago," said Louis. He took a deep breath and continued. "He was a cool guy. I am really sorry."The marshal looked over to where Alex and his friends were sitting and said, "I heard you had an argument with him last night. Is that true?"

Louis smiled and said, "It was just a friendly discussion--oh, I remember now. It was just for a beer. But when I bought this place, I invited all the staff to stay and work for me." Then he sighed and said, "I was so sad to lose a good waiter like him."

At that time, he noticed a nearby waiter listening to them. Therefore, he glared at him threateningly. The marshal's eyes were on Louis as he carefully studied his reaction, and then he asked, "What time did he leave here last night?"

"I think it was about two."

"Who was here at that time?"

"I was with the entire staff," Louis said after a pause. He was beginning to get scared, so he tried ways to ward off the marshal's suspicion. "Is it possible he committed suicide?"

The Marshal said immediately, "He was stabbed with a broken bottle in an alley."

Louis said with a sigh, "Oh, my God." He dropped his gaze to the bottle of Jack Daniels and shook his head from side to side.

The marshal stood up and said confidently, "I will find the murderer, you can be sure of that." Then he walked out.

Louis carried the whiskey bottle to the cash register and stood there, drumming his fingers. He went outside, lit a cigarette, and paced in front of the saloon, his mind searching for a way out of his dilemma. Soon Alex came out and asked, "What are you doing out here? Come back inside."

Louis grabbed his collar. "Stupid, this is all your fault."

"What?" said Alex fearfully.

"The marshal came around here asking questions about Brandy."

Alex looked at him warily and his shoulders raised a little to indicate that what happened was through no fault of his. Louis's eyes darted around. "You'd better get inside. I'll tell you what to do later." Alex went inside the saloon while Louis stood by the post, chain smoking. He knew the marshal would ask all of his staff about what had happened the night Brandy was killed. And he felt sure when he was interrogated Alex wouldn't be able to answer all his questions and act normally. He thought it over and finally decided to send Alex away New from York City before the marshal could interrogate him, placing the suspicion squarely on Alex. He suddenly thought to send him to Italy, where Alex had lived for twenty years traveling there as a youth with his mother. He was visiting his Italian stepfather, before returning to America eighteen years ago when he was thirty years old.

The saloon closed at one o'clock in the morning, and Louis and Alex headed to the old shipyard in an old Chevy pickup he had bought that day for twenty dollars. Alex knew Louis was mad at him, so he sat quietly.

Without looking at him Louis said, "The marshal asked me lots of questions about the boy you killed. He also asked me some questions about you. I think somebody may have seen you last night."

"But nobody was there," Alex said. "I am sure nobody saw me."

Louis shouted angrily, "How are you sure that nobody saw you? You were drunk last night."

Alex became silent again and just listened.

The marshal will interrogate everybody in the saloon, including you, and sooner or later this will lead to your arrest." Then he sighed. "You were always problematic. Even as a child you were in trouble all the time."

Alex tried to think clearly, but it was no use. Finally, he asked for Louis's help. "Tell me what I should do?"

Louis turned to him finally and said, "You must go back to Italy. If you stay here, you will be arrested, and you will get me in trouble along with you."

"Italy!" Alex said worriedly.

"If you stay in this country the marshal will track you down like a hound dog. I think Italy is the best place. You already know the language and everything. Plus it's far enough away for you to be safe. You can come back after a couple years. It should be safe for you by then."

Alex thought about it. Everything Louis said made sense "How will I get there? I don't have any money."

"Don't worry, I'll pay your way, and I'll give you enough money, so you won't have to work for a few months over there."

"When should I leave?"

"Tomorrow. You can hide out at my house untill then." Then he drove directly to the old shipyard.

Chapter 8

After four days, when Laura saw no sign of Peter, she decided to speak with the marshal. It was mid-morning, and she sat Katherine in the buggy and headed toward the police station. Five minutes later, on the way there, she saw Peter's friend, Robert Brown, the one who had lent Peter the diving suits. He was driving toward them, and as soon as he recognized her, he waved and pulled over. Laura stopped the buggy immediately and said to Katherine to stay put and she ran across the road to talk to him. As Robert got out of his car, she asked anxiously, "Do you know anything about Peter?"

When Robert saw her worry, he smiled, and said, "As a matter of fact, I came to ask you the same question."

"He went to Boston four days ago, and he hasn't come back yet. I went to Boston to Samuel's tackle store two days ago, the place he was supposed to do his shopping, but Samuel didn't know anything about him either."

Robert looked puzzled. He thought of what Peter had told him, which was totally different than what Laura was talking about. He asked, "Did he tell you that he was going to Boston to shop at Samuel's?"

"Yeah, that's what he told me. I am so worried. What could have happened to him? Today will make four days since he left."

"But he told me something different." Robert took a deep breath. "He came to my shop five days ago and borrowed two diving suits. He said he was going to give somebody diving lessons, and he would bring them back in two days. Did he mention anything like that to you?"

"Diving suit! This is the first I've heard of it," said Laura, her concern mounting.

"Yeah, it was exactly five days ago that he borrowed them from me."

Why didn't he tell me about it? Why did he lie? Laura asked herself. Who did he go with? For a moment, it occurred to her that he was seeing another woman, but she quickly dismissed the idea. This impression gave way to a host of unanswered questions. "Did he tell you his friend's name? I mean the person he was going with."

"No, I didn't ask him," Robert sighed. "I have to talk to you about something important. I found one of the diving suits in a flea market this morning."

Laura's eyes were wide. She swallowed with difficulty, her mind filling with horrible possibilities. "Oh my God, what has happened to him?"

Robert shook his head anxiously. "I hope he is all right."Are you sure that it was the same suit you gave to Peter?"

"I always mark my diving suits."

"Who was selling it? Do you know him?"

"That's a good question," said Robert. "I was in a flea market this morning and I saw that crazy boy, Patrick, was selling my diving suit. I think you know him."

Laura quickly said, "The boy who always has his dog with him?"

"That's him. He said that he had found it at the seaside."

Patrick was an odd boy. He was sixteen years old and lived with his grandmother in the old shipyard. Everything he found in the area he sold at a flea market and gave the money to his grandmother. Laura seemed to know him well.

"Do you know the house?" asked Robert.

"I just know that they live in that area."

"No problem. We can ask around," said Robert.

"I wish we knew who went with Peter."

"Don't worry, I am sure when we find his grandma, we can get more information from her," said Robert, and then he bit his lower lip and squeezed his eyes shut and continued, "The boy told me that he found the diving suit early in the morning when he was out running with his dog toward the sun."

"What do you mean?"

"I mean that we should go east of his grandma's house and check along the shore."

"He is just an odd boy. Did you believe him?" said Laura.

"He is odd, but he can sound like a wise man sometimes," said Robert emphatically. "Whatever. Let's go to there right now."

"Okay. First I need to take Katherine home and leave the buggy."

"I'll follow you."

While Laura and Katherine waited at the house for Robert, Katherine grew excited at the prospect of riding in Robert's car to see her father at his friend's house, which is what her mother told her. So she stopped asking questions. As they stood in front of the house, watching the road, they saw Robert walking toward them. He seemed downtrodden. "I am sorry, my car broke down. I don't know what the problem is."

"What should we do now?" Laura asked.

"I don't know. I will a mechanic look at it. It won't start."

"How long will it take?" asked Laura.

"Probably two hours," Robert said. "As soon as it's fixed, I'll come back here." Then he left for his car.

Laura thought of the story Robert told her, and the fact that Peter was missing. With every moment that passed, she grew more and more worried, and she began to wonder if she would ever see him again. She took Katherine inside the house and waited for Robert until two o'clock. The situation was becoming unbearable, so she decided that she and Katherine would go to where they talked about without him. She looked out through the window. "If we wait for him any longer it will soon be too late." Then they went outside, got in the buggy and headed toward the old shipyard.

Laura focused on the road ahead. All she wanted was to get there as soon as possible and reach Peter before it was too late. Katherine was thinking of her father and expecting to see him very soon. She had missed him, and she wanted to tell him about all that had happened while he was gone, including the story of her necklace. She was wearing it, having tucked it inside her dress. She turned to Laura and said with a smile, "Mom, don't tell Daddy about the necklace. I am going tell him that I lost it." Then she laughed. Laura smiled a little and returned her attention to the road.

At three o'clock in the afternoon, they reached the old shipyard. Laura asked the first person she saw about Patrick's Grandma's house, and very soon they were there. It was an old wooden house situated on the coastline like many houses in that area. Laura quickly dismounted the buggy, went and knocked on the door and stood waiting. Nobody came. She knocked again and called, "Hello is anybody in?" but there was no reply. She turned around and saw Katherine looking at her. She asked loudly, "Isn't Daddy there?"

"I don't know," Laura, answered wearily as she knocked on the door one last time. She looked around, but there was nobody to be seen.

"Where's Daddy?" Katherine asked.

Laura walked to the buggy and tried to disguise her worry, so she answered, "We had better ask somebody else." She stood there looking at the sea. It was calm and the sun was still shining on the beach. As she lost herself in the scenery, she suddenly recalled Robert telling her to look, for Patrick had found the diving suit on that side of the house. As she scanned the distance carefully, she saw somebody far down the beach. She said, pointing, "Look! Then she mounted the buggy and sped toward the lone figure.

As she got closer, she made out a black man and a boy working in a fishing boat by the water's edge. Before they reached them, the man slid the boat in the sea and the boy ran up the shore to a house. Katherine said excitedly, "That's Daniel. I know him."

"Daniel?" Laura said.

"I mean that boy," Katherine said, pointing. "He is George's friend. I met him when I came with George and his mom to see his grandma."

"The man in that fishing boat is probably his father," said Laura.

"Yes, you're right."

"Let's go to see Daniel first," said Laura, and they went to his house.

Daniel was standing by the window, looking out at them, as the buggy pulled up in front of the house.

He recognized Katherine and went outside. "What are you doing here, Katherine?"

Katherine smiled. "We came here to see my dad."

Laura interjected hastily, "Can I talk to your mom, please?"

"I don't have a mother," said Daniel vaguely. "She died many years ago."

"I am so sorry," said Laura.

"My dad says she is in heaven."

"Of course, your dad is right," said Laura, and she turned to the sea. "When will your dad be back? Will it take long?"

"He is going to be back in one hour."

Laura looked into the distance toward the east and thought of all the horrible things that might have happened to Peter. Thinking it might be too late if she waited for Daniel's father to get back, she decided to try to find somebody else who could help her find Peter. She turned to Daniel and said, "We are going to that side to see the shore. We will come back in half an hour. I want to talk to your dad." Then they got into the buggy and headed eastward.

Laura's eyes searched the shore for clues to her husband's whereabouts. She stopped occasionally, and from her place in the buggy, examined the small bits of wood and other objects brought in by the tide. After twenty minutes, she stopped and stared at the far shore, and seeing nobody, she looked back at Daniel's father's boat in the sea and thought he was probably their best chance after all, so they returned the way they had come. The grooves made by the wheels and the prints of the horseshoes on the seashore captivated Katherine. It was her first time to see such things, and she looked back at where they crossed the wheel prints of the buggy. As they came up the beach, Daniel ran toward them and cried, "Look, my dad is coming. Let's go see how many fish he caught today." Then Laura and Katherine followed him in the buggy.

Sam got angry when he saw them, for he did not like strangers to see his fish. He believed that it robbed him of all his blessings, especially when a woman saw his fish. Even his wife, when she was alive, wouldn't come to his boat to see his catch. On that day he hadn't caught enough fish and was angry as he landed on the beach. He barked at Daniel, "Who are they? What do they want here?"

"That lady is looking for her husband. She wants to talk to you about him," answered Daniel.

Sam looked at them grumpily for a moment, took a deep breath, covered the fish basket, and told Daniel to take it to the backyard. Daniel took the fish basket, and as he passed by the buggy, he asked Katherine to go with him to see the fish, so they walked up the shore to the house alongside one another, and Laura slowly approached Sam and stood by his boat. "Hi."

Sam was mildly irritated, and working in the boat, he did not lift up his head and said nothing, acting as if he did not hear her. Laura got closer and said, "Hello, sir."

Sam picked up his head heavily and said, "Hi." Then he returned to his work.

"My name is Laura Vincent. I am looking for my husband."

As Sam worked, he said, "I'm listening."

"He came to this area a few days ago and he hasn't returned."

"Why did he come here?"

"To teach his friend diving."

Sam stopped working, stood up and looked into her eyes. He quickly remembered Louis and Edward Wilson, the man who was with him, and the diving suit in his boat, and he thought he must surely be this woman's husband. He asked, "Did your husband tell you about his friend? Do you know his name?"

"No, I don't even know who he went with. I just heard about it today from a friend of his--the same person who lent him the diving suit. Then she told him Robert's story of finding the diving suit in a flea market.

When Laura finished, Sam asked, "Is he sure it is the same diving suit that he gave your husband?"

"Yes, he is."

Sam sighed deeply and shook his head from side to side and turned back to the sea and stared at the place he had seen them that day. "I saw somebody with Louis a few days ago. It was the first time I had seen that person."

"When did you see him? Tell me, please," urged Laura.

Sam sighed, hung his head and thought about argument he would have with Louis very soon for the information that he was giving her.

"Please," Laura begged. "I have been looking for him for four days. I don't know what to tell my daughter. Please help me." Then she began to cry.

Sam turned to his house and looked at Katherine standing in front with Daniel, looking at the fish in the fish basket. He pursed his lips and after a few moments he looked at the signs of his net and said, "It was about four days ago that I saw Louis and that man in the sea by my net, and there was a diving suit in their boat I just saw them for a minute, then they went to the other side."

"Who is Louis?" Laura asked eagerly. "You know him, right?"

"Yeah, that's his house," Sam said, pointing to a house a quarter of a mile away. At that moment a blue Chevrolet pickup stopped in front of the house and a man got out and went to the backyard.

"Can you describe the man who was with Louis that day?" asked Laura.

Sam squinted his eyes a little and said, "He was middle-aged and he had a mustache. He was sitting in the boat so I can't tell you how tall he was."

Laura said in a rush, "That was my husband, Peter. I know it was!" Then she looked at Louis's house and said seriously, "I am going to go ask him about Peter. He knows where he is."

Thinking of the woman's safety, Sam said, "I think you better talk to the marshal first."

"No, I am going to talk to him right now." Then she walked up the beach to Katherine and they got in the buggy and went to Louis's house.

The sun was westering with an orange blush. She knew that the darkness was closing in and she didn't have much time to get back home, but she had to talk to Louis. It might be her last chance. She did not tell Katherine what was going on, although she knew she could not disguise the reality of the situation from her for very long. She would have to tell her everything if Peter did not show up that night. Katherine was thinking of her father and becoming curious about his long absence. "Mom, do you think we are going to see Daddy in that house?"

"I hope so, answered Laura.

"Why doesn't he come to see us?"

Laura sighed painfully. "He will come, my dear. Don't worry."

As the buggy was approaching Louis's house Laura's heart beat faster and faster and her body trembled. She was afraid of what she might learn about Peter. As they got closer to the house, Katherine said quickly, "Mom, I know this house. Daddy, Mr. Wilson and I came here a few days ago.

Do you remember? I told you about it that night? I am sure this is the same house."

Laura remembered the night when Peter and Katherine had talked to her about it, and she said thoughtfully, "Yeah, I remember."

"The owner of that house is Daddy's friend," said Katherine.

Now Laura was confused. Could she trust Louis? On the one hand, she thought of him as her husband's friend, but on the other, she recalled the stories she had heard from Robert and Sam about Peter and she grew suspicious. She felt like she was losing her mind.

They stopped in front of the house next to the Louis's truck, and she set the brake and wrapped the lines around a rod by the seat and told Katherine to stay in the buggy until she came back, and then she herself approached the house. A pall of fear had settled on her, her feet felt heavy, as if she were dragging a heavy chain behind her, and she felt that something was pulling her backward. She knocked on the door and called, "Mr. Louis." She stood waiting. Nobody was in the house. Louis and Alex were in the backyard, talking about Alex's trip to Italy. As soon as they heard her voice, Alex asked in horror, "Is that the marshal? Is he here to arrest me?"

Louis instantly feared that all his plans would be ruined. He hid Alex in his boat and then went to peek from the corner of the house, where he saw a little girl sitting in a buggy and a woman standing at the front door calling his name. He had never seen them before and he wondered how she knew his name. Still they did not appear to present a threat to him, or so he told himself. So he walked toward Laura and said with a smile, "How can I help you?"

Laura stepped toward him and said abruptly, "I am looking for my husband, Peter."

Louis froze. Now he felt the danger around him, though he tried to ignore it. "Peter? I don't know anybody by that name."

Laura's lips snarled and her eyes were fierce. Before she said anything, she turned to check on Katherine, who was watching them. Laura composed herself, turned back to Louis and spoke slowly. She leaned forward tensely and said, "You went to the sea with Peter four days ago, and yet now you tell me that you don't know him. Your neighbor, Sam saw you that day. Tell me, where is Peter? What has happened to him?

Louis turned to Katherine recognizing her when she was inside Edward Wilson's car and was playing with the steering wheel in front of his house. He turned to Laura, smiled and said calmly, "I am not the one you are looking for. Louis is in the backyard. Look, this is my truck. I came here to get some money he owes me." Then he pursed his lips, paused for a second, and continued. "Now I understand why he sent me to talk to you."

"Is he in the backyard?" Laura asked.

As she moved toward the backyard, Louis obstructed her path. He looked earnestly into her eyes. "I know you are worried about your husband, but you had better stay with your daughter and let me go get Louis."

Laura looked at him with intensity in her eyes and said nothing. Louis went quickly to the backyard. Before he ever reached Alex, he had devised a way to get rid of Laura. He approached the boat and called, "Hey, get out of here."

Alex stood up quickly and asked with fear, "Who was it?"

Louis sighed deeply and said, "Do you know who is here? The wife of the guy you killed two days ago, and she knows that you are the one who killed him."

"What did you tell her?" Alex interrupted him. "You didn't tell her I was here, did you?"

"She already knew you were here."

"Who told her that?"

"She said my neighbor Sam, that black man, told her."

"What should I do now?" Alex asked helplessly. "Where should I go?"

"We have to kill her before she tells somebody else."

"Did she come here by herself?"

"She is here with her daughter. She is very little, maybe five years old."

"Do we have to kill the girl, too?"

"No, we may need that girl. I will tell you what to do with her later, but for now we have to take care of her mother."

Suddenly, Laura appeared in the backyard looking at them with predatory eyes under the mistaken impression that Louis was the one in the boat. She approached and looked into his eyes distastefully and said, "Where is Peter?"

Alex climbed out of the boat and chuckled. "Who is Peter? Who is she talking about?" he said, looking at Louis. Louis slowly moved and stood behind Laura. As soon as she grabbed Alex's collar, he attacked her from behind, put his hand over her mouth, and began to laugh loudly in order to muffle her weak cries for help. Alex laughed as well, so all Katherine heard was their laughter. As Laura struggled to get away, Louis gestured with his head toward the barrel full of water that was next to the boat, and they pulled her over to it and dunked her head under the water. When they were sure she was dead, they hid her in the boat, and Louis walked to the front of the house and over to the buggy.

Katherine sat holding her doll in her arms, looking at the corner of the house for mother. As Louis came toward her by himself, she thought her parents might have seen each other in the backyard and were waiting for her there. Louis approached her slowly. His eyes were cruel, but the rest of his face tried to appear welcoming. "Hi, pretty girl, I am Louis. What is your name?"

Katherine looked at the long burn mark on his face and the spot of blood in his eye and replied, "Katherine."

"Oh, your daddy has told me about you many times. I remember that day you came here with him."

Katherine recognized him. She nodded gently and asked, "Is my daddy here?"

"He was here earlier, but he went somewhere," Louis said with a smile. "My brother and I are going to go meet him today." Then he put his hand on her shoulder and said kindly, "You know, Katherine, your dad is one of my best friends."

"Where is my mom?" Katherine asked.

"Oh, your mom…" Louis paused and pointed. "She went to my neighbor's house. That black man. She told me that she left something over there and she will be right back. She also told me to take you into the house until she comes back."

Katherine looked into Louis's eye and focused on the spot of blood there. Something was wrong. She said politely, "I didn't see her go over there."

"She took a shortcut from the backyard. That's why you couldn't see her from here. Let's go inside. It is getting dark. Your mom will be back in a minute." Then he hugged her, took her in the house, and sat her on a chair. "I am going to get my brother from the backyard so we can go meet your daddy. You just wait for me here." He left the room and closed the door behind him.

Katherine looked around the house. There were two broken wooden chairs in the corner and a broken glass on the floor. On the table were a few dirty plates and some half-eaten pieces of bread. The squeaking of mice could be heard from the kitchen. It was a cold house. Katherine had never seen such a place, but she did not mind, for she knew she would not be there for very long.

The afternoon waned and gave way to the night. Alex was still waiting in the backyard when Louis returned. When he saw him, he asked hurriedly, "Where is the girl? Are we going to kill her?"

"No, I told you that we need the girl. I have an idea. I will tell you what to do." Alex listened to him, with clueless desperation.

"I thought about it all this time," said Louis confidently. "I think she should accompany you to Italy."

Alex looked at him bewilderedly. "What do you mean? You want me to take her with me?""Listen to me," said Louis cautiously. "You know the marshal is looking for you, and he has probably notified other police stations to be on the lookout for you. But if you change your clothes and take this girl with you, they won't recognize you."

"You are a genius," Alex muttered. He rubbed his thick hands together and stuttered breathlessly, "I will take her with me and sell her over there in Italy. I have a good customer for her, who will give me five bucks." Then he smiled wistfully. "Maybe I can trade her for some bottles of beer or whisky."

"You can do whatever you want with her when you get to Italy."

Alex scratched his stubbly beard and chuckled. "Don't worry; I know how to take care of her."

Louis looked around and said, "Listen to me, her name is Katherine and she doesn't know her father is dead. I told her that he is our friend and we are going to meet with him tonight, so she agreed to come with us."

Alex nodded his head in agreement.

"You should know her father's name is Peter," continued Louis.

"He was not Brandy?"

"His family knew him as Peter." Then he put his hands on his shoulders and said, "You go inside the house now and shave. Get ready and wait for me there."

"Where are you going?"

"I am going to get your suit. I forgot to bring it this afternoon. By the way, in case she asks for her mom, just tell her that we went to buy something for her dad and we will be back soon. She believes you are my brother and don't forget to be very nice to her." Then they cautiously went to the front of the house, and Louis got in his truck and drove away.

When Katherine heard the sound of the engine, she immediately went to the window and looked outside as the truck pulled away. She noticed the buggy was still in front of the house. She felt lonely and scared. Just then the door opened and Alex clomped in. His eyes searched the room and found her standing by the window looking at him. He said with his friendliest face, "Hi, Katherine."

Katherine looked at him with fear. She had never seen such a horrible face. He was like a monster. She asked, "Where is my mom?"

As Alex looked at her, he tried to recall what all Louis had told him. He chuckled and said, "Your mom and my brother went to buy something for your daddy. They will come back very soon, and we will all go to see your daddy together."

Katherine grew very scared at the thought that she was alone in the house with this horrible man. She looked out the window into the darkness, wondering why her mom did not take her with her. Why didn't she tell me she was leaving?" Then she remembered that Alex was her dad's friend and she should not be afraid of him. Alex went to her and closed the curtain. "Come, Katherine, sit down. I want to get ready before your mom and my brother come back." He put his hand on her shoulder and pushed her gently to the chair.

Katherine sat quiet as a stone and looked down at her doll in her arms. One of her eyes was always on the door and her ears listened for the sound of the truck.

An hour later Louis returned. As soon as Katherine heard the truck she ran to the door. But before she could open it, Alex ran up to her and said firmly, "Don't open the door. You just stay here and let me see who it is." Then he walked outside and closed the door behind him.

Louis climbed out of his truck and asked, "Where is the girl?"

"She is inside."

Louis turned and saw her looking at them through the window. "Did she ask you about her mom?"

"Yeah, but I told her that two of you went to buy some stuff for her daddy--that's what you told me to say."

Louis walked to the front door, pulled out a key from the pocket of his pants, locked the door, and walked to the backyard. As Alex followed close behind he asked, "What do you want to do with her mom?"

"We need to make sure nobody can find her," answered Louis.

"We can bury her."

"No, the dogs will dig her up." Louis took a deep breath. "I know. We can weight her down and throw her in the sea." His eyes went to a large rock that was on the ground next to his fishing boat. That one should be heavy enough to do the trick."

They went over to a little rowboat in one corner of the backyard by the fence and moved it to the water's edge.

Katherine stood by the window, her eyes searching outside for her mother. She looked carefully at the truck. "Where is my mom?" she asked herself. "Why didn't she comeback?" As she was looking outside, she saw two people pulling a little rowboat to the sea. Louis noticed her and said, "The girl sees us. I will go inside the house and try to put her to sleep. You take the boat to the water and wait for me there." Then he walked to the house, and Alex did as he was told and dragged the boat to the water's edge.

When Katherine heard the door, she stepped over to it and stood waiting. Louis entered with a smile on his face, holding out some wrapped candies. "These are for you." He hugged her and sat her on the chair.

Katherine looked up at him questioningly. "Where is my mom?"

"She didn't come with me." Louis smiled and squatted in front of her and said, "I took her to buy some gifts for your daddy, and she is waiting for us in the train station to go to your daddy. But before we go, I have a little job outside to do. It will take only a few minutes."

Katherine looked at the burn mark on his face and the spot of blood in his eye for a long time without saying anything.

Louis quickly unwrapped a candy, put it in her palm and continued. "I better go finish my job so we can get ready and go to your mom as soon as possible. She is waiting for us." Then he stood up, went to the window, closed the curtain and said, "You'd better not look outside at this time of the night. Just sit here and eat your candy. I will be back pretty soon." Then he went out, locked the door behind him and walked to the water's edge to the boat, where Alex was. Alex had taken Laura to the boat while Louis was inside the house with Katherine.

As soon as he saw Louis, he stood up and went to him.

"She is in the boat."

Louis went and looked into the boat for a second and asked, "Where is the rock?"

"What do you mean?"

"Stupid, we need that rock to weight her down, the rock that I showed you in the backyard."

"Oh, yeah."

"Go, bring it, and don't forget to bring some rope. It is in the fishing boat."

"I know where it is." Then he ran up the beach to the backyard, and soon he returned carrying the big rock on his shoulder and the rope in his hand. They put everything in the boat, slid it into the sea and got in, and Louis steered the boat carefully. The gentle wind blowing softly from the bay to the sea pushed the boat gently in the direction Louis was headed. It seemed that everything was with them.

After five minutes, Louis looked at the shore to estimate the depth of the water, pulled the paddles out, put them in the boat and said, "Here it is deep enough." Then he tied Laura to the rock and together they threw her overboard, the heavy rock pulling her body down to the bottom of the sea in a short time.

Louis looked at the bubbles that came to the surface for a few seconds and said with venom, "Go to your dear husband."He turned his face to the shore, looked at his house, and thought of Katherine, and then he drove the paddles into the water, rowing the boat back to the beach. Very soon, they landed and hauled the boat to the backyard. Louis's eyes searched the darkness like an owl's, and he went over and picked up a crowbar that was leaning against his house.

Alex was standing beside him. "What are you going to do with that?"

"We have one more thing to do before we go back inside the house."

"What is that?"

"We got to kill that black man."

"What are you talking about?"

"Sam, my neighbor," Louis said, pointing to Sam's house with the crowbar in his hand.

"Why do you want to kill him?"

"He is the only one who knows that the little girl and her mom came to my house today. He could get us in a lot of trouble."

"Yeah, you are right," said Alex, and he grabbed the crowbar from his hand and shifted it quickly and sniffed the air and nodded his head in agreement. Then they made their way toward Sam's house. When they got there they carefully moved to a corner of the house, stayed there and looked around. When Louis was sure nobody was around, he moved slowly to the window and peered inside through the curtain, which was slightly open. Sam sat on the floor in the living room by the fireplace, repairing a fishing net. There was nobody else to be seen, and Daniel was asleep in the bedroom. Louis kicked the ground with his foot to attract his attention; then he repeated it quickly so that it sounded like somebody was running outside. When Sam noticed the sound, he stood up, picked up a stick and walked out. Louis quickly stepped back to the corner, deeper into the shadows, beyond where Alex stood, and lay on his back on the ground. Alex stood ready, swinging the crowbar back and forth. Sam opened the door slowly and he looked first at his boat, which was near the water's edge. The night was dark, but he could see that his boat was safe. He closed the door and went to make sure nobody was inside it. Just then, he heard a faint sound on the side of the house, and he turned and saw a dark figure lying on the ground, moaning weakly. He held the stick tightly in his hand and called, "Who is there?"

Louis moaned and said a weak voice, "Help."

Sam stepped cautiously toward him and asked, "Who are you? What are you doing in here?"

The man's face was obscured by the darkness, but Sam could hear moaning and see the figure stretching out his hand a weak voice saying, "I am dying, please help me."

Sam stepped over to help, until he stood over the figure. Louis had covered his face with his jacket. Sam bent down and asked, "What is the matter?" At that point, Alex attacked him from behind, bringing down the crowbar on Sam's head until he fell on the ground. The blood oozed down like a little brook, and soon Sam stopped moving. Louis stood up, grabbed the crowbar from Alex and hit Sam several more times to make sure he was dead. Then, they walked down the shore and threw the crowbar into the sea and then returned to Louis's house. However, before they went inside, Louis told Alex to take the buggy away.

Katherine was sitting on the chair, listening to the splash of little waves on the beach and the occasional sounds of seagulls. She was crying softly, for she was alone without her parents. She suddenly heard the sound of the horse and buggy, and she quickly went to the window, opened the curtain and saw someone walking in front of the horse, holding the rope and leading it eastward. Just then, the door opened and Louis entered, holding a bag and a suit in his hands. "I am sorry it took so long, Katherine, but we are going to leave now. My brother just took your buggy to his house, so that his family can take care of the horse while we are away. He will be back in a minute and then we can go to your mom."

Katherine was standing by the window, looking at him without saying a word. Her eyes were still wet from crying. Louis approached and put his hand on her shoulder and said, "You should be happy that you are going to see your parents."

As Katherine looked up at him, the door opened and Alex entered. Louis handed him the suit and said, "Come on, put it on. We don't have much time. Katherine's mom is waiting for us in the train station." Alex quickly changed his clothes in the other room, and he returned to the living room, stood in front of the mirror and looked at himself smiling. It was a dirty mirror, covered with oily fingerprints, and it had a long crack running from the bottom to the top. He tightened his belt, combed his hair with his fingers, and put on the glasses that Louis had brought it for him. He looked at himself for a long time. He seemed mesmerized by his own appearance. He looked back at Louis, chuckled and said proudly, "I really look different." Then he picked up a half-eaten loaf of bread from the table, wolfed it down, drank from a jar and belched loudly while smiling. His silver tooth glimmered.

"It is time to go," said Louis. Then he held Katherine's hand, and they all walked outside to the truck and he sat her in between he and Alex, and he sped toward the city.

He knew it would be risky to go to the central train station downtown, as someone or even the police might recognize them. He knew he was close to finishing his job of sending them out of the country, and he did not want to take a chance to ruin all his plans, so he took another road to get to the next station, which was five miles out of the city. When they got there, he pulled over in the darkness a little past the station and looked down at Katherine, who was looking all around, expecting to see her mom. He told her to stay in the truck and got out with Alex and they walked toward the station, where he told Alex everything he needed him to tell her while they were travelling to Italy, for he knew Alex on his own would not be able to come up with plausible answers to all of her questions. Louis looked all around the station, and when he was sure there were no policemen there, they went back to the truck and he opened the door and said, "Your mom is coming on the train from downtown. We will wait for her in this station. She will arrive in ten or fifteen minutes." Katherine looked at him without complaint, thinking it might be disrespectful if she asked him too many questions. Her eyes searched the darkness through the windshield, and it seemed she had no choice but to accept what they told her. Wanting to prepare her for her trip to Italy as well as cover his own tracks, Louis looked around and said, "Katherine, listen to me. You shouldn't talk to any strangers before you see your mom, because the police will put children in jail if they find them travelling around without their parents. You have to be careful, and you should call my brother 'Dad' while we are waiting for your mom." Katherine looked at him with fear in her eyes and nodded her head in agreement.

"Good," said Louis. "Now, I'm leaving to park my truck at my house. I will join you at the train station in a few minutes before your mom comes." Then he took her out of the truck and drove away, and Alex held her hand as they walked to the train station.

It was a small station. There were three men and a woman sitting on benches waiting for the train, and their heads turned to them as they walked up. Alex looked at them for a few seconds and continued to an empty bench away from where they were. He was glad to see there were no policemen there. Katherine looked up at a big round clock that was hanging from the ceiling on platform three. It showed 10:20pm, which was past her bedtime. She was cold and hungry, and her mom's face appeared before of her eyes, waving at her from the window of the train. She imagined her mother giving her a warm hug and something to eat. Little did she know she would never see her mother again. She kept looking at the tracks waiting for her mom.

The train finally arrived at 10:45pm. Katherine was so happy, she stood up and peered anxiously at the windows of the cabins to see her mother. The train stopped and a few people got out. Alex held her hand and said, "Let's go."

"Where is my mom?" asked Katherine.

"She is on the train. Let's go find her." Alex pulled her after him onto the train.

When the passengers got on, the train whistled and left the station, headed to the city of Boston. Katherine' eyes were on the door of the cabin. There were two men sitting in front of them, and she was afraid to ask Alex about her parents in front of strangers, for she was afraid she would be arrested by policemen if they found out she was without her parents. She remained awake for the entire trip, eager to see her mother. The train reached Boston at 4:55a.m. The central train station in Boston was the last stop, and all of the passengers got out. Katherine looked around as Alex led her by the hand through the crowd. As soon as they got off the train, she asked, "Where is my mom?"

Alex had almost forgotten about her mother. He looked around, smiled vaguely, cleared his throat, spat into the street and tried to remember what Louis had taught him to say. "I didn't see her either. It is very hard to see her in this crowd. Don't worry, we are going to see her in the port in ten minutes. You know, Katherine, we need to take a ship to get to the place where your daddy is." Then he called a taxi and did not let her ask another question, and they headed to the port of Boston.

Soon they reached the port, where they walked over, sat on an iron bench and waited for the booths to open to buy their tickets. Katherine looked around to make sure nobody was around to hear them. The ships were easily seen in the lights of the port, and a few employees were working about hundred feet away. "This is like the place I came with my mom and Edward Wilson a few days ago," Katherine said to herself. Then she looked around for her mother and asked him, "Where is she?"

Alex looked around as he was trying to think of something to tell her. "She should be on her way here."

Katherine looked at the ships and thought of her father overseas. "Where is my daddy?"

Alex was ready with an answer. "Your daddy is in a nice place. I am sure you are going to love it. We are going to take one of these ships to go there soon."

Katherine looked at him for a long time, and then she looked all around for her mother. She was cold and hungry, and lonely, and she began to cry. "I want my mom."

Afraid she would draw the attention of the police if she kept on crying, Alex said, "Your mom should be here in the next few minutes." Then he took off his coat and put it around her shoulders. "I know you are cold. Put this on. It will keep you warm."

Katherine dropped her head down without saying anything and cried quietly. Apparently she had no choice but to wait for her mother with Alex, and because he was her father's friend she should listen to him. As she sat on the bench, squeezing her doll against her chest, she kept her eyes on the lookout for her mother. She was very tired, and in a little while, as she was thinking of her house and the cozy bed that waited for her there, she leaned against Alex and fell asleep. When Alex was sure that she was asleep, he laid her on the bench and covered her with his coat. He stood up, lit a cigarette, threw the match without blowing it out and began pacing. He smoked nervously, his eyes searching every nook of the port as they waited to board the ship and leave the country forever. For an hour, he chain-smoked until he finished the pack of cigarettes, then he inspected the pockets of the coat that was covering Katherine, but there were no more cigarettes there. He sat on the bench beside her, and as soon as he made contact with the cold iron bench, he turned his face to her and stared at his coat. Then he reached over to the coat, removed it carefully from her and put it on. It was cold and Katherine hadn't enough clothing. She wore a long dress and a jacket that her mother had made for her. She was cold and curled up like a little bird in it's nest. Dewdrop covered everything outside, and her rubber boots glimmered in the lights of the port. She had never before spent the night outside. The stars were shimmering faintly, gradually giving way to the light of the sun.

By sunrise, a few people had arrived at the port. When the booths opened at 7:00a.m., Alex was the first in line to buy tickets, and after making the purchase he returned to where Katherine lie on the bench. She was still asleep, still in the same position. At that time, a woman headed to the booths stopped and looked down at Katherine and said to Alex, "I think she is cold. Don't you have anything to cover her? She will get sick."

Alex was scared, and for a moment, he thought that she had recognized her. He took off his coat, covered Katherine and gazed at her without saying anything.

"That's better," said the woman, who smiled and continued to the booths.

Alex's hands searched nervously for a cigarette in his pockets as his eyes followed her, but he found nothing. He noticed a shop open by the booths, and he quickly went and bought three packs of cigarettes and came back and lighted a cigarette and began pacing again. He did not wake her up for he didn't want her to ask him about her parents and risk ruining his plan before they got on the ship. She slept until she awoke at 10:30am by the noises of the large crowd that had gathered in the port. The ship was scheduled to depart at 11:30am, and the passengers were in the port getting ready to board. Katherine sat on the bench looking around, and soon she remembered where she was. She saw Alex standing in front of her, looking at the ships as he smoked a cigarette. "Mr. Alex, where is my mom?"

Alex bent over her, put his hand on her shoulder and said, "Hush, don't ask me about your parents in here. Your mom was here while you were asleep, but she didn't want to wake you up. She went in the ship to check out the cabin and to store her suitcase." Katherine was very happy to see her mom soon, and her eyes went to the ship.

Ten minutes later Alex said, "You know what, we'd better get on the ship. Your mom might not find us in this crowd. We can see her on the ship." He drew her gently, holding her by the wrist, and they went aboard with the last passengers.

The deck was filled with passengers waving at their friends and relatives in the port. The sea was calm and the sun was shining in a clear sky, and it promised to be an enjoyable trip. However, none of these things interested Katherine, not without her parents. Her eyes searched and her ears listened for any sign of her mother until the ship departed from the port and went away from the city of Boston, though she was still hoping to see her mother in another part of the ship very soon. For Katherine the trip was a boring one without her parents, and she was very sad and cried secretly at night. She looked for her mother everywhere on the ship. She did not ask anybody about her parents for fear of Alex, and she stayed away and kept quiet when somebody approached to talk to her. She had lots to say, but she just waited for the moment that she would get the opportunity to see her parents again in a new land.

Chapter 9

After twelve days, the ship arrived at the port of Liverpool in the middle of the day. Katherine's eyes were searching for her parents as Alex pulled her among the crowd of people. She looked around outside at the port and the city from the deck. It was a new and different land. Alex led her out of the port and called a taxi to take them to the train station. Before they got into the taxi, Katherine asked him, "Where is my mom?"

"We are going to see her in the place where your daddy is," said Alex, and they got in the taxi and headed to the train station.

Alex leaned back against the seat, looking outside victoriously. There was nothing more to fear, and he was proud of himself for getting them this far without any problem. Next, he would sell her to somebody in Italy.

As Katherine was thinking of her parents, she noticed the inside of the car was different than the cars in America. She looked at the driver and said excitedly, "The steering wheel is on the right side."

As Alex was looking ahead at the road, he answered dryly, "Yeah, it is."

The taxi driver looked at Katherine in the rearview mirror and said, "You are very clever. You realized that difference right away. Yeah, in England, the steering wheel is on the right side." Then he turned to Alex and said, "Your girl is very clever."

Alex kept looking outside without saying anything.

"It is a long trip from America," said the driver. "How many days were you on the ship?"

"I counted them. It took about twelve days," answered Katherine.

Alex sensed danger, afraid that Katherine might say something about her parents. He turned and frowned at her and said, "You talk too much."

Katherine saw his anger, and she dropped her head and kept quiet.

"Twelve days! You must be so tired," said the driver, who waited for a response.

Alex looked outside angrily and ignored him. When the driver saw this, he just drove and kept to himself.

In a few minutes, they reached the train station, and Alex and Katherine got out of the car. Then, Alex bent over her, put his heavy hand on her tiny shoulder and said, "I told you many times, don't talk to strangers, but you don't listen to me at all. If somebody finds out you are not my daughter, you will be reported to the police and they will put you in jail... and you will put me in big trouble along with you."

For the first time Katherine sensed something strange about his behavior, although she thought that it was through some fault of her own.

Alex continued. "Listen to me. If I see you talk to somebody just one more time, I will leave you and go my own way."

Katherine was very scared. She was alone and helpless in a new land, and she couldn't go anywhere by herself and it appeared Alex was the only person who could take her to her parents. She began to cry, "Please don't leave me alone. I won't talk to anybody, I promise. Please don't leave. I want to go to my parents."

"Don't cry. Wipe your tears and follow me," Alex hissed at her, and he turned away from her and walked to the train station. Katherine wiped her tears away and trotted after him.

In ten minutes, they boarded a train to the southern city of Dover. There was a port there, so they could go to Calais, France by ship, and it was the best way to go to Italy. At 5:00pm, they reached the port of

Dover, and in two hours, they left the port bound for Calais, France.

Katherine obeyed his every word without question. She didn't even dare to look into his reproving eyes. She sat with elaborate silence the entire way. In her mind, sometimes her parents were near and sometimes they were far away. She had a lot to say, and she was waiting for the moment that Alex would let her talk.

In a few hours, they got to the port of Calais, and after that they went to the city of Paris, where they caught a train to Italy that arrived at 1:00a.m.

It was a long trip for Katherine, and she was very tired. She sat quietly until the train reached the station in the city of Genoa. Alex was so happy to be finally at liberty. He laughed loudly and said, "This is the city where your parents are. Now you can talk as much as you like."

Katherine looked around at the people getting out of the train. She said, "I think my mom is with my daddy." It was the first sentence she had spoken in a long time.

"Sure," said Alex laughingly. "We'll just take a taxi and go to them. In the next few minutes you are going to see them." They walked out of the train station and into the street.

Katherine was very happy after going so long without seeing her parents. The people she passed in the street looked at her with kindness and familiarity, but the language they spoke was totally alien to her. Some of the old people said to her smilingly, "Ciao, bella." After hearing the same word a few times, she became curios and asked Alex what it meant. Alex paused and then answered, "Don't mind what those stupid people are saying." Then he called a taxi and they went to a neighborhood outside the city called Tor San Lorenzo.

They arrived there at 5:30 in the afternoon. Finally, they got out of the taxi. Alex stretched his arms and his joints popped, and he threw his hat and glasses away and said, "I don't need those anymore. Now let's go see your parents."

Katherine looked at the hat and the glasses on the ground. She began to feel scared, but the feeling quickly passed when she thought about seeing her parents.

She looked around as they entered a narrow, rutted road. It was an old neighborhood with a stony road, and there were a few houses lining the road. It was very quiet and depressing to her. After five minutes, she saw an old woman standing in front of a house, smiling at her. Her face was motherly and benign and her eyes twinkled with friendship. She was a small woman with a soft voice. Her name was Rosa, and she was nearly seventy and had been living in that neighborhood for all her life.

Alex went to her and asked, "Do you know if Stefano and his wife, Carla, are still living in this neighborhood?"

Just then, Rosa's dog came from the backyard, stood beside her and gazed at Alex. It was a big, white dog called Bianco, and he did not take his eyes off him, as if he sensed Alex was a bad person. Rosa suspected him as soon as she heard the names, Stefano and Carla, for everybody knew they had a bad reputation. She looked at him carefully. His clothes were clean, but his rough face and cruel eyes and smile did not look right. "Is that her father? He might be a smuggler and intends to sell her to them, she thought to herself. She looked at Katherine compassionately and smiled a little. Katherine smiled back, as if she had finally found somebody who understood her.

Alex took a step toward her and asked again, "Do you know them?"

"You mean the people who keep the gypsy kids in their house?" asked Rosa.

Alex laughed a little. "Oh, yeah."

Rosa nodded without saying anything.

Alex turned to Katherine. "Let's go. It is getting dark." He walked down the road and Katherine walked after him.

Ten minutes later, he stopped halfway across a little stony bridge and pointed. "See that two-story house? Your mom and daddy are waiting for you over there."The house was a quarter a mile away and was hard to see.

A little nighthawk was stalking a mouse that had come out to take a little piece of bread on the bridge behind them. Katherine quickly turned back and sensed danger. Dark seemed to bring with it scary things.

"Let's go," said Alex. Then they walked toward the house.

The house was a place that was used to train gypsy kids for beggary and pick-pocketing. Everything they got they brought back to the owner of the house, Carla. None of the residents of that neighborhood would associate with her, and they stayed far away from her and the gypsies.

Katherine's eyes searched for lights in the house from afar. It was dark, and it looked like nobody was living there. It was dark when they got there.

127

Three gypsy girls ages seven, ten, and eleven stood in front of the house, waiting for their two friends, who had gone to steal some firewood from the backyard of a neighbor's house. The other gypsies were inside the house.

When Alex and Katherine approached, Alex asked, "Hey, do you live here?"

The ten-year-old, whose name was Vanessa, stepped forward and asked, "Who are you? What do you want here?"

Alex said angrily, "Where is Stefano? Is he inside? I want to see him."

The girl chuckled. "Stefano? You're a little late. He died a couple years ago." The three girls formed a half-circle around Katherine, and the older one asked, "What is your name?"

Katherine looked at them without saying anything.

The girl looked up at Alex. "Can't she talk?"

"She doesn't understand Italian."

"Where is she from? Are you going to sell her to Miss Carla?"

"It is none of your business. Tell me, where Carla is?" said Alex.

"Miss Carla is in the house," the girls answered together.

"Tell her Alessandro is here, Stefano's partner," said Alex.

The three girls ran inside the house quickly.

Katherine looked at the house. It was not like she had imagined. It was an old, stone house, and the front yard was filled with trash. She saw two bats hunting some moths in the weak light that came through a worn-out curtain, their dark furry bodies beating against the glass of a second-floor window. Katherine shivered a little and looked around her into the darkness and then quickly turned her face to the door and waited for her parents to come out and hug her. The door opened and the three girls came out and said, "Come on in. Miss Carla is waiting for you upstairs." The girls ran upstairs and stood behind the door of Carla's room, waiting for them.

Alex went up the wooden stairs and Katherine followed him. The steps creaked as they were stepped on, and they threatened to break under Alex's heavy tread. There was only one candle upstairs on the rail, shimmering its light onto the stairway, which was the only ingress to the rooms of the house. Carla's room was the first room at the top of the stairs, so she could monitor all associations from her room.

Once upstairs, a door opened and an ugly girl in her twenties came out and looked at them for a second and said curtly, "Come on in." This was Carla's daughter. Alex and Katherine stepped inside and stood in the middle of the room in front of a wicked-looking woman. This was Carla. She was sixty-two years old and had long, gray hair that was unkempt. She sat on an old rocking chair and gently teetered back and forth. Her right hand held a coin, which she rolled back and forth over her knuckles, making it appear and disappear, and making it spin and sparkle in the light of the candle. But her eyes were as steady and cruel and unblinking as a hawk's eyes. Katherine stared at her with anxiety and fear. Then she turned around, hoping to see her parents. Everything was strange and scary. A few scraps of loose wallpapers were hung here and there, and some parts of the wall were covered with cartons. There were no pictures on the wall, and all the gypsies were clad in dirty old dresses. To Katherine everything seemed unwelcoming and cold. Her eyes searched every corner, and she looked up at Alex with frightened, questioning eyes and waited to hear from him about her parents. Alex looked at Carla and said, "The girls told me that Stefano died two years ago. What happened?"

Carla said carelessly, "He was always sick--he is better off dead."

Alex nodded.

"Where have you been? Nobody has seen you in a long time," said Carla.

"I went to America to stay with my cousin, Louis, when I was released from the prison in Genoa."

"Why did you come back here?"

"I didn't want to live there anymore."

"You are well dressed. Did you bring any money with you?"

"Hah, money?" Alex smiled and took off his jacket. "Even this suit is borrowed."

"Don't you have any place to go? Or were you expecting to stay here tonight for free?" asked Carla angrily.

Alex knew he had to pay her a tribute so that she would let them stay in her house, so he smiled and put his hand on Katherine's shoulder and said, "I brought this girl for you. She is so smart. I think she can be the smartest girl in this house."

Carla stared at Katherine coldly. Her eyes were hard and cruel and bitter. She asked listlessly, "Who is she? Is she your daughter?"

"She is an orphan. Her name is Katherine, but you can call her whatever you want. She is a gift for you."

Carla hummed under her breath and nodded, seeming to be satisfied.

Katherine did not understand what they were talking about, and panic welled within her. "Where are my parents? What is going on in this house?" she asked herself. She looked up at Alex and saw a contemptuous smile on his face, and when she could not wait any longer she finally asked him, "Where are my parents?"

Alex burst out laughing and did not stop for a long time. Carla asked, "What is going on?"

"She wants her parents," answered Alex as he was laughing.

Katherine asked again, "Where are my parents?"

"Your parents? They're dead. Louis and I killed them and threw them into the sea, so you want to know where they are. They are at the bottom of the sea, that's where."

Katherine froze, looking up at him. She remembered the night that she was in Louis's house, looking at them through the window, pulling the boat toward the sea. Everything went dark in front of her eyes, as it seemed she was having a nightmare. It was the worst thing she could ever imagine.

"Everything I told you was lie, continued Alex. "You will never see your parents again."

Katherine burst into tears, and she cried hoarsely, "Murderer!"Then she kicked at his legs and punched him in the stomach with both hands.

Suddenly Alex's expression grew dark and dangerous. His face lost its smile and all the cruelty that was hidden in him came into it. He grabbed her hands and held them in one of his and with the other hand he pinched her chin between his thumb and forefinger and said cruelly, "Hush and listen to me. You don't have anybody to help you here."Then he threw her on the floor.

Carla's daughter picked up her doll from the floor and threw it to Carla and Carla snatched it out of the air and cried, "Take her to the other room."

Alex kicked Katherine in the back and said, "Come with me."

From the floor, she shouted through her tears, "No, no..."

Alex grabbed her dress and dragged her behind him while Carla's daughter and the three other girls walked laughingly along with them. As Katherine writhed on the floor and struggled to release herself, she called desperately for help. Alex dragged her to the room where the other gypsies were, and he stood over her and said, "This is your room. Look, you are just like everyone else here, and like everyone else you are going to go begging with them to make money for Carla tomorrow." He left the room, and Carla's daughter slammed the door after him.

Katherine lay on the ground crying. She picked up her head and looked around. It was a long room with a big window that was covered with tattered curtains, dust and cobwebs obscuring the glass, lit dimly by two candles, and there were twenty gypsies ages two to eighteen, and two of the girls held babies in their arms, and everybody was looking at her. Katherine turned away and continued weeping. She thought of the word orphan, feeling crushed by the future that Alex had described to her. All possibilities had ended, there was no escape, life had no meaning to her anymore. The girl who was named Vanessa and the two girls who were with her swarmed around her like hyenas around a corpse. Suddenly Vanessa noticed the necklace that Katherine was wearing, and she bent over her and stroked it with her fingers. As Katherine realized what she was doing, she grasped her necklace tightly and held it. When Vanessa saw her resisting, she cried, "Give it to me. I don't want to rip it off the chain." Then she brought up her knee and felt around on Katherine's chest and she held her down on the ground by the neck with one hand while the other hand tried to open the chain. The two other girls held her hands and helped Vanessa to wrench away the necklace. Katherine cried, "No, no!" Her hands grappled limply toward the necklace, but it was in vain. She was helpless to get her necklace back. Vanessa put on the necklace, turned to the gypsies, and said smilingly, "See how nice it looks on me? I am going to sleep with it on tonight." Then they all burst out laughing.

A sense of helplessness and hopelessness swept over Katherine. The night was cold and bitter, and there was no warmth to her life at all. It seemed that all was over for her.

Thirty minutes later, when her cries grew weaker, she heard the shriek of an owl from outside, and she picked up her head and looked around. There was nobody else in the room. They had all gone downstairs for dinner. She drew herself to the wall next to the door and leaned against it and stared fearfully at the dark glass of the window and quickly dropped her head down and covered her eyes with her crossed arms and sat there for a long time and cried herself to sleep. She slept there all night. She had nightmares several times, waking with a start as she saw herself in that long room and the gypsies in front of her and all she could do was cry weakly. What good was life for a little girl without her parents? She thought and saw her future as cold and aimless and full of dangers. The room was cold, and she had nothing to cover herself with. She crouched on the floor, leaned her back against the wall, and fell asleep.

Chapter 10

The next morning at 7:00, Katherine was jolted out of sleep by Carla's cry. She was standing in the doorway, screaming, "Get up, get up, why are you all still sleeping? Come on, get in the truck quickly!"

All the gypsies bolted out of bed and ran outside. Katherine thought she was in a nightmare. She sat by the door hugging her knees, frightened, looking up at Carla, then she quickly looked away. Carla called to Vanessa and the other two girls "Take off her dress. Nobody will give her a penny with her looking like this!" Then she walked away. The three girls undressed Katherine by force and dressed her in a long worn-out dress with holes in the knees, and then they took her outside. Katherine was crying, but she could not resist or even protest.

Carla had started the box truck. The body of the truck was severely battered, and the engine sizzled and creaked as she gave it some gas. Carla quickly moved to the back of the truck to make sure everybody was inside. Most of the gypsies were sitting in the truck, and as her eyes adjusted to the dimness, she noticed one of the boys was eating something. He was ten years old. He was eating a cookie. Carla cried, "Hey, you, what are you eating there? Come here."

The boy dropped the cookie and did not move. Carla cried again, "I said, what are you eating?" and she climbed in and searched around in the truck and found the cookie and took the boy out of the truck, pulling his ear with her grimy hand, and said angrily. "I told you all many times that you got to bring me everything you find, but you, stupid boy think you can eat this cookie without telling me. It is your last time to hide something from me." All the gypsies were looking at her without saying anything. Carla cried, "You got it?"

"Yes, Miss Carla." All the gypsies answered together.

Carla nodded as she was swallowing the cookie, and she turned her head back to Katherine, who stood behind her looking into the truck at the gypsies with tearful eyes. Carla approved of the dress that she was wearing, which made her look like the other gypsies.

Carla cried, "Why are you standing there just looking around? Get in the truck, come on." Then she pushed her into the truck.

The truck was a little high, and it was hard for Katherine to put her foot on the broken step to climb in. Vanessa grabbed her hand from the truck and pulled her up roughly. Katherine's legs were gouged by the iron step, and she screamed with pain, but nobody seemed to care. Carla quickly slid the door down behind them, and the truck clanked toward the city of Genoa.

It was dark inside the trailer. Katherine could only make out dark figures around her. They pushed her against the door on purpose every time the truck hit a bump in the road, then they laughed. She cried because of her legs, which were bleeding and burning with pain. Thirty minutes later the truck stopped at its destination. It was a quiet place, where Carla liked to drop the gypsies off in the morning and pick them up before dark. As soon as Carla slid open the back door, the gypsies rushed down, pushing one another out of the truck, but before Katherine could get out by herself, Vanessa kicked her and she fell to the ground, her knees and palms hitting the stones and bleeding more as she cried out.

Carla kicked her again as she turned to Vanessa. "Keep your eye on her, and teach her well. I will see you here at five o'clock." She got in the truck and drove away.

The gypsies broke up into four groups and moved to different parts of the city. Katherine went with Vanessa and the two other girls. She took a little comfort when she saw people in the street. She expected them to look at her with the same welcoming kindness as the day before, but they did not. In their eyes, she was just another gypsy, in her ragged dress, and so the people were cautious and they frowned at her when she stared at them or walked close to them with the other gypsies. There was no help in her new world at all; nobody could even understand what she was saying. She feared everybody, and she had no choice but to follow these gypsies.

At 9:00a.m, they went to a fresh market that was named, "Buon Appetito Amigos." It was the biggest fresh market in Genoa, and many people purchased their fresh vegetables and fruits at that time of the day, which made it the best time for pick pocketing. The youngest girl stayed with Katherine under a tree next to a shop while the other one and Vanessa moved among the crowd. They were experts at recognizing their victims, and very soon, they approached an old woman standing in front of the shop looking at fruit. As they reached her, the girl who was with Vanessa hustled the woman from the side, and when the woman turned to her, Vanessa quickly snatched the purse from her bag from the other side. The woman did not even realize what had happened. Katherine looked on, scared, and frozen in position. She was looking at them with wide eyes, wondering what would happen next. The girls and Vanessa quickly went behind a tree, opened the purse, took the money from it and threw it into a trashcan. Then she turned to Katherine and said with a smile, "Watch and learn."

Katherine did not understand what she was saying, but she could tell they were happy with their success, as they patted one another on the back. Vanessa continued. "Good start. It's going to be a good day." Then they all went to the other side of the market, where it was just as busy. While they were walking, Katherine noticed a man as he pulled his hand from his pocket, and his money fell to the ground. Before the gypsies noticed, she walked to the man and touched his hand and pointed to the money. The man looked, felt at his pocket, and quickly bent and grabbed his money. Then he put his hand on Katherine's shoulder and thanked her. Katherine looked up at him with questioning eyes. The man looked at her dress and took pity on her, and he asked kindly, "Do you need some money?"

Katherine looked up at him, thinking he might be able to help her, but how could she ask him with the gypsies standing so close by, glaring at her angrily. Suddenly, Vanessa ran to her and took her by the arm, drawing her through the crowd. She stopped behind a shop and hit her over the head several times along with the two other girls. Vanessa shouted, "Stupid, you found money and gave it to that man?"

The youngest girl said, "Miss Carla will kill her for that."

"She deserves to be punished," Vanessa added. As they all proceeded to beat her, Katherine dropped her head defenselessly.

At 12:30p.m.the gypsies gathered in a small park. It was the place where they ate their lunch and took a short break before they started their afternoon work.

Everyone ate something except for Katherine, who sat in a corner under a tree, watching them eat. She hadn't eaten in nearly twenty-four hours, and her lips were cracked from cold and thirst, so she wet them with her tongue. She saw two gypsies drinking water from a faucet in the park, and when they were done, she went over and drank deeply before returning to her place under the tree. As she was looking at the gypsies, one of the boys who was punished by Carla in the morning, said, "Hey, didn't you get anything to eat?" Then he picked up his bread, threw it onto the grass near her and said, "You can have it today, but you've got to get your own lunch tomorrow."

Katherine was starving. She looked down at the bread for a few seconds eagerly before reaching her hand toward it, but before she take it, Vanessa jumped and grabbed it and turned to the gypsies and said, "No, she can't have it. None of you will give her anything to eat. She has to learn how to get her food by herself." Then she took a few steps toward them and continued. "You know what she did today? She found some money and gave it to a man instead of taking it to Miss. Carla."

The gypsies gasped fearfully. Some of them said, "Miss. Carla will get so angry." Some said, "She is not going to give her anything to eat for dinner."

Vanessa added, "She is going to teach her a lesson with that long stick tonight."

All of the gypsies were familiar with that stick, for they had been punished with it many times and all knew the pain it could inflict. Vanessa sat among the other gypsies, grabbed a slingshot from a boy, fitted the leather pouch with a stone and shot it at Katherine. The first stone struck her rubber boot, the next stone, which was shaped like a lentil, hit her on the arm, and all the gypsies laughed. The wound stung like a hot coal. "Ouch," she cried. She turned to them helplessly with tearful eyes and then she closed her eyes with pain and dropped her head down.

How long must I stay with these people? She thought, foreseeing her future as dark and grim.

After a while, Vanessa and the two other girls took her to a busy shopping center. The girl who was ten years old, sat on the ground and stretched out her legs and the youngest one lay down on her side and put her head on her friend's feet and began to shiver, pretending to be sick. The other girl called out, "Please help us. My sister got the flu, and we don't have money to buy any medicine for her. She is going to die if we don't get it for her. Please help us." From time to time, when no one was looking, they looked up at Vanessa and a hint of a smile appeared on their faces. Katherine was standing next to Vanessa and looked down at them. She had never seen such scheming in her life, and it surprised her. A short time later, when they received no sympathy from the people, Vanessa took her finger and tore at a hole that was on Katherine's dress at the knee and said, "You can beg better now." Then she grabbed her by the hand and made her lie on the ground and demanded that she act like the other girls, but Katherine refused and released herself and stood a few feet away from them. Everything they were doing, was bad and she could not accept any of it. Vanessa attacked her like an angry cat, pulling her hair and hitting her over the head several times, and then she returned to the girls, but her eyes never left Katherine.

Katherine hung her head in defeat. She brushed her hair out of her eyes and touched her scalp, which was burning with pain, as she stood by a trashcan on the sidewalk, looking at the people in the street. Some of them passed by without paying any attention to her, while others looked at the tear on her ragged dress, which made her blush inwardly. The word "orphan" sounded hurtfully in her head. For a moment, she smelled the pizza from the shops around, and it made her hungry again. Then she saw it, through the papers in the trashcan--a large piece of pizza. At first, it seemed like a picture to her, then she cleared her eyes and looked carefully. It was a Margherita pizza, and there was dirt on it. It looked like it was dropped on the ground after it was bitten into. She hesitated to take it, although her eyes were on it the entire time. Finally, she seemed to have no choice if she wanted to survive, so she decided to take it. Before she moved to the trashcan she looked back, and she saw the others were still sitting on the ground. When she was sure they were not looking, she slid closer to the trashcan, slowly moving one foot and then the other until she stood over it. Now was her chance. Without drawing their attention, she grabbed it and hid it behind her back, and then she turned around and began to eat as fast as she could. She swallowed some of it without chewing, finishing the pizza without the gypsies noticing.

The next thirty minutes passed quickly, then three more stops in the city, more pandering, more pick-pocketing, until 5:00p.m., when they all gathered at the place where Carla had dropped them off, and they headed back to Tor San Lorenzo.

When they reached home, Carla opened the back door of the truck and went to her room, where Alex and Carla's daughter were waiting, and all the gypsies followed. Alex was looking at the gypsies, who approached Carla one by one, and he asked laughingly, "Did they have a good day?"

As Carla was collecting the money, she said, "I don't know."

"How about Katherine, the girl that I brought?" asked Alex.

At that time Vanessa said angrily, "That princess? Do you know what she did today? She found some money in fresh market and gave it to a man."

Alex immediately turned to Carla. She stopped counting the money, her face exploding with anger, and her right hand went behind her chair to grab her stick.

Vanessa continued. "She disobeyed everything that I asked her to do today. I was going to teach her some of our tricks, but she would not listen to me at all." Before she finished, Carla cried out in a guttural voice, "Alessandro, come with me. It would be better for me if you brought some cats instead of her. They at least would get some mice in this house." Then she walked to the room where Katherine was, and Alex and her daughter and the gypsies ran after her.

Katherine was sitting next to the door when she heard footsteps coming toward her. The door flew open and Carla stood in the doorway. She was holding a long wooden stick, and her rage-filled eyes went down to Katherine. Alex and her daughter appeared next to her. Katherine was very scared, and she dropped her head quickly and crouched against the wall. She knew they were going to punish her again. Alex walked inside, stood over her and said angrily, "You found some money today and give it back? You didn't bring it for Carla?"

Katherine preferred to tell him the truth. Maybe then, they would change their mind and wouldn't punish her. So she picked her head up slowly and said meekly, "The money that I found, it belonged to him. I saw it drop from his pocket' that's why I gave it to him."

"Shut up." Alex pulled her hair and cried, "You have to learn that everything you find, it is for Carla,. Do you understand?"

As Katherine was crying, she said helplessly, "Yes, sir."

Carla pushed Alex aside. "You stand back. I am going to teach her a lesson that she will never forget." Then she began to hit her. Katherine squirmed around her on the floor. Carla hit her hands and arms when Katherine tried to shield herself from the blows. Her feet were the only parts of her body that were protected, as she wore her rubber boots. Everybody was looking at her and enjoyed seeing her suffer. Nobody heard her cry from outside the house, and her cries were meaningless to those inside the house. Then Carla turned to Alex and said, "I will kill her if she does it again." Then she left the room. Alex squatted down beside Katherine and said, "Hey, orphan, did you hear what she said? She will kill you if you do it one more time."

Katherine put her face on the floor and cried without saying anything. Alex pinched her chin with his cruel fingers and picked her face up a little and said, "Look at me, nobody will give you a room and food for free You got to earn them, understand?"

For a few seconds, Katherine looked up at his face and his silver tooth glimmering in the light of the candles, then she closed her eyes. Carla's daughter was standing over them, she took Alex's arm and pulled him away, whispering, "It is enough for tonight, Let's go to my room."

Katherine, her mind racing, with fear, thought, Is this really my life? The street was so harsh, and there was nowhere to run." She cried herself to sleep in the same place as the night before, without a blanket, next to the door.

Chapter 11

The next morning she was jerked awake by the sound of Carla calling out, and for a moment, she looked up at her then quickly looked away. Vanessa grabbed her hands and cried, "Come on. Why are you sitting there? Let's go."

Katherine climbed painfully to her feet. Everybody could see the look of anguish on her face. Her body ached, and she had to force herself to follow them downstairs. When she went out of the house, Carla was already in the truck, cranking the engine. It seemed something was wrong and it wouldn't start. She got out, popped the hood and touched all the wires to make sure they were connected. They were dirty with oil and dust. She cleaned her hands with a rag, then she got back into the truck and tried again, but it still would not start. Some of the gypsies asked, "What is wrong?"

Carla smacked the steering wheel with her palms and said, "I don't know what the hell is wrong with this old truck." Then she got down, touched the carburetor and said, "I think it has a fuel problem. I have to find somebody to fix it." She looked at the road and said, "You know what? I can't find anybody now. You have to go to the city on foot."

The gypsies looked at one another as they estimated the mileage in their heads and talked about the distance they would have to walk. Suddenly, Carla cried, "Did you hear me? Go now! Move it! I will pick you up in the same place at five o'clock."

Everybody answered together, "Yes, Miss Carla." Then they headed toward the city. Katherine was standing outside behind the truck, looking at the gypsies walking in the road. She did not know what was going on. Vanessa ran to her, grabbed her dress and took her to the others. Now Katherine understood she had to walk with the gypsies somewhere. She considered the place where she was yesterday, and although it seemed too far in her mind, she followed them anyway.

After a few minutes, she saw an old woman standing on the porch of a little house, holding an apron and looking at them. It was Rosa, and her big white dog was standing beside her. Katherine remembered her from the very first time Alex brought her to that neighborhood. She stopped in the roadway, staring at her, and Rosa's warm smile let Katherine know she understood very well Katherine's plight. She may have pitied her when she saw her in that ragged dress as she walked down and stood on the stairs and looked at her wounded legs and thought to herself, Poor little girl. She was worried as she thought of the child's bleak future.

As the gypsies were walking up the road toward the city, Vanessa looked back to make sure Katherine was coming. She saw her standing in the road, looking at Rosa, and she cried, "Hey, Princess, what are you doing there? Come on, we can't wait for you all day."

As Katherine followed the gypsies, she looked at Rosa standing on the porch, waving at her with her apron.

The gypsies were walking fast, and Katherine trotted behind them to keep up. It was a long journey, and they had to stop several times to rest their feet. Along the way they raised their hands to try and get a ride from the trucks that passed, but nobody stopped when they recognized them as gypsies. Katherine was so tired, her body was weak, and she ached all over, and whenever she stopped to rest, Vanessa would hit her with a stick so she would follow them. Finally they reached the city around twelve o'clock, and they split up into four groups. At one o'clock they gathered at the same park to eat their lunch. Katherine had nothing to eat, and none of them gave her any of their food. She sat dejected on the grass under a tree, looking down at her wounded legs. A big fly buzzed around her wounds, and sometimes she moved her hands to keep it away. Her body was heavy with pain, and she felt it all the time. The gypsies were tired, and they lay down on the grass to rest after they finished their lunch. Vanessa came to Katherine, pushed her with her knee and said, "Get out of my sight. I am going to take a nap right here." Then she lay down on the grass, pulled out Katherine's necklace from her pocket and said with a smirk, "Thank you for the necklace, Princess. I love it." Then she quickly returned it to her pocket.

One of the boys said, "Hey, why didn't you give that to Miss Carla yet? I am going to tell her."

"I will give it to her tonight," said Vanessa.

"She is going to be angry if she finds out that you have had that necklace for two days. You'll get punished for sure," said the boy.

"She won't give you anything to eat tonight," another boy said.

Vanessa quipped, "Shut up. That is not going to happen because you're not going to say anything. Now, we had better get some rest. We don't have much time." Then she turned over and lay on her stomach, yawned and closed her eyes, her chin braced on her crossed arms.

Katherine sat on the grass a few feet away, her eyes fixed on Vanessa's pocket, when suddenly she saw the necklace drop out onto the grass. She felt happy for a moment as she looked around to make sure nobody was watching. The necklace glistened in the grass, and she could not take her eyes from it. The faces of her parents came before her eyes, and she became sad. That necklace was the only thing of value that had come from them, and it belonged to her. So she decided to get it back. She waited for a long time to make sure all the gypsies were asleep, and then she proceeded, knowing any wrong movement might draw their attention. After fifteen minutes, when she saw no stirring from them, she lay as rigid as a tree limb, and silently, warily, like a snake, she reached out cautiously, got the necklace, pulled it to her and then slipped back to the place where she was. She quickly looked around and considered to hide it in a safe place. The park was not a good hiding place for it might be lost there. She looked down at the pocket of her dress, but it was not a good place either, for the gypsies could find it there easily. For a moment, she looked down involuntary and her eyes settled on her rubber boots. Her boots were the only things that she carried with her all the times and they were the safest place to hide the necklace at that time, so after looking around at the gypsies she hid it in her right boot. As her foot touched the necklace, she felt the encouraging warmth of her family. She did not know what would happen next; she just wanted to hang onto the necklace. She sat there for nearly twenty minutes, until one of the boys woke up and cried, "Hey, wake up, it is getting late."

Vanessa stirred and awakened, sat and looked up at the puffy, wind-driven clouds and warned, "It looks like rain."

The boy said, "I hope it don't rain before we get home." Then all the gypsies walked out of the park. As they were leaving, Vanessa checked her pockets and she cried, "Where is my necklace?" She ran back to the park and looked all around, and after a few minutes she returned to Katherine and the two other girls in her team and said, "Somebody has stolen my necklace."

"Did you search the place where you slept?" asked the little girl.

"Yeah, I did, but it was not there."

"Let's go back and search together. I am sure we can find it," said the other girl, and the three walked to the park and pulled Katherine by the arm after them.

Katherine was very scared. She stood in the middle of the park watching as they searched in the grass all over. After five minutes, Vanessa's eyes went to Katherine and she cried, "Hey, you were beside me the entire time I was asleep." She rushed toward her and looked in her pockets.

Katherine had dropped her head down and she did not move at all. She was careful not to move her feet even a little, so that their eyes would not be drawn to her boots. When Vanessa didn't find the necklace, she hit Katherine on the head, and she went to her friends and searched in their pockets despite their protests. Then she turned to the road and said, "One of those kids has stolen the necklace, I just know it." Then they all left the park with Katherine.

They went to a busy part of the city, sat Katherine down on the ground and handed her a piece of carton with "Help, we need food" written on it and made her beg, but Katherine didn't want to cooperate and she threw it away. The girls pushed her down on the ground and tried forcing her to beg, but she disobeyed again and even threw up her hands to defend herself. It was the first time she had stood against them seriously, as if she were learning how to defend herself in that new land. She stood up, walked over to the sidewalk and looked at them. The girls stormed up to her and hit her over the head repeatedly, and then they sat on the ground to beg but kept their eyes on her. Knowing that she would be punished by Carla that night and worried about having her necklace found by them and taken from her forever, she decided to run away. She looked around at the streets, but it was new ground and she did not know the way. A cold wind struck her, blew up her hair and ruffled her dress. She pushed back her hair with one hand and held her dress down with the other as she looked up at the clouds, which were thickening and curling southward. It was very cold, and the chill breath of the wind went into all the houses of Genoa. "Where can I find shelter away from the gypsies? Who can help me?" she asked herself. She noticed an old blind man standing across the street, holding a walking stick and asking help to cross. His lips fluttered a little and a weak voice came from between them, a voice that trembled, and the jerkiness of his movements and scuffling of his heels were obvious. Katherine ran toward him and helped him to cross the road. The gypsies were looking at her, and before the man thanked her, three of them reached him, clustered around him and searched his pockets for money. Not finding anything, they took Katherine by the arm and quickly left the area.

They went to different places but they were having no luck. At this rate, they would be taking nothing back to Carla. At five o'clock, they went to the place where Carla was waiting to pick them up. She was standing in front of her truck and looking nervously at the road, waiting for some of the gypsies who were late. As soon as she recognized Vanessa and the girls, she took a few steps toward them and asked loudly, "Didn't you see Jovani?"

"Jovani? What has happened?" asked Vanessa.

"One of the boys told me he was chased by a man when he stole his wallet. I hope he was not caught," said Carla.

"Don't worry about him. He is too fast for anybody to catch him," said Vanessa.

Carla turned her face to Katherine, who stood behind Vanessa, and she asked, "Did she get anything today? Was she better than yesterday?"

Answering Vanessa said, "She just disobeyed everything we asked her to do."

Carla looked at her with eyes threatening for a few seconds and said, "Get her into the truck. I know how to punish her tonight."

Katherine did not dare to look into Carla's eyes. She knew they were talking about her and she thought about the long wooden stick and the cold house. Carla felt a raindrop on her face, and she looked up at the cloud-laden sky and said, "We can't stay here long. I don't know what the hell Jovani is doing."

"Look there he comes," Vanessa suddenly cried.

Carla's eyes went to the road, where she saw Jovani running toward them. It was getting dark, but he was recognizable. She cried angrily, "Where the hell were you?"

Jovani approached and handed a wallet to Carla and said breathlessly as he was looking back at the road, "I was chased by a man, but I lost him a few blocks back."

"We have to leave this place right now. Come on, get into the truck." Carla's eyes searched around carefully. They got into the truck with Katherine quickly, and Carla closed the door behind them and drove away toward Tor San Lorenzo.

It was raining now, a few gusty rain showers sat first, that gave way to a strong, steady rain. The rain pattered against the roof of the truck. Katherine was still planning to run away, but she knew it would be hard to find shelter in the rain in the dark, especially when her every move was watched by eyes that were on her at all times. Her necklace was all she thought of. She touched her boot and felt warmth, her boot was still the safest place to hide it. It was raining hard, and Carla couldn't see the way well, although the wipers were on high. The bumpy road was not visible, neither were the ditches nor the sides, and Carla had to drive slowly and carefully.

They finally got home at seven o'clock. Carla quickly got down, slid the back door up and cried, "Close the door behind you." Then she ran into the house. The gypsies rushed in after her as fast as they could, and Katherine was the last one to get out of the truck. She stood in the rain between the house and the truck and saw herself alone, and she realized that it was a good time to runaway. She looked back at the truck to make sure nobody was there, she turned her head to the house and the door swinging on rusted hinges, squealing and banging in the wind, and nobody was there either. She remembered Carla's eyes for a moment, and she knew she would be punished with her long stick, and she might lose her necklace forever. She looked at the uncertain way, and the darkness made her afraid, but she remembered her necklace, the only thing of value she owned. Her will hardened, her eyes went to some weak lights in the distance, and she thought that any of those houses would be better than Carla's. Then she broke into a sprint through the dark rain in the direction that she was brought by Alex. She trotted, slopping through the gravely mud of the road. The rain slanted and swirled under a cold and gusty wind. After a few minutes, she reached the little stone bridge and she stood there to rest a little. The necklace was under her foot and she could not run well, so she pulled off her boot and held the necklace in her hand. As she looked down at it in the dark, thunder crashed and lightning illuminated the night as bright as day. For an instant, she thought she had been seen by the gypsies, but a strobe of lightning brought on temporary blindness, and after blinking a few times to clear her vision, another peal of thunder sounded and she looked at Carla's house for the last time. She bent over and pulled on her boot quickly to get as far away from that place as possible. She suddenly heard strange sounds coming from under the bridge, like stray dogs fighting to keep a place away from the rain. Katherine was very afraid, and her grip tightened on the necklace. She ran toward the closest light, which was shining in front of a little house. As she got there, she knocked on the door and stood waiting; after a little while, the door opened and an grumpy old man stood in the doorway with his hands on the door frame and looked down at her for a few seconds and drunkenly cried, "Hey, gypsy, what the hell you are doing in front of my house? Did that old devil kick you out?"

Katherine looked at him and said panting, "Please help me."

"What damn gypsy language are you talking?" the man cried. "Get out of here, you dirty thief." Then he raised his hand as if to strike her.

Katherine promptly fled down the road. She never thought the man would treat her like that, and gripped by panic, she ran faster still. The blackness of the night and the chilled rain enfolded her, weighing her down with fear. When she reached the next house she knocked on the door and waited, but there was no answer. As she knocked, again she saw the curtain moved a little, but still no one opened the door or turned on the light. In time, she grew sad, discouraged that nobody would help her. She was so tired, so she remained where she was to rest a little. The wind brought voices to her ears, and she thought of the gypsies. She knew that along with Carla and Alex they would come looking for her as soon as they found out that she was not in the house. She became increasingly worried that she would be exposed by the dim light of a lantern hanging in front of the house. Slowly she made her way to the back yard, her eyes frantically searching the shadows. She turned her gaze to the black thing that was by the wall, struggling to recognize it. Thunder crashed and lightning illuminated the backyard. An empty barrel had been overturned. Katherine crouched against the wall beside the barrel. She saw the glimmer of her necklace in the dark and she remembered her parents and began to cry. How will I get through this night? What sorts of things might happen to me?" These frightening thoughts and more came to her mind. Again, thunder crashed and roared, and a magnificent lightning bolt lit the sky, but when the light faded, it left an image of a monster in her head. Every noise evoked panic, and every object was a threat. The creak of the branches in the wind brought the strange and fearful forms of storybook monsters before her eyes, and for a moment, she wanted to leave the place and return to the front of the house, but she remembered Carla and the gypsies and chose to stay there and keep her necklace. She closed her eyes and cried silently.

When Carla noticed Katherine was not in the house, she sent Alex and the gypsies outside to search the neighborhood. She grew angry as she talked and her voice rose, everybody noticing the flash of anger in her eyes. She slapped the long stick against her palm and waited in the house.

Eventually they reached the house where Katherine was hiding. She was crouching beside the house in the back yard crying when she suddenly heard sounds. They were coming closer. She was sure it was the gypsies and that now it was too late to leave. Katherine shivered with fear, trying to stay as still and silent as possible. She thought it was all over and her necklace would be gone forever. They were in front of the house now. Remaining crouched, she glided her body across the house, and reaching the barrel, she pushed it with her right shoulder until it fell over on the ground. At that moment thunder crashed and lightning flashed, and Katherine saw the barrel was open on one end and a snail was stuck inside it. When the light faded, an image formed in front of her eyes, and she realized the safest place to hide was inside the barrel. So she quickly got into it and turned it upside down over her. She caught her breath sharply and listened to the voices, which were coming toward her. Finally, they arrived at the back yard, till they stood right next to the barrel, but the darkness and rain were with Katherine, and they paid no attention to the scuffed areas around the barrel. Katherine's eyes were squeezed shut, as she remained contorted beneath the barrel, holding her breath, her heart thundering in her chest. Her fingers had closed over her necklace tightly. As she stay frozen there for what seemed like an eternity she heard the voices and footsteps begin to go away. Finally, she released her breath and opened her eyes, but she still did not move a muscle. All she heard was the sound of raindrops on the barrel and the creak of branches in the wind and sometimes the roar of thunder. Thirty minutes later, when she was sure that they were gone, she came out from under the barrel. It was still raining hard, as Katherine rose from her crouching position and moved to the corner of the house and looked around before creeping gently to the front, the light of fear in her eyes. She peeked very carefully from the corner of the house. There was no sign of the gypsies. She turned her attention to a house that was about three hundred feet away, and then she ran toward it. When she got there, she stood in front of the door and glanced around before knocking, looking back at the road to make sure the gypsies were not coming. When there was no reply, she knocked again and called out for help, but nobody responded. She looked at the next house, but it appeared to be deserted. A hopeless lethargy settled in her. She was cold and disappointed; every road seemed like a dead end. After standing forlornly in front of the house, looking at the road with tearful eyes, she heard a dog barking in distance, and she remembered the old woman, Rosa, and new hope came to her. Rosa's warm smile appeared before her eyes, and without any hesitation, she ran toward her house her necklace tightly grasped in her hand.

Rosa's dog, Bianco, was sitting on the porch barking aimlessly, and as soon as he saw Katherine approaching from a distance he stood up and went to the stairs and stood there, staring at her curiously without barking, for he sensed no danger from her at all.

Katherine was running on the road toward Rosa's house when she saw a big white dog standing on the porch, looking at her. Immediately she recognized it as Rosa's dog. She stopped in the rain and gazed at him, not daring to get any closer than about forty feet, thinking that maybe Rosa would come out and see her. Bianco recognized Katherine, too, and he went to her. He stood beside her, looking up at her, wagging his tail and licking her cold, wet hands. Katherine froze, looking down at him timidly, but her fear soon went away. Bianco went upstairs and waited for her to follow, and knowing she could not stay in the rain for long and that she had to call Rosa and get help from her before the gypsies returned, she walked slowly up to the front door as her eyes stayed glued on Bianco. She knocked on the door and waited, confident that Rosa would let her in. For the longest time she stood there, and she grew worried again and began casting glances all around, on the lookout for the gypsies. She knocked on the door again and fearfully called, "Please open the door… Please help me."

As the seconds ticked away, she fell into despair, and all her worries returned, for she had come to believe Rosa was her only hope on that scary night. Her body trembled and her teeth chattered with the cold, and she knew she could go no farther in the rain. She sat exhausted next to the door, looking at Bianco, and then she rested her forehead on her crossed arms and thought of the awful things that might befall her that night. At least on Rosa's porch she could feel a little safe and less lonely, with Bianco there, even though she knew the light of the tin lantern hanging over her head could put her in danger with the gypsies.

Rosa was baking cookies to deliver to some of the sweetshop keepers in the city of Genoa tomorrow. It was only source of income, and she had been doing that job for many years. Rosa was a little hard of hearing, and she did not realize anyone was at the door until Katherine had just knocked for the last time. She wiped her hands and went to the door, but before she opened it, she looked out the window and saw Bianco and a blurred little figure crouching next to the door. Immediately Rosa recognized the little girl, and she said to herself, "That's the girl who was here with that man a few days ago, the one with the gypsies, I wonder if she escaped from Carla's house." She quickly opened the door, and Katherine jumped up and turned to her with tearful eyes. Rosa smiled at her, her eyes soft and warm on her like before. She looked at her shivering in her wet dress, the water dripping from her hair. "Poor little girl, come on in." Then she put her arm around her shoulders and guided her inside. Rosa led Katherine over to the fireplace while she went to the bedroom to look for something she could wear. Katherine looked around the small house, which apart from the living room where she stood had one bedroom and a tiny kitchen, where garlands of red peppers and garlic were tacked up to the wall and two bottles of olives stood on the shelves. The light from the candles and the crackling embers in the fireplace dispelled the darkness in the house. Rosa eventually returned holding one of her smallest dresses, although it was still big on Katherine. As Katherine was changing into it, Rosa noticed the bruises on all over her body and she knew Carla had put them there. Rosa took pity on the sad child. She sat her close in front of the fireplace and added more wood until there was a roaring fire. Katherine felt safe and warm, and she was happy that she could save her necklace. She held it out to show Rosa. Rosa looked at the icon, glimmering in the light of the tall dancing flame, and she said with a smile, "It is beautiful."

Katherine clutched the necklace against her chest and said, "It is mine. They had stolen it from me."

Although Rosa did not understand English, she realized what the girl was talking about, she nodded her head gently, held her tightly and kissed her on the cheek. "I know this is yours," she said kindly. Then she went to the kitchen and returned with round tray holding half a loaf of bread and some mashed potatoes that were left over from dinner and a few cookies, along with a glass of water, and put them on the floor in front of Katherine. She handed the bread to her and told her to eat. Katherine was famished and ate everything. Rosa sat beside her, observing her all the times. She knew the girl had suffered at the hands of the gypsies and was scared of the outside world, so Rosa stayed close to her. After she finished her food, she rested her head on her feet and covered her with a blanket, and Katherine fell asleep in front of the fireplace within minutes. Soon thereafter Rosa heard her dog, Bianco barking furiously. She went over to the window where she saw a few dark figures skulking in the back yard, like wolves in search of prey. Rosa recognized Alex and the gypsies and she watched them until they disappeared in the dark. She checked the door to make sure it was locked before returning to Katherine's side. Around midnight, Rosa was awakened by Katherine's cries of, "No, no, this is my necklace." In her dream, Katherine saw Alex and Carla standing outside, eyeing her sinisterly through the window. Rosa checked her forehead and found that she had a high fever, so she quickly brought a bowl of cold water and a towel and stood over her dipping the towel into the water and placing it on her forehead until the fever abated. She took the opportunity to wash her feet, too. She stayed awake all night long nursing her, knowing her illness was serious and that she would need to see a doctor. So at dawn, as Katherine lie sleeping, she set off in her buggy to fetch Dr. Mario whom she had known for many years. He lived between Tor San Lorenzo and the city of Genoa, and because he was the only doctor in the area. He was in high demand and kept very busy. Fortunately, he was home when Rosa got there, and during their journey to Tor San Lorenzo in his car Rosa told him about Katherine's illness.

Katherine was still asleep when Rosa and Dr. Mario arrived. They knelt beside her, and Dr. Mario touched her forehead. "Her fever is too high." He opened his bag, took out a stethoscope and two bottles of syrup and asked Rosa to bring a teaspoon. Rosa quickly complied and sat beside Katherine and stroked her face gently, calling softly, "My dear, wake up. The doctor is here."

Katherine stirred weakly, and her eyes fluttered open. Rosa put one hand on her back, held her hand with the other and helped her to sit up. It was then that Katherine saw the man in front of her, and she turned fearfully toward Rosa, who gave her a reassuring hug and said, "This is Dr. Mario. He is going to give you some medicine so you will feel better." As Katherine looked at the stethoscope on his shoulder, Dr. Mario asked, "What is your name, pretty girl? I am sure it is a nice one." Rosa's mind searched for a name, and finally she said, "Angela."

"It is a nice name," said Dr. Mario who then examined her deliberately for a few minutes and turned to Rosa. "She has the flu. I have some medicine here that should help her to recover in two or three days." He smiled and handed Rosa the syrups and left.

Rosa stayed at home nursing Katherine back to health. She did not even deliver her cookies to the shopkeepers in the city.

Two days later, as she was preparing breakfast, she saw Katherine get out of bed and smiled. Rosa hugged her tightly and cried happily, "Thank God you are well, my little angel."

Just then Katherine heard the sound of a truck passing by the house, and she went to the window and looked outside. It was Carla's truck heading to the city. She backed hastily away from the window and leaned back against the wall, looking at Rosa with fear in her eyes. Rosa hugged her and said, "Don't be afraid, my dear. You are with me. I won't let anybody hurt you." Then she led her to the kitchen for breakfast.

Katherine was very afraid Alex and Carla would kidnap her again, and for the next few days she made no sound in the house and trembled with fear at any sounds from outside, especially the sound of Carla's truck which she heard every day which brought back bad memories. Rosa's heart went at the sight of such sorrow in her. Sometimes, she looked at her crooning as she played with the dolls and she wept secretly. She was always kind to her and she tried to do things to make her happy. She took Katherine to the city whenever she went to deliver her cookies to the sweet-shopkeepers, and she always bought her something. Her behavior had a profound effect on her, and Katherine came to know herself as a member of Rosa's family. It was a new life for her. Rosa was all she had in the world, and her little home was the only safe place for her, a refuge from the dangers of the world outside.

Chapter 12

Six months passed. Katherine and her family were all forgotten by New Yorkers, except for Edward Wilson, who still moped away inside for his friend's death and the disappearance of his family. However, he had a clarity in his dreams that Katherine and Laura were still alive and they would come back some day, and he would give them Peter's share of the treasure they had found together, in this way he could make up for his bad past a little and disburden himself of some of his sins. Nevertheless, Louis Wilson still sought to possess half of Peter's share, and he thought it was high time that Edward relinquish his friend's share given such a long absence of Katherine and her mother.

One evening Louis went to Edward's jewelry store. Edward was sitting behind his desk when the door opened and Louis entered. There was nobody else in the store. Louis approached him and said with a smile, "Hi." Then he made himself comfortable in a chair across the desk from Edward and crossed his legs. Edward looked at him in wonder for a few seconds without saying anything. He asked himself, is he here to borrow money? However, he owns his own saloon and makes enough money himself. He should not have financial problems. He thought hard, but he could not discern why he had come.

"If I didn't know better I'd say you aren't very happy to see me," said Louis.

"What do you want?" asked Edward dubiously.

Louis smiled and said causally, "I came here for the rest of my share."

"What do you mean? What share are you talking about?"

"You once said you wanted to give Peter's share to his family, right?"

Edward took a deep breath, dropped his head down and said, "Yeah, I am still waiting for them."

"It's been six months since they disappeared, and in all that time not one person has seen them. Why are you still waiting for them?" said Louis. "Forget about them, and let's split it."

"That share belongs to his family, and I intend to give it to them."

Louis pursed his lips and snorted angrily. "Do you think I am stupid? You know better than anyone that his family will never show up, and you are planning to keep that share for yourself."

Edward stood firmly his ground. His eyes hooded, his cheeks drawn taut, he said loudly, "I don't want to hear any more nonsense from you! Do not forget that you lost the bet and you were supposed to help us bring the treasure to the boat for free. Now, get out of my store."

Louis knew Edward would get physical with him if necessary, so he left there shaking his head and vowing his revenge. Edward stood his ground until he left the store, then he sat down and thought about Laura and Katherine. One moment they seemed lost to him forever, but the next he would recall his dreams and rekindle his hope as he saw them on a bright road in front of him.

That night, he dreamt he was searching for Laura and Katherine in a jungle. After hours of searching he sat down on a log to rest by a stony road. It was getting dark, and his eyes were on the road, searching for them. Suddenly he saw two dark figures on the road. They wore long black hooded capes that covered their bodies from head to toe. They were long in coming in the dusk, and a little girl was following them. As they passed him by, he recognized the little girl as Katherine. Edward jumped up and called out, "Katherine."

Katherine stopped and turned her face to him and said with a smile, "Hi, Mr. Wilson."

"What are you doing here? Where are you going?" asked Edward.

"I am going to go to my daddy."

"Where is he? Where is your mom?"

Katherine looked at the two men and said, "They know where my mom and dad are, and they are going to take me there."

Edward turned his head to the two dark figures. They glanced sideways at him as they silently walked away. Their faces were not recognizable, but they seemed somehow bad to him, as if they were not to be trusted. They looked back at Katherine and gestured for her to follow them. At that time Katherine said loudly, "I am sorry, Mr. Wilson, I have to go. It is getting late." Then she ran to catch up with them and they melted into the darkness.

Edward cried, "No, they are lying to you...Don't go." As he was saying this, he felt a hand on his shoulder, and he quickly turned around and saw his friend, Peter, smiling at him.

"Are you alive?" asked Edward with fear.

"Of course, I am alive."

"Where is Laura?"

"She lives in the same place I do. We don't live on the earth anymore."

"I mean, I mean…" Edward continued.

Peter put his hand on his shoulder, interrupted him, and said with smile, "Please go and find Katherine, she is very lonely in this world. Bring her with you and take care of her." Then he took a deep breath and added, "You will always be my best friend."

Edward looked back at the tall dark tree trunks in the darkness for a moment and was scared. He turned his face back to Peter, but he saw nobody there. Edward ran toward the woods and shouted, "Katherine, Katherine, don't go with them." He could only see a jungle with black columns of tree trunks and ghosts that had surrounded him. He jumped crying from his nightmare and was jolted awake. His wife, Mary, leaped up with his cry and asked, "What happened? Are you all right?"

"Yeah, I am fine. It was just a nightmare," Edward said, panting. "You can go back to sleep." He drank a glass of water that was on the nightstand next to him and lay quietly on the bed and thought of his dream all night long.

Chapter 13

Four years passed, and Katherine was eleven years old. She and Rosa still lived in the same house, and every day she still heard Carla's truck reminding her daily of Carla's evil face, Alex's giant face with his silver tooth, and Louis's cruel face with the burn mark and the blood spot in his eyes. The details stayed fresh in her mind, as if no time had passed since those awful days. She still hid herself most of the time, she never stood by the window or on the porch, and the door was always locked when she was alone at home, but she was happy to be living with Rosa. She had learned many things from her, including how to speak Italian and how to cook and bake, and she had begun to help Rosa with her orders from the shopkeepers of the city of Genoa. Rosa would take her to the city whenever she went to deliver the cookies, and Katherine covered her head with a scarf, so Carla and the gypsies would not recognize her. They lived happily with each other and everything was going well, but one day it came to an end when Rosa was attacked by a rabid dog. It was a hot afternoon in August, and Rosa was coming back from visiting one of her neighbors when it happened. Her dog Bianco was about two houses away, and as soon as he heard Rosa's cry and the wild clamor of barking, he raced to her like a bullet and attacked the strange dog. He fought off the sick dog away, which limped away yelping with agony. Rosa's left leg had been bitten. She bent down and with a rag wiped away the blood. The wound was deep and painful, and soon the rag was soaked with blood.

When she got home, she told the story of what had happened to Katherine, who quickly brought a cloth and wrapped her leg, urging her to see Dr. Mario. But Rosa refused.

The next morning upon opening her eyes to the first rays of the sun Katherine looked over to Rosa, who was sleeping in bed next to her. It was 6:30, which was odd because usually Rosa woke up before sunrise. She looked at her and listened to her breathing for a few seconds and then she went into the kitchen to prepare breakfast. Thirty minutes later when she saw that Rosa still had not woken up, she went over and stood next to her and with her small hand touched her shoulder as she called gently, "Grandma, it is seven o'clock."

Rosa opened her eyes slowly. "Good morning, my dear."

"Breakfast is ready," said Katherine.

"I can't eat anything now," Rosa said weakly, and she moved her leg under the blanket a little, sending a surge of pain through her. "Don't wait for me. You go ahead and eat your breakfast."

"You are not all right," said Katherine worriedly.

"I have a fever," Rosa said, touching her forehead. "I think I am getting the flu."

"Let's go to Dr. Mario."

"No, no need to do that. I have all the medications I need. They are on the shelves."

Katherine went to the kitchen and rummaged through the shelves. "Which one is for flu?"

"Hold on, I'll get it myself," said Rosa, and she got up and went to the kitchen. Her leg was so painful she nearly had to drag it. She did not know the dog had rabies and just took the medicine that was for the flu. Antifebrile was the only thing that worked on her, and it reduced her fever a few hours and helped her stay out of bed.

The next morning Katherine let Rosa sleep late because of her illness. She did her chores and got all the cookies orders ready while she waited for Rosa to wake up.

It was almost 10:00a.m.when Rosa opened her eyes, looked around and tried to move her leg. It was even sorer than yesterday, when she turned her face to Katherine's bed and saw she was not there, she called out to her.

In the kitchen, Katherine heard her name being called, and she quickly went to Rosa. "Hi, grandma, how are you doing today?"

Rosa took a few seconds to clear her throat and wet her lips and said, "I need some water." Then she sat up in bed while Katherine went to the kitchen. Katherine brought her a glass of water and sat on her bed next to her and said, "I got all the orders ready for today."

"I am not feeling well today. We will do it tomorrow, when I feel better." She drank the water and touched her face and forehead with one hand. "I still have a fever. Hand me my medicine."

"You need to see Dr. Mario," said Katherine.

"I don't need the doctor. He is just going to give me the same medicine I am taking it now. I have the flu, is all," Rosa said languorously. "I will be out of bed in a couple of days."

Katherine looked at her doubtfully and said, "You will get well soon?"

Rosa stood up, trying to act, as she was not sick, and she walked to the kitchen. However, she could only trudge and move sluggishly, unable to steady herself for very long, and after that she took her medication and returned to bed.

The last teaspoon of antifebrile was taken by dusk, and Katherine grew worried when she could find no more of it. She knew Rosa would get worse without the medicine, and she returned to her, lighted a candle and set it upright on a heart-shaped stone that Rosa had found a few years ago. She sat on the floor by her bed and looked at her face in the dancing candlelight. Very soon Rosa's fever returned, settling all over her body. Katherine stayed up with her, dipping a cloth in cold water and squeezing it and putting it on her forehead. However, the fever remained, and Rosa spent a very bad night.

It was a bad night for Katherine, too, but she stayed awake and did her best to nurse Rosa back to health. She was very tired, and by dawn, leaning against Rosa's bed, she fell asleep, failing even to hear Carla's truck that morning. Outside on the porch, Bianco, stared at the door, waiting for his breakfast, But he heard no sounds coming from inside the house for hours. At 12:30 p.m. Katherine sensed a movement and her eyes opened. She went to Rosa found that saw her face was puffy and red, her eyes were sealed shut with dried mucus, and she shivered feverishly. Katherine knew immediately she was worse than before, and she called out, "Grandma."

Rosa said nothing.

"You need a doctor." Katherine put the wet towel on her forehead. "The medicine is not helping. Let me go and bring Dr. Mario to see you."

Rosa shook her head. Katherine took the pot to the kitchen, changed the water and continued mopping her brow with a wet cloth waiting for Rosa to relent. After twenty minutes Rosa became unresponsive, so Katherine paced back and forth patiently and finally declared, "I am going to go to bring Dr. Mario here." She covered her head with a scarf and headed outside. Rosa heard her, and she opened her inflamed eyes barely and reached her hand out, but Katherine was gone with the buggy.

Katherine pushed aside her fear of the outdoor world. Rosa's life was the most important thing to her in the moment, so she pulled her scarf tightly, hiding her face It was six miles to Dr. Mario's house, and getting there was all she was thinking of.

When she reached the doctor's house she jumped down from the buggy, knocked on the door and called for the doctor panting. The doctor's wife opened the door, looked down at her and said, "Hello. What can I do for you?"

"Where is Dr. Mario? My Grandma is very sick. She is dying."

"He left for the city thirty minutes ago, he went to the Leonardos' pharmacy to get some medicine."

"When will he be back?"

"I am not sure. It may be a matter of hours."

Katherine looked at the road for a second and said breathlessly, "It is going to be too late. Where is the pharmacy? Would you give me the address?"

"Yes, of course. It is located in Del Papollo square." She brought a piece of paper and wrote the directions. Katherine grabbed the paper, leaped into the buggy and headed off toward the city.

Rosa's suffering face never left her mind, and she wished for wings to fly to the doctor so he could heal Rosa as soon as possible.

Finally, around four o'clock, she reached Del Papollo square. It was one of the main square in the city and at that hour was a very busy place. As she got to the pharmacy, she stepped down from the buggy and ran inside.

Three customers sat waiting for their prescriptions, and a man about fifty years old, wearing a white cape searched the shelves behind the counter. The three customers turned their faces to Katherine at the same time, and seeing the worry in her face, they realized something awful had happened to her.

Katherine approached the counter and asked anxiously, "Is Dr. Mario here?"

The pharmacist turned around. "Dr. Mario? He is not here. What do you want?"

"I need him to come with me to see my Grandma. She is very sick, with a high fever. She is dying."

"He was here earlier, but he was called to a serious case."

Katherine continued seriously. "Can you tell me where he has gone?"

"I don't know the address, but I think you better wait for him here. He should come back to pick up some medicine."

Katherine dropped her head down, began to cry and said helplessly, "My Grandma is dying."

"Where is she now?" asked the pharmacist. "Where is your house?"

"I came from Tor San Lorenzo."

"Where? Tor San Lorenzo? It is far. How did you get here?"

"I came with our buggy."

"Where are your parents? Do they know about it?"

"I don't have parents. I live with my Grandma," said Katherine as the tears poured from her.

"Oh, poor girl, sounds like her Grandma is the only one that she has," said a female customer.

A man sitting next to the woman sighed and said, "Oh man, it is too hard waiting for a doctor at this time." The other two customers nodded their heads in agreement.

"You can't do anything now. You had better wait for Dr. Mario. He will show up in thirty minutes, that is my best suggestion."

Katherine dropped her head, walked to the door and stood next to a bench crying.

The others pitied her, and as Katherine stood by the door crying, she suddenly heard a car horn honking, followed by the squeal of a horse, and it was then she remembered she hadn't tied up the horse. The horse reared and ran away. Katherine darted into the street and tried to stop it, but she couldn't reach it in time. As she was running, her scarf blew. She halted for a moment, trying to catch it, but she missed it, turned, and continued chasing the horse, which stamped madly, running straight down the road. The frightened people stayed on the sidewalks, some of them ducking into shops. Women and the children screamed, and mothers held their children about them. Nobody could stop the mad horse. Katherine lost sight of the horse after two blocks, and when she stopped and asked a newsman, he pointed down the street, so she kept on running. After four blocks she had to stop, catching her breath in the middle of the crosswalk, looking around hesitatingly, Katherine was too tired to run, so she walked down the road searching everywhere for the horse. After an hour, she realized she was far from the pharmacy, so she turned around and headed back to the pharmacy to see Dr. Mario. Rosa's face came before her eyes again, and Katherine said to herself, "It might be too late; she might not be alive by now." She looked around feeling lonely and began to cry, as one by one the doors seemed to close in front of her. While she was walking, she heard, "Hey, Princess." The voice was familiar, there was anger in it, and it startled her. She turned around and saw three teenage girls sitting on a short wall by the sidewalk. Their faces and dresses reminded her of long-ago memories. They were the girls who used to live with Carla, and one of them was Vanessa. She recognized her and said loudly, "I told you, it's the same girl who escaped Ms. Carla's house a few years ago, and that necklace that she is wearing, it is the same one that she stole from me. Let's get her." then they ran toward her.

Katherine was terrified, and she broke into a run on the flagstones in the road, her tearful eyes searching for somebody to help her, but it was a quiet road and there was no one around.

The faces of Louis, Alex, and Carla and a dark future in captivity came in front of her eyes, and she ran as fast as she could. As she looked back to see how close her pursuers were she tripped on a stone, fell, and in no time, the gypsies captured her. Katherine cried for help as she struggled to get away, but they all held her down and would not let her go. Vanessa kicked her in the back and cried, "Thief! Give me my necklace back." Then she asked the girls to hold her so she could take the necklace herself. Katherine was holding the necklace tightly and crying for help. At that time, Vanessa cried cheerfully, "Hey, look, here comes Miss Carla."

All eyes went to Carla's truck, which was coming down the road toward them, and after a few seconds, she swerved and came to a stop in front of them and shouted, "What the hell is going on here?"

"Miss Carla, this is the girl who escaped from your house a few years ago," said Vanessa loudly. "The girl who was brought by Alessandro, and this the necklace that she stole from me."

"What?" shouted Carla, and she got out of the truck immediately, stood over her and angrily studied her face. Katherine looked up at her evil face and her hair that was in disarray as always. She was exactly as Katherine remembered. Carla opened the back door of the truck and cried, "Put her in before somebody shows up."

Katherine cried, "No, no, I am not going with you." She screamed for help, hoping some of the townspeople would hear her. The girls dragged her on the ground to the truck and were trying to force her in when a car stopped across the road. It was a black Alfa Romeo, and two men in black suits got out of the car and walked toward them. They were about the same size and the same age, and they carried black slouch hats, and they looked very serious. Carla and the girls put her down quickly. The men approached and looked at Katherine for a second and then one of them said to Carla, "Hey, you old devil, what are you going to do with this girl? Let her go."

Carla said smilingly, "She is my granddaughter. I am going to take her home."

"Why did you hit her?"

"Sometimes, punishment is necessary." Carla smiled and put her hands on Katherine's shoulder gently.

Katherine suddenly cried with terror in her voice, "No sir, she is lying, she is not my Grandma, they are going to kidnap me."

"Shut up," said Carla covering Katherine's mouth and refusing to let her talk.

"You know what? She stole that necklace from us and we want it back," said Vanessa.

Katherine held the necklace tightly and tore Carla's hand away from her mouth. "No, that is a lie, this is my necklace and they are going to steal it from me. Please help me, please."

"She is not going with you so leave her alone," said the man to Carla.

"I told you, she is my granddaughter, I need to take her home."

"Shut up. My boss eyes never make a mistake. You do not have any relationship with this girl. Now, you and your gypsies better get out of here before my boss gets angry," said the man.

Carla turned and saw a man sitting in the back seat by the window, smoking cigar, and he was looking out straight ahead through the windshield. He wore a black Italian slouch hat and his left fingers were working mechanically, precisely, on the door beside him. There was a shadow on his face and he was not recognizable. He was Ivano Rossi, leader of the gang responsible for many bank robberies and jewelry heists in the city of Genoa. He was fifty-five years old and had never married. He dyed his hair black twice a week. He never repeated himself when he gave instructions, and because all his guys knew it they listened to him carefully whenever he would talk to them.

Carla guessed he was an underworld figure, and if that were true, she knew that she should not mess around with him, so she quickly gathered her girls and drove away without saying another word.

The two men led Katherine to the car, and one of them opened the back door and stood waiting. Katherine stood looking at Ivano. He put his cigar in the ashtray on the door, turned his face to Katherine, and said with a smile and with dignity in his voice, "Did they hurt you?"

"I am fine. Thank you, sir, for your help."

"You better get in the car. It is not safe to be alone in this area."

Katherine sat down next to him, and before the car moved, he asked, "What is your name, pretty girl?"

"Angela," Katherine said quickly.

"It is a beautiful name. Where is your house, Angela?"

"Tor San Lorenzo," Katherine said with concern.

"You came all the way from Tor San Lorenzo? How did you get here?"

"I came with my buggy."

Ivano saw fright and worry in her eyes. He took a few seconds before he continued. "Can I ask what you are doing here?"

"I came to take Dr. Mario to Tor San Lorenzo to see my Grandma." Katherine began to cry. "My Grandma is very sick, she is dying, sir."

"Where are your parents?"

"They died a few years ago. I live with my Grandma."

"I am sorry," said Ivano, and he dropped his head down and released his breath and asked, "Where is the doctor now?"

"He should be in the Leonardos' pharmacy."

Ivano peered out for a second and told his driver to take the shortcut to the pharmacy and in no time they were there.

Katherine and one of the men got out of the car, at which time Dr. Mario came outside.

Katherine cried, "Dr. Mario."

"I have been waiting for you a long time. Where have you been? Tell me what is wrong with Rosa?"

"She is very sick, she has high fever." Katherine grabbed his hand, imploring him to hurry.

"Let's go in my car," said Dr. Mario.

Katherine looked back at Ivano and said, "Let me say goodbye to them." She ran to the car and said, pointing, "He is Dr. Mario. He is going to help my Grandma. We are going to go in his car. Thank you very much for your help, sir."

Dr. Mario walked over and looked at Ivano. "Hello."

"Doctor, Angela is going to be in my car. We will follow you," said Ivano.

"All right," said Dr. Mario, and they all drove toward Tor San Lorenzo.

Dr. Mario drove fast to get to his patient as soon as possible, and Ivano's driver stayed about a hundred feet behind the doctor's car at all times. Ivano's eyes were always on Katherine, who was crying. He seemed to make a decision about her, a decision he had never made before in his life. Time seemed to pass slowly for Katherine, her tearful eyes on the road at all times. She was afraid that they wouldn't get to Rosa on time.

They reached Rosa's house in fifteen minutes, Ivano's car coming to a stop ten feet behind Dr. Mario's car. Katherine got out quickly and hurried inside, followed by the doctor, holding his little bag, and one of the Ivano's men walked after them. Ivano and the other man remained inside the car.

Rosa was in her bed, her eyes half closed, and she was barely breathing. Katherine put her arms about her neck and cried, "Grandma, I came back. Dr. Mario is here. You are going to be fine."

"Let me see," said Dr. Mario, and he sat on the edge of the bed and touched Rosa's face and looked in her eyes and put the stethoscope to her chest. It was clear to him her illness was serious, and he was afraid it might be too late to save her. Her body was hot, so he removed the blanket from her and asked Katherine to open the window.

"Why didn't you come and get me earlier?" asked Dr. Mario."I tried to, but she wouldn't let me."

Dr. Mario noticed her leg that was wrapped up and swollen, and he asked, "What happened to her leg?"

"A dog bit her a few days ago."

"A dog! Oh, my goodness." He gasped. "She got rabies from that dog."

"She is going to be fine, right, doctor?" Katherine asked timidly. "You won't let anything happen to her, right?"

At that time Rosa's right hand went toward Katherine and her body shook a little. She inhaled sharply and deeply, and she died. Katherine ran to her and shouted, "Grandma, no, don't leave me." She turned to Dr. Mario. "Please, save her. Please."

Dr. Mario took the stethoscope from his neck, dropped his head and said, "It is too late. I am sorry."

"No, no, don't say that," Katherine screamed, and she put her face on Rosa's chest. "Grandma, don't leave me, I am so alone. Please don't leave me."

Ivano's man was standing in the room, looking at the scene, and he went out to tell Ivano all that had happened. A minute later, Ivano and his man entered the house to hear an explanation from Dr. Mario.

"It was too late," said Dr. Mario. "She got rabies from a dog a few days ago. There was nothing anyone could do."

Ivano sighed, took a few steps toward Katherine and stood over her, looking down at her thoughtfully. His eyes shown with volition. Katherine's scream turned into moans, as she thought of the dangerous and lonely future that awaited her, her bright future fading forever from her view. "How can I live in this house alone?" she asked herself. She thought fearfully of the oncoming night. It would be cold and scary to be with Rosa's corpse in the house. Then she thought of Carla and the gypsies, and she was terrified to be taken by them in the night. It was then she felt a hand on her shoulder, giving her a warm and trustworthy squeeze. It was Ivano. "You are not alone, Angela. I am here." Then he turned to Dr. Mario and said, "I will adopt her as my daughter." Dr. Mario and Ivano's men looked on proud of their boss. Katherine felt his support, a bulwark against loneliness and abuse. She sensed the guarantee of a future of comfort, free of fear of Alex and Carla and the gypsies and all other bad people.

Chapter 14

Ten years later, Louis, the murderer of Katherine's parents, gambled away all his money and property in his saloon one night. With no house, his family went to stay in the rental house of a friend. They blamed him all the time and people said that he finally got the life that he deserved. Louis locked himself away in his friend's house for forty-eight hours trying to find a way to get his life back. Finally, out of necessity decided to approach his brother, Edward Wilson.

The next evening, he went to Edward's house with his wife, Emily. It was 8:00p.m. when they got there. Louis rapped the iron doorknocker three times and stood waiting. In a short time the door opened and an old man of sixty stood in front of them. He was the servant and had been with Edward for fifteen years. His name was Bernard. He said politely, "Good evening. How may I help you?"

Louis knew that he had to be nice to everybody, even the servant of the house, if he wanted to get anything from Edward. "Please, tell Edward his brother Louis and Emily are here."

Bernard was shocked for a moment, because it was his first time to meet Edward's brother. He said humbly, "Yes sir, let me tell Mr. Wilson." He left the door open while he went to relay the news.

Edward and his son, George, were in the living room, talking business. Now, sixty-five years old, Edward was the richest man in America. His wife, Mary, had died two years earlier from breast cancer. George was twenty-four and helped him in all of his affairs. As Bernard entered the living room, George asked quickly, "Is Daniel here?" as if he were waiting for somebody. Bernard approached and said, "No, sir." Then he turned to Edward and said, "A gentleman is here to see you. He says that he is your brother."

At those words, Edward and George felt a wave of resentment rising in them. Edward and Louis had not had anything to do with each other. Even when Mary died, Louis did not come to the funeral or even send his condolences. Edward narrowed his eyes and was thoughtful for a second. "My brother?"

His name is Louis, and he is with his wife, Emily," answered Bernard.

Edward stood up and said harshly, "What are they doing here?"

George stood up after him and said angrily, "What do they want?"

Edward took a breath, and after a few moments, he said to Bernard, "Bring them in."

Very soon, Bernard went to the door and led them to the living room.

Edward and George stood in the middle of the room, eyeing them coldly. Louis and Emily stood a few feet away. Everything was set, and they both knew what to do. They said remorsefully, "Hi." Then Louis walked quickly over to Edward, hugged him tightly and said, "I am sorry, brother. Please forgive me. I have not been a good brother to you."

"We're so sorry," said Emily tearfully. Louis continued. "I dreamed of our father last night. He told me to come to you and ask you to forgive me. I realize my mistakes, and I want to make up for the past. I swear to God, I want to live honesty. I want to be a good brother to you for the rest of my life Please forgive me."

Emily added, "God knows, he has changed. I have never seen him like this before."

For Louis and his wife, it did not matter that they took God's name in vain for their own benefit. Edward and George were reticent, regarding them with the piqued look. But Louis and Emily were confident their charade would work, and they hung their heads silently, waiting. Edward sighed and put his hand on Louis's arm. "Have a seat." He seemed to believe that they had really changed, and he forgave them. When George saw the reaction of his father, he followed suit as always and forgave them as well. Louis saw satisfaction come over Edward's face, and he was very happy. For a minute, nobody said anything. Edward looked at Louis and asked, "Where are your children? How are they doing?"

"They are fine," Louis said quickly before Emily could speak.

"You had three children, right?" asked Edward.

"Yeah, two boys and one girl," answered Louis. "They are very good children and they help us a lot." Emily nodded her head in agreement.

"Are they married?" asked Edward.

"No, they are not," said Louis, and he looked at George and smiled. "I am sure George is a big help to you."

George smiled and said nothing. Edward replied, "Yes, he helps me in all my work."

At that time Bernard and a young black man entered the living room, and the man said, "Hi."

He was Daniel Smith. The boy who lived in the old shipyard with his father, Sam, by George's Grandma fourteen years ago, the child whose father was murdered by Louis and Alex on the night that Katherine was kidnapped by them. He was

George's best friend and a sailor on one of Edward's passenger ships that traveled between Europe and America.

George stood up and said, "Where have you been? You are late."

"I thought I'd arrive for dinner on time," Daniel said. Everybody laughed, and then George made introductions. As Edward sat on the couch, he said to Louis and Emily, "His father was Sam Smith, the person who was your neighbor in the old shipyard, about fourteen years ago. Daniel was a little boy then."

Louis and Emily studied Daniel carefully, Louis remembered the night that he killed his father, alongside of Alex, and he grew scared. Soon he collected himself and said to Daniel, "Mr. Smith, how are you doing? We are very pleased to meet you."

For a moment, Daniel looked at the burn mark on his face, and he remembered his childhood and Louis's family as the bad people of that neighborhood. But soon he put it out of his mind and said, "Good to see you, too."

"Young sailor, we are proud of you," said Louis.

"Yes, we really are," said Emily.

Edward looked at them and said, "Dinner will be served in a few minutes. Would you like to join us?"

Louis and Emily looked at each other and Louis said hesitatingly, "We don't know." They seemed to want to stay.

"Did you already have dinner?" asked Edward.

"No, not yet," answered Louis and Emily together.

"All right, you can join us. There is plenty of food for everybody," said Edward, and he turned to Bernard. "Serve dinner, please."

Louis and Emily were very happy to see Edward trusted them, and they were sure that he would accept their request and help them out generously.

Most of the dinner conversation was about Daniel's trip, and he shared many things he had experienced. He spoke of the huge icebergs that he saw in the Atlantic Ocean. George and Edward were fascinated. They had never experienced such a thing before, and they listened to him passionately.

"It was like a mountain. It was the biggest iceberg that I have ever seen in all my trips."

"Did you see it during the day or at night?" George asked.

"It was in the day," Daniel replied. "I remember, I saw another huge iceberg very close to our ship, and that was at night. Fortunately the watchmen saw it and we managed to avoid hitting it."

"Do you see them on every trip?" asked George.

"No. Usually, you can see the icebergs during these months more than on other months of the year."

"I think traveling in these months is more interesting for you," said George.

"Oh, yeah, it is very interesting," answered Daniel.

Now, George was very interested to see the icebergs, and he felt a surge of exhilaration for a moment and said, "I'd like to see them."

"You can come with me on the next trip," said Daniel.

"Oh, no, I can't," George said with a smile.

"Why not?" asked Daniel.

"Yes, why not?" asked Edward.

"We have a lot of work to do," George said to Edward referring to their business.

"Don't worry about it," said Edward. "I think it is a good time if you want to take a while off. It would be a good experience for you."

George dropped his head and thought for a few seconds and asked Daniel, "When is your next trip?"

"Within the next five days."

"I can get some work done before that," George said thoughtfully. "All right, I'll come with you."

"That's great!" Daniel said enthusiastically. "I am sure you will enjoy it."

Edward nodded his head gently in agreement, as he looked at George.

As Louis was listening to them, a plan formed in his mind. It would ensure a good future for him and his family, and he was sure that it would work. A few minutes after dinner he said goodbye and left. Once they were outside the house, Emily said, "Hey, stupid, why didn't you ask for the money?"

Louis chuckled. "If I ask him tonight, he would realize that we only came to his house for the money, not for him."

"When do you want to ask him about it? Did you forget that we don't have anything to eat?"

Louis thought of his plan for a second and grinned. "I have a better idea."

"What is your damn idea? Tell me quick."

"I am going to possess all Edward's belongings," said Louis.

"What? Are you crazy? Do you even know what are you talking about?"

"Didn't you hear? George is going to Europe with that black guy."

"So?"

"I am going on that trip with him, too."

"To Europe? Are you crazy?" Emily said angrily. "How are you going to get there? We don't even have money to buy food for us, now you want to go on a trip."

"Listen to me. I will go on that trip with George, but he will never come back to America."

"What do you mean? Do you want to kill him?"

"Yeah, I am going to take Simon and Tiffany with me. They can help with my plan."

"What about Edward? What do you want to do with him?"

"That is your job, you and Dennis. You two stay here and take care of him."

"How?" asked Emily.

"Don't worry, I already have a plan. Once we kill them, I, Louis Wilson, Edward's half-brother and only surviving relative, will be the legal heir of his entire estate."

Now Emily was happy.

The next evening, Louis went to the Edward's house alone. Bernard opened the door for him and led him to the living room, where Edward was. He entered smilingly and said, "Good evening, brother. I want to talk to you about something."

Edward gave him a questioning look and waited for him to go on. Louis smiled and asked, "When do George and his friend go to Europe?"

"I think they leave in four days. Why do you ask?" said Edward.

"You know, brother, I have never been to Europe. Now that I am old enough I want to see some other countries before I die."

Edward smiled a little and nodded his head, happy that his brother wanted to go on a trip with George. For a moment, it occurred to him to accompany them as well. He looked benevolently at him and answered, "Not a problem. You can go, too."

Louis stood up and said happily, "I am sure we are going to have a good time. Thank God I have this chance to take this trip with my nephew."

"I'm sure you two are going to have a great time."

"All right, brother, I've got to go," said Louis. "I have lots to do to get ready for the trip." Then he walked out hurriedly.

Edward believed every word Louis said, convinced he had changed.

Chapter 15

Four days later, on April 16, at 10:00a.m., Louis and George departed from the port of Boston bound for England in one of the Edward's ships, the Destiny. It was the ship that Daniel worked on since he was hired as a sailor. Louis's daughter and his youngest son were with him, while his older son, Dennis, stayed with his mother in New York City to kill Edward. Everybody in his family was happy with his plan and to possessing Edward's belongings. During the trip, they were extremely nice to George, going out of their way to show their kindness and faithfulness as real relatives, so that they could gain his trust, even pretending to enjoy his company. But George did not like spending time with them and always had an excuse to reject their requests politely so he could spend most of his time with his friend, Daniel. For this reason they felt humiliated, especially when they saw how much respect was paid to him by the ship's staff. The fire of vengeance burned in them, but they could not do anything about it yet, and would have to be patient and nice to him until an opportunity presented itself for them to execute their heinous plan. Louis was watching out at all times what George did and where he was, he studied all parts of the ship in order to choose the best place to kill him on the way back to America.

After seven days of sailing, they arrived to the port of Liverpool in England. Louis tried to take advantage of George in the last moments before he got off the ship. George was standing among the passengers on the deck, looking down at the port; Louis approached him anxiously and said, "Somebody has stolen my money."

"What?" asked George, and his brows furrowed. "Somebody stole your money?"

"All my money was in my wallet and it was in my cabin."

"Who do you think did it?" George asked thoughtfully.

Louis turned to the passengers who were getting off the ship and said angrily, "He probably has left the ship by now."

"How much was in your wallet?" asked George.

"Three hundred bucks, all of the money that I brought with me on this trip. I am an idiot to put all of my money in my wallet." Louis looked around and sighed. "I need that money to buy gifts for my family and friends, and to take Simon and Tiffany with me to some of the European countries. If we don't see them this time, we will never get another chance." Then he dropped his head and began to cry.

George looked at him sympathetically for a while without saying anything. "If my father was here, he would help his brother," he said to himself. He took a deep breath and said, "Don't worry; it is going to be all right. How much do you need?"

As Louis was wiping his tears, he said, "I just need three hundred dollars. I promise to pay it back as soon as we get back to New York City."

George dropped his head and said to himself, "It is a lot of money, but he is a relative and I should trust him. Besides, this is the first request he has made from me. All right, I will get the money for you. I will be right back."

After ten minutes, George returned and handed Louis an envelope and said, "That's three hundred dollars."

Louis's greedy fingers touched the envelope and he hugged George and said with delight, "Thank you, George, thank you so much. I am so lucky that you were here, otherwise..." With that he shrugged and returned to his cabin, where Tiffany and Simon were waiting for him. As he entered, they quickly asked, "Did you get the money from him? How much? How much?"

"I just got fifty bucks is all," said Louis.

"Give me twenty bucks," said Simon.

"Twenty bucks! No, we need the money to go to Italy."

"Italy!" said Simon and Tiffany together.

"Yeah, I have to bring my cousin, Alex, with me on this ship. We need him to help us kill George."

"What? You want to bring him here? We don't need him. The three of us can kill that boy by ourselves," said Simon angrily.

"You skinny dogs are blind and don't see his muscles. He is very strong, and he is always with his friend. We need at least one person to help us with this job." Then he took a few steps in the cabin and added, "Maybe we have to kill his friend, too. I may bring on one of Alex's friends with to make killing them easier."

"I think you want to share Edward's belongings with your cousin and his friend," Simon said, chuckling.

"I just want to bring them onboard so they help us to kill those boys. That's all. Alex and his friend will never get to America. I will kill them before that."

"When will we go to Italy?" asked Tiffany.

"Right now."

"I want to stay on the ship," said Simon. "Give me some money."

Louis brought out a five-dollar bill that he had already prepared for him, and said, "Come on."

Simon looked at the money and complained, "What the hell is this? You know that I smoke, and I like to go to the saloon every night. This money is nothing."

Louis searched in his pocket, brought another five dollars out and rumpled Simon's hair and continued chuckling. "Take it and don't say anything else."

Simon grabbed the money and walked out without saying a word. Then Louis and Tiffany got out of the ship and went to Italy.

Chapter 16

The years passed quickly for Katherine. She turned twenty-one, she was living with Ivano, and she was happy in her life. Although it was a long time since she was taken from her homeland, she still thought about it. During the seasons, sometimes she stood by the window in her room and looked up at the migrating birds in the sky and she became homesick. There was a feeling in her, like going, like flight to the land where she was born, the place where she belonged. "How can I get there?" she asked herself. "How can I tell Ivano about it? Would he help me? Or he would be mad at me?" First, she thought to tell him about her past, but it was very hard for her to do that after ten years living in his house. She felt guilty and she was afraid.

One night as she was playing piano in memory of her parents in her room, Ivano entered. As soon as she heard the door, she stopped playing, stood up and said, "Hi, Papa."

"Have a seat, my dear. I like this music. Go on," said Ivano with a smile.

Katherine smiled a little, sat on the bench and continued to play. In a few minutes, her parents' faces came before her eyes as always when she played the same music. Memories of her childhood came one after another, and at last, she was left with her parents' absence, and then she felt lonely. She needed Ivano to be with her at that time and listen to her. She wanted to put her head on his shoulder and cry and tell him the story that she had kept from him for years. It had taken a long time to get her courage up, and now it was time to tell him. As she was playing, she began to cry, but she wanted to finish the piece in order to please him.

Ivano was standing over her, watching her fingers, enjoying the music that she was playing so skillfully. There was a little smile of pride on his face. Suddenly, Katherine stopped playing with a whimper. Ivano was shocked for a moment, and he put his hands on her shoulders and asked, "What is the matter? Why are you crying, my dear?"

Katherine raised her head, looked up at him and said, "I need to tell you something."

Ivano's mind raced to identify what it could be, wanting to kill and destroy whatever was hurting her. He asked restlessly, "What is it?"

"Something that I never told you."

Ivano looked at her shame-filled and downcast eyes and said tenderly, "Tell me, my dear."

"I was kidnapped fourteen years ago, and they killed my mom and dad."

Ivano narrowed his eyes and asked, "Who did it?"

"Louis and Alex--they killed them for no reason."

Ivano sat her on the bench by the piano and handed her a tissue and asked her to tell him what all had happened to her. Katherine wiped her tears and told Ivano everything. She relayed her story from beginning to end. Even though fourteen years had passed, she had not forgotten the bitter memories of those years, or the faces of those who had done her wrong. It was all still clear in her mind. When she was finished, she waited for Ivano's reaction, still thinking that he might get mad at her.

Ivano was standing over her, listening to her carefully, and Katherine's speech and the pain in her heart ignited the heart of Ivano. It was plain to see the nature of the anger that burned in him; it was the anger of revenge. The burn mark on Louis's face and the blood spot in his eye, and Alex's silver tooth were the first things he questioned her about, although he tried to hide his anger and do something to make her happy. So his demeanor softened, and he raised gentle hands to her shoulders and reassured her, "Everything is going to be all right."

Katherine raised her wet eyes and looked at him for a while, and she felt there was no anger in him for her and she felt glad. Then Ivano added, "Would you like to go back to your homeland?"

Katherine looked at him, smiled shyly and dropped her head down, thinking of the years that he had been taking care of her.

"I know you like that," Ivano said kindly. "Don't worry; I will come with you to set up everything for you there."

At that time, Katherine gave a happy cry, hugged him and thanked him. She knew that Ivano would do whatever he said, and he would never change his mind about it. She was very happy, to think that she would see her homeland again soon.

Louis's cousin, Alex, was still living in the city of Genoa, although his life, as always, was not a good one, filled as it was with stealing stuff from others, shoplifting, drinking beer, eating leftovers found in dumpsters, and being altogether useless. He lived in the basement of a house that belonged to an old woman, his rent only four dollars a month. But even with that he was always out of money, always behind, and often he paid his rent in stolen goods.

Fourteen years had passed since he kidnapped Katherine and taken her to Italy, and he no longer thought about her.

One day at 2:00p.m., he was in a saloon, sitting in the corner against the wall, drinking beer, when suddenly two of Ivano's men entered. All heads turned to them and all conversations came to an abrupt end, as if everyone knew whom they were. The two men walked directly over to Alex without saying a word and stood in front of him. "Alessandro?" one of them asked with a smile.

Alex waved his hand listlessly at the fly on his face and said, "Yeah, what do you want?"

"My boss wants to see you. He wants to make you an offer," the man said.

Alex asked stubbornly, "Who is your boss? Where is he?"

"You will see him," the man continued. "He has a job for you, and I am sure you will find his offer acceptable."

The other man spoke up, saying, "You are strong, which is just what is needed for the job. You don't want to miss out on this opportunity."

Alex procured his own beer and studied their suits for a while, and then he toyed with the thought of being a member of the group. Finally, he decided there was not anything wrong with their offer, his little brain deducing that any offer would be better than the life he had. His face took on a smile of security, and he greedily sucked down the beer, draining the bottle to the last drop. "Let's go see the boss," he declared, and he followed them out.

After ten minutes of driving, they reached a rundown factory in a quiet neighborhood. There were no houses or people to be seen. Alex got out of the car and looked around before following them into the factory. There was a rusted iron door, which screeched when they opened it. Inside there was no light, only sporadic streaks of sunshine through the crevices of the rusted sheeting of the roof. Alex looked around and said with a chuckle, "Can't your boss afford something nicer?"

At that time a car pulled up outside, followed by the opening and closing of car doors. Sounds like a few people are joining us; surely the boss is among them. Alex thought. Then three figures filled the doorway. Alex turned to one of the men who was beside him and asked, "Which one is your boss?"

"I'll let him introduce himself," the man answered slowly. Then both men said hello to Ivano, and they took a few respectful steps toward him. Ivano did not need to ask them about Alex, for he was sure they brought the right person. He walked over, stood in front of him and scrutinized him suspiciously in streaky sunlight that fell on his face. One of the men walked outside to stand guard, and the other one stayed next to Ivano. The last two men moved slowly behind Alex. They did not look at each other. They knew their job well and did not need to seek confirmation. Alex turned his head a little to see Ivano's face better, but the light was very dim and he could not quite make it out. He said with a nervous titter, "So you're the boss? I understand you have an offer for me."

"Shut up," Ivano said gruffly. Alex looked back at the men behind him, who stood looking at him threateningly. He was confused momentarily wondering if he were drunk or perhaps dreaming. "What the hell is going on here?" He twitched his eyes, then he felt a little tremor.

Ivano walked slowly and he did not look directly at him. "We are going to go back to fourteen years ago when you kidnapped a little girl from America and brought her to Italy. Do you remember that?"

Alex thought about that for a while, and finally his little brain kicked into gear. He was very scared. He shivered and said nothing.

"I don't ask a question twice," Ivano added.

"Yes, sir, I remember."

"What happened to her parents?" Ivano asked.

Alex dropped his head and answered miserably, "We killed them."

"Why?"

Alex began to flounder."It was not my fault... It was all his idea... I mean, my cousin, Louis."

"Where is he?" asked Ivano.

"He is in America, in New York City."

Ivano walked in front of him saying nothing. , Then he looked at him directly and said, "You are going to lose your tongue or your ears today for the things that you did to that girl. Which do you prefer?"

Alex's mouth dropped open in terror and remained open while his brain sought for something to say, then he cried, "Please, don't do it. It was not my fault."

Ivano looked down at his wrist watch and said, "I will see you again in ten days." Then he looked at his men and gestured toward Alex and left the factory without saying another word.

Alex took a few steps toward him, crying, "Please, forgive me." Nevertheless, Ivano's men stepped in front of him and barred his way. Alex saw no sign of forgiveness from Ivano, so he turned to Ivano's men, hoping they might put in a good word for him with their leader. The two men who had brought him there smiled as though something were about to happen.

Alex resigned himself to the inevitable and asked helplessly, "What should I do?"

Both men took out a switchblade and waved it at him, and one of them said, "If I were you I'd choose to keep my tongue."

Alex looked at them for a few seconds as he was crying and nodded dumbly in agreement. The two men cut his ears off without ceremony, and the blood spilled all over his face and neck and onto his shirt. He screamed like a monster, deafening shrieks that filled the room. All the creatures in the vicinity seemed to be still for a few beats, as if sensing danger, and many of them fled the area as fast as they could. Ivano's men walked outside quickly, got into the cars and drove away with their leader.

Without anyone around to help him, Alex found his own way home. He could not stop thinking about the day he would see Ivano's men again, and along with the severe pain, he suffered greatly. He thought dark and brooding thoughts. There was no escape for him anywhere. Ivano's gang controlled all the roads. His only option seemed to be suicide. With nothing else to live for, he started drinking to dull the pain.

Chapter 17

As evening fell and it became dark, he heard a voice from outside, somebody calling his name. "Hey, Alex, open the door."

It was his cousin, Louis. He was there to take him to the ship. Alex had a bandage on his wound and could not hear very well. At first, he thought that Ivano's men had returned for him. He was terrified, feeling as if there was nowhere for him to escape. Louis knocked on the little window of the basement and called loudly, "Hey, it's me, Louis, your cousin."

The voice sounded familiar to him, so he got closer to the window and listened carefully through his fear.

" Damn it, open the door. It's Louis," he called, trying to see him through the window.

Alex peeked out through the old dirty curtain and saw a man looking at him. It was too dark to make out who it was. Louis called again, "Hey, Alex, I came here to see you. Open the door."

Alex held up a candle and looked at him carefully to see better. Louis put his face to the iron bars in front of the window and waved his hand.

Alex studied his face in the light of the candle for a few seconds, and as it dawned on him who it was, he felt happy, for Louis was good in these situations. So he quickly opened the door and looked at him and Tiffany and asked frighteningly, "What are you doing here? Who is this?"

"This is my daughter, Tiffany."

Alex pulled them in and locked the door behind them. "Come in."

"What the hell is going on here?" asked Louis.

Alex sat on the chair and took the hat from his head and said, crying, "They cut my ears off... I don't have ears anymore."

Louis got closer, looked at the bandage around his head in the light of the candles carefully and asked, "What happened? Who did this to you?"

"That girl's relatives, that's who."

"Who are you talking about?"

"The girl whose parents we killed fourteen years ago."

Louis looked at him thoughtfully and he became very scared. He studied Alex's face anxiously, and the danger and fear he saw there began to infect him. He became unsteady on his feet, so he sat on a chair and dropped his head down without saying anything. He wished he'd never come to Italy, and now all he wanted to do was to get out of that place as soon as possible, before he started losing appendages, too.

"What girl?" Tiffany asked. "Who are you talking about? Why did you kill her parents?"

"It was a mistake," said Louis, looking at the floor.

"It was your idea," said Alex angrily. "It was all your fault."

"Damn it, did you forget you were the one who started it?" said Louis.

"Someone tell me what is going on here!" demanded Tiffany.

"I told you, we made a mistake," answered Louis angrily. He turned to Alex and asked, "How did they find you? Did you tell them anything about me?"

"Yeah, I told them everything," Alex said. Then he told him all that had happened. When he finished, he glared at the burning candle on the table, and began to cry again, nodding his head gravely. "It's over. They are going to kill me. Even if they don't kill me, they will cut my tongue off." Then he sighed noisily. "I'd rather die than live without a tongue."

Louis felt the danger closing in on him. That house was not safe, and he needed to get out of that dreaded place soon. However, he needed to take Alex with him to kill George, despite the trouble that he would make for him. He stood up and said, "There is another way to get rid of that gang."

As Alex whined miserably, "There is no way. I am going to bump myself off."

"You can come with us to America," said Louis.

Alex looked into his eyes helplessly and heaved a great sigh, and dropped his head down.

"What are you thinking?" Louis touched the crump on the table and looked around. "What kind of life do you have here? Friendless, alone, living like a stray dog. Is this what you want? Come on, come with me and begin a new life in America."

Alex looked at him and shook head. Louis tried to reassure him. "What do you think? You think that I want to trick you? I just want to help you. Remember, you have to act fast because they are going to kill you, man. Come on, you won't lose anything by coming to America."

Alex began to feel encouraged and even hopeful, and his face showed it. He only wanted to be free of Ivano and his men. He stood up, hugged Louis in a frenzy of thankfulness and said, "Thank you. You always were good to me. I will come with you. Let's get out of here right now."

Louis put five dollars into his pocket and said, "You are going to need this. Now listen to me well. Tiffany and I will go first, and then you leave the house ten minutes after us. We will meet you at the train station. You've got to be careful—don't get too close to us on the way." Then he and Tiffany left the house quickly.

Chapter 18

Katherine was very happy to be returning to her homeland after fourteen years. She had been waiting restlessly for that moment, and now it was only three days off. Ivano assured her that he would come with her to America, but something was bothering her, an unexpected feeling of doom, and she wished it would go away.

At 10:00a.m., she came downstairs, and saw Jonluka and Paula, the old servant couple of Ivano's, looking at her sadly. She had never seen them like that before. They seemed to have a bad news, the thing that she worried about, maybe something worse than that. Katherine stepped down toward them, her eyes fixated on them. There was a newspaper in Jonluka's hand and they looked at each other for a second, then he reached out his hand and handed it to Katherine.

"What has happened?" asked Katherine as she grabbed the newspaper quickly and glanced at the headlines. In big letters it read, INVISIBLE MAN KILLED. Ivano Rossi, known to many as the Invisible Man, was killed in a bank robbery last night in the early morning hours along with twenty-five of his men…Forty-two policemen were also killed in the shootout…

Katherine stood there shocked. It was like a nightmare. Her body trembled, and everything became dark in front of her eyes. Paula put her hands around her shoulders and sat her down on the stairs. Katherine began to cry saying, "No, no…" She could not believe they were talking about the same Ivano in whose house she had been living for ten years. Memories flooded her mind of how good and fatherly he had been with her and everything he had done for her over the years. He had supported her completely, and she was never afraid of anything since he came into her life, but now he was gone forever, leaving Katherine all alone again. She wondered how she would ever get back to her homeland by herself. The faces of the bad people from her past came before her eyes for a moment. Yet she was determined to go even if it meant being without Ivano in that land. "She should go to her homeland, the place where she belongs," she heard him say in her head. Time was short, and she still had to get to the Destiny in time, so her will hardened and she decided she would go by herself. She went up to her room, grabbed her suitcase, went downstairs and said to Jonluka and Paula, "I want to go to America."

Jonluka and Paula stood there looking at her, sad to hear her decision. Nevertheless, it was up to her, and it was clear nobody could change her mind.

Paula's thin lips curled. "Go with God, my dear." Jonluka nodded his head in agreement. Paula gave her a double embrace and kissed her on both cheeks. "We will miss you." Then Katherine hugged them, thanked them and went out disconsolately, hearing Paula's cry as she left.

There would be a lot to face going on such a trip alone, a lot she could not predict--nobody could say what might happen. In claiming her own future, she had taken control of her destiny.

She remained vigilant throughout the duration of her trip, staying mindful of her surroundings. It took longer than planned to get to the city of Liverpool. It was 10:30a.m., and the Destiny was scheduled to depart for America in an hour. Katherine stood outside the train station waiting for a taxi. She put her suitcase down and looked around. The place was foggy, the streets filled with people. She stared at the smoke coming from the chimneys and thought of the time that she had passed in that city with Alex. A taxi stopped in front of her. The driver was a tiny man of forty-eight, with short, red, curly hair and a long mustache. He asked, smiling, "Can I be of service to you?"

"I want to go to the port," said Katherine.

The driver got out of the car, grabbed her suitcase, put it into the trunk hurriedly and said, "You want to go to America, right?"

Katherine nodded her head. "Yes, sir."

"Come on, get in the car. You don't have much time." The driver opened the door for her. "The ship is going to depart at twelve o'clock." He held the door until she got into the car, and then he drove away quickly toward the port.

"How long will it take to get there?" Katherine asked.

"Usually it takes about twenty minutes, but I can get there in ten," said the driver. Then he sped up a little. He was talkative and had a lot to say while he drove. He looked at her in the rearview mirror and continued. "I can drive very fast, but I have to be careful. I have family, you see, five children. And if something happens to me there will be nobody to take care of them." He sighed and added, "You know, it is very hard to make a living doing this, so I have to work hard for them. I haven't had a vacation ever since I got married. It's always work, work, work…And here my wife is, pregnant again. Oh, my God, it is going to be even harder with another baby. I will have to work twenty hours a day." Then he shook his head and sighed. "Twenty hours every day is too much for me and this old car.

I'm not sure which one of us will break down first. Only time will tell."

Katherine was watching the road without saying anything, counting the seconds until they got to the port. As they slowed down at a crossing, the car shut off. The driver turned the key, but it would not start back up. He slammed the steering wheel with his palms and said angrily, "Damn it, not again."

Katherine asked with concern, "What is it?"

"Carburetor, it's not the first time." Then he got out of the car and opened the hood.

Katherine looked at her watch and became worried. She turned to the driver, who was whistling while he worked, seemingly in no hurry to fix the car. Katherine got out and asked, "How long will it take to repair it?"

"I am working on it." The driver stopped what he was doing and said, "Don't worry, I will get you to the port on time. I remember the last time the car broke down, I was taking a family from the port to the train station, a mother and three kids. Her oldest one was a boy, ten years old. He helped me fix the car. He was a very clever boy and knew a lot about cars. The other two children were girls. They stood with their mom, watching us the entire time."

At that point, Katherine lost her patience and interrupted him. "Please, just concentrate on fixing the car. I really can't miss my ship."

"Oh, yeah," said the driver and he continued working.

After ten minutes, the driver got into the car and tried unsuccessfully to start it up, so he looked out at her and said disappointedly, "I don't know what is wrong with my car. I can't fix it. I am sorry."

Katherine stared straight ahead for a few seconds and asked, "How far is the port from here?"

"Not too far. It is only five minutes by car. Of course, you can get there by foot, too." He pointed down the road and added, "Keep going straight. It'll take you straight there."

"Thank you," said Katherine, and she got out, grabbed her suitcase and stood waiting by the road for another taxi.

She raised her hand for every cab that passed, but all of them were carrying passengers and none of them stopped. After ten minutes, she turned and saw the driver who had brought her this far and he was still working on his car. "It's getting late. My only chance of getting to the port on time is to go by foot," she said to herself. She seized her suitcase and headed quickly down the road, the heavy suitcase banging against her knees. Desperate to be on her way to America, her mind grasped onto the idea that after the Destiny set sail there would never be another ship to America. After ten minutes of running, she slowed down and started pulling her heavy suitcase behind her. Her feet were heavy and she was panting with the effort, and still she saw no sign of the port. She thought, Maybe I'm going the wrong way. At that time, she heard a car coming up from behind, and she quickly turned and raised her hand and called loudly, "Port." The car passed by her like all the others.

Katherine was beginning to believe she really would not get to the port on time when the car that had just passed by stopped and began backing up. When it reached her it stopped, and the driver got out of the car and said as he opened the trunk, "We are going to the port; you can come with us if you like." Then he grabbed her suitcase and put it in the trunk.

"Thank you, sir. Thank you very much," said Katherine.

"You should thank this family. They asked me to give you a ride." Then the rear door opened and a woman of about forty said, "Come on in, we are going to the port, too."

Katherine got into the car and it continued down the road. It was a Jewish family inside the car. A middle-age man sat in front and his wife sat by Katherine. Their daughter and son, ages twelve and ten, sat next to the mom.

"Thank you all," said Katherine.

"Are you a passenger on the Destiny," asked the woman.

"Yes, I am going to America," answered Katherine.

"We are too."

"Do you think we can get there on time?" said Katherine

"Don't worry, we will make it in time," said the man.

"I see the port from here," said the driver. "You are not going to miss your ship."

Two minutes later, they reached the port, and after thanking them again, Katherine made her way to the ticketing booth, holding her suitcase.

There were other late-arriving passengers, but thinking that she was the last one, she pushed her way through the crowd, burst through, strode to the booth, bought her ticket and got aboard the ship. In a short while, the Destiny whistled and departed the port, bound for America. Katherine was standing on the deck among the passengers, looking at the port as the ship sailed away. She remembered past times with Rosa and Ivano, those who saw her through her years of loneliness, and the tears rolled down her cheeks. As she wiped her eyes, she noticed a little girl of about six with sunshine gold hair, looking up at her. Katherine smiled at her and turned her face to the port again. The girl asked, "Are you crying for your mommy and daddy?"

Katherine turned quickly to her, paused for a second and said with a smile, "Yeah."

"Where are they now?" asked the girl. "Are they in America?"

It was then the girl's mother, who was standing beside her, interrupted. "Tina, it is not nice to ask her such a question."

Katherine touched her head gently, smoothed her hair and smiled. "Tina, you have a nice name."

"What is your name?" asked the girl.

"My name is Angela."

"I am Margaret, and this is my son, Arthur," said Tina's mom as she put her hand on the shoulder of the boy standing next to her.

"My daddy is in America. He is in New York City," said Tina. "We are going to see him and maybe even live there forever."

Katherine smiled and said, "That is good."

"Are your mommy and daddy living in New York City, too?" asked Tina.

Katherine paused for a moment and replied, "Yeah."

Margaret said, "Tina, did you forget what I told you just a minute ago?"

"She can't be quiet. She can talk nonstop till tomorrow," Arthur said to Katherine.

Then everybody laughed and together they walked through the crowd toward the lower levels of the second class to their cabin.

There were 1,300 passengers on board, most of them in second class; among them were many different nationalities migrating to America dreaming big dreams. Katherine was the only one who was returning to her homeland after years away.

Chapter 19

Alex was lying on the bed in his cabin in the Destiny, thinking of lvano and his gang, when the door suddenly opened. He jumped down from the bed and stared at the door, afraid that lvano's men had found him and were there to finish the job, but it was only Louis. "God damn it, you scared me," said Alex. "I thought those bastards were here to kill me."

Louis said chuckling, "You are not in Italy anymore. You don't have to live in fear. Open your eyes. You are on a ship, going to America. They will never find you."

Alex gave a great sigh of relief. "Yeah, you are right."

"Where are the foreigners who were in your cabin?" asked Louis.

"They went to the storeroom to do some gambling. They asked me to go with them, but I said no."

"Storeroom!"

"Do you want to join them?"

"Of course I do. I haven't gambled since I left America. Come on, let's go." They walked down the corridor to the storeroom. Along the way, Louis coached Alex in what to say about him. When they got to the door of the storeroom, he listened through the door and said, "You go inside. I will be right back."

"Where are you going?" asked Alex.

"I just want to tell Simon and Tiffany where I am." Then he walked upstairs to the first class area and to his cabin.

Simon and Tiffany were waiting for him in his cabin and as Louis entered, he said with a chuckle, "We are going to have the dinner with George in two or three days. I'm hoping we will have a chance to kill him at that time."

Simon said angrily, "I am sick and tired of pretending to like him. I can't do it anymore."

"Fool. We have to be patient." Louis turned to him. "Do you think I can bear spending time with that spoiled boy? We have to act as if we love him like a relative. Just think about all the wealth that will be ours. We are so close to having the life we have always dreamed of." He paused and took a deep breath. "I know a good place to kill him--the stern. Then we can throw him overboard for the sharks. That way nobody will ever find his body." He turned to Tiffany "You've got to be on your toes."

"What should I do?" asked Tiffany.

"You've got to pretend that you have fallen in love with him."

"He doesn't even pay any attention to me."

"I know, I know, everything you say is true, but we have to be patient. You just get him to the stern after dinner--tell him you want to talk to him about something important. Try to keep him there as long as you can. We just need a few minutes to finish the job."

"Don't worry. I know what to do," said Tiffany.

"I am going to fill Alex in," said Louis, and he left the cabin to join Alex and the others.

Louis entered the storeroom holding two six-packs of beer. All eyes went to him. "Hello, my friends." He knew how to treat people right when he needed to. Alex ran over, grabbed the beers from him and said cheerfully, "My friends, this is the man I was talking about. He raised the packs. "You see his generosity."

The foreigners arose with alacrity and remained standing out of respect. They were two Hungarians and two Albanians who were middle aged, and two swarthy Moroccans who were slightly younger. Louis stepped up and said, "I am Louis."

One of the Hungarians quickly said, "I am Barnabas."

The other Hungarian followed. "I am Zsombor."

Louis looked at their huge bodies and said, "It is very nice to meet two such strong men."

The two Albanians made the next introductions. "Hi, Louis, my name is Armend."

The other one said, "I am Bujar."

"What a good fortune that I have met such good, strong friends," said Louis and he turned to the two Moroccans.

The taller of the two, the one with the tough face and mustache, took two steps toward Louis and said, "I am Osman."

"Hi, Osman," said Louis.

Then the other one introduced himself. "I am Jamal."

"You look like each other. Are you related?" said Louis.

"Yeah, he is my cousin," answered Jamal quickly. "Mr. Louis is very perceptive to notice that about us."

"Yeah, he really is," said Alex. "I am sure he is just the man to solve all your problems."

Louis studied all of them, in case he could use them somehow in his plan, so he asked, "Problems! What kind of problems do you have? I will be happy to help if I can."

"All of them are going to America for work," said Alex, "but they don't have anybody to help them find a job once they get there."

Louis sighed and said, "It is very hard to find a job in America without a reference, but you don't need to worry about it. You all can work in one of my factories in New York City."

Alex jumped in the middle, holding the beer and handing the bottles around and said, "See? What did I tell you? Now drink your beer and forget all your worries."

Then Louis continued. "I will help you get everything you need to make a good life for you and your families."

A flame of joy lit up in all their faces, which now shone with happiness. They all felt understood by their new friend, and soon they settled into a trusting relationship that made them proud to have a friend and a boss like him. Their faces swung appreciatively toward him. "Thank you, Mr. Louis."

Louis shook his head selflessly. "What good is money if one doesn't use it to help those in need."

All of the men nodded politely, and then Louis added, "My friends, that is the way it should be--I help you today and you help me tomorrow."

All of them nodded in agreement and said together, "Yes, you are right."

Louis knew they would trust him now, that he had them right where he wanted them. At that time, the door opened and somebody stood in the doorway, looking at them. All heads turned. It was Simon. Louis recognized him right away, and he said to the men, "This is my son. I will go and see what he wants and be right back." Then he walked over to Simon, put his hand on his back, pushed him gently out of the room and closed the door behind them, saying angrily, "What the hell are you doing here?"

Simon smiled and said, "What was that all about?"

"None of your business. How did you find this place anyway?"

"It was easy. I just followed you."

Louis's eyes searched around for a second, holding Simon's arm, and he said, "Get out of here."

Simon knew him very well, and he could take advantage of him in that situation, so he asserted boldly, "Give me some money if you want me to leave here now."

"Money! I gave you ten bucks three days ago. What did you do with that?"

"What do you think I did with that chump change? I spent it in the first night. You know what, I won't leave here until you give me another five bucks."

Louis glared at him for a while; then, he took five dollars out of his pocket, threw it at his face and said, "I wish I hadn't brought you with me on this trip."

"Simon bent down and grabbed the money from the floor and said, "Too late." Then he walked away.

One of the ship employees who was a Chinese sailor was watching them from the end of the corridor, and as Louis sneaked into the storeroom, he followed him.

All of the foreigners were waiting ceremoniously for Louis. As he walked back in he said. "I am sorry, my friends, I had an important telegram from New York City."

At that time, the door opened and the Chinese sailor entered and looked at them for a few seconds and said, "Who are you? What are you doing here?"

"We just needed a quiet place to play cards," Louis answered in a friendly tone. The sailor looked at the beer and cigarette in their hands and said, "You can play in your cabin."

"The cabin is not big enough for all of us. On top of that, we don't want to bother the other people with our noises at this time of the night."

"This place is perfect," said Alex who sat on a wooden box, holding a beer bottle in one hand and a cigarette in the other.

"You can't smoke in this place. You could start a fire. You have to put out your cigarette right now," said the sailor seriously.

"Yes sir, we won't smoke in here anymore," Said Louis humbly. He looked around at the others and continued. "Did you hear what this gentleman just said? Please put out your cigarettes." The sailor remained until they had all put out their cigarettes, then he left the storeroom.

Louis stepped into the middle of the room and boasted, "If he knew who I was, he wouldn't dare talk to me like that."

"Why didn't you introduce yourself?" asked Alex.

"Forget about it. Let's just play cards and enjoy the company of our new friends," said Louis.

They all stayed in the storeroom until 3:00a.m. Everybody gambled his money away that night, except for Louis, the only winner. However, before they left the place, he gave all their money back to them in order to prove his generosity. As they left for their cabins, Louis asked Alex to meet him upstairs in the stern in ten minutes; then, he quickly walked upstairs by himself and waited for him.

It was cold outside. Louis had one foot on the lowest rail and his elbows on the top bar, while he smoked his cigarette and looked down at the sea, thinking about how he could use the foreigners in his plan. After a few minutes, Alex came from behind and called, "Louis?"

Louis turned back quickly. "It's me."

Alex approached and asked, "Do you have a cigarette?"

Louis stretched his hand. "This is the last one, but you can have it."

Alex grabbed the cigarette and lit it quickly, the match illuminating their faces for a moment. Then he leaned over the rails. Slightly drunk, he sighed with abysmal comfort and chuckled, "Oh, man, I am very happy that I am not in Italy anymore. Those bastards will never find me now."

"Think of the hell you'd face if you stayed there."

Alex put his hand on his shoulder and added, "Thank you. You saved my life."

Louis had been waiting to hear this from him. "You know, Alex, you are my cousin. We need to help each other."

"Sure, I will do anything for you, man," said Alex.

"I have something I think you can help me with," said Louis.

"You name it."

Louis threw the cigarette butt into the sea and sighed. "Do you remember my half-brother, Edward?"

Alex thought for a few seconds, and asked, "Your brother?"

"Yeah, my half-brother, Edward Wilson, the owner of the jewelry stores in New York City."

Alex thought for a while and answered, "Yeah, your brother, I know who you are talking about."

"Now he is the richest man in America. Do you want to know how he got so rich?"

"How?" asked Alex.

Louis sighed and shook his head. "We found a treasure together a few years ago, but that bastard cheated me out of my share and he kept it all for himself."

"But you both found the treasure together, right?" said Alex. "Why did you let him keep all of it?"

"I told you, he cheated me. He took the treasure home and told me that he would give me my share the next day, but when I went to get it he denied we'd ever found any treasure."

"What?" said Alex angrily. "That bastard should be punished."

"It is not fair." Louis sighed. "I suffer inside when I think about the way he treated me--my own brother! How could he do that to me?"

"If I were you, I would kill him."

"I finally decided I would get my share from him no matter what."

"Don't worry, I will help you. Just tell me what to do."

"I am going to take everything he owns."

"How?"

"He has no wife and one son, who will be his only heir after his death. But if I kill him and his son, I will be next in line to inherit everything."

"Oh, man, that's smart."

"We've got to kill his son first. Do you know where is he now?" said Louis.

"Where is he?"

"He is on this ship."

"What do you mean?"

"His son, George, is onboard this ship right now."

"Is his father here too?"

"No, he is in New York City. His son came on a vacation."

Alex brought the switchblade out of his pocket. "What are you waiting for? Let's kill him."

Louis grabbed the switchblade from his hand and opened it deliberately, fondling the blade and smiling. "We will kill him soon and throw him into the sea for the sharks. I will tell you when." Then he sent him to his cabin, and he left the place a few minutes later.

Chapter 20

It was the Destiny's third day at sea. The sky was clear the sun had fallen on the ship and warmed it up, and a gentle wind was blowing. Some of the passengers were walking and some were sitting on the wooden boxes and the warm boards of the deck and enjoying the sun. Katherine walked up to the main deck with the little girl, Tina. They walked among the people and then they stood at the port by the rails and looked out at the sea. Tina brought a paper box of colorful balloons out of the pocket of her jacket and said, "Let's blow some up and release them in the sky."

"Wow, you have a lot of balloons there," said Katherine.

"I think we should release two balloons every day until we get to America."

Katherine picked a red balloon from her hand and began to blow it up.

"Don't blow it up too much, or it will pop," said Tina, and she handed her a string.

Katherine grabbed the string, tied the balloon quickly and said, "I think we could blow up more." At that time, she released the balloon, which moved through the air by the gentle wind among the people toward the stern. Katherine and Tina ran laughing to catch the balloon. Every few seconds, the balloon touched the floor and bounced back into the air again. Everybody was looking at the balloon and the two girls that were running after it. A few people reached out to try to catch the balloon, but they missed. Katherine was running ahead of Tina, and she ran faster when it got close to the stern because she did not want to lose it. As she was running, she saw a man standing by the rails at the end of the ship, looking outward. It was George Wilson, and he was the only one left who could catch the balloon. Katherine called loudly, "Sir, please…my balloon."

George turned around and looked at Katherine, then at the balloon coming toward him, so he immediately jumped and caught it in the air before it got away. Katherine stopped in front of him panting, and she said, "Thank you very much."

George reached out, handed it to her and said, "You are welcome."

As Katherine took the balloon, they stared at each other for a long time, their eyes shining with excitement, their hearts pounding faster. As if it were a new experience for both of them. George smiled and said, "I am George."

"I am Angela," said Katherine smiling, and they shook hands.

At that time, Tina caught up with them and said, "You caught it."

"Almost got away forever, but then George here caught it," said Katherine.

Tina looked up at George and said, "Thank you, sir."

"You're welcome, pretty girl," said George. Katherine thanked him again and she walked toward the port alongside Tina.

George's friend, Daniel, was on the quarter deck, looking at George, staring at Katherine walking away, so he walked down to him and said with a chuckle, "Did you finally find the girl of your dreams?"

George smiled and dropped his head and did not say anything.

"I saw the whole thing. Tell me what happened?" said Daniel.

"I rescued their balloon."

"Did you ask where is she from?" asked Daniel.

"No."

"Where is her cabin?"

"I don't know."

"Well? Why don't you go and talk to her?"

"She was with that little girl. I prefer to talk to her when she is alone," said George as his eyes searched for her among the other passengers.

"I remembered something," said Daniel thoughtfully. "I saw her in the morning in front of the ship. She was by herself, looking at the sea. It was about seven o'clock."

"Are you sure it was the same girl?"

"Oh, yeah, I am sure. She was wearing the same dress."

George's eyes were still searching for her and he did not say anything.

"You know, George, if I were you, I would wake up early tomorrow and wait for her on the deck. She may show up there," Daniel suggested.

George paused for a few seconds and said, "That's not a bad idea."

"All right, let's go eat something. I haven't eaten all day." Then they walked up to the restaurant together.

George could not get Katherine out of his head. He went to the deck several times that afternoon and stayed there for hours hoping to see her, but she didn't show up. He remembered the moment they met. That night, he awakened at intervals, looked at the clock and paced in his cabin for a few minutes before going back to bed. The moments passed slowly and the night was long, as he restlessly waited to see her in the morning.

Katherine was thinking of George too, and she was inclined to see him again.

The next morning at the daybreak, Katherine emerged on the deck like on the previous day, and walked to the front of the ship and stood by the rails, looking up into the blue sky. It was clear and not a cloud was to be seen. She looked at the sea rippling and sparkling below, and her gaze went into the distance. Her blond hair, disarrayed in the wind, gleamed in the sunlight. She put her hands on the top rails, closed her eyes and felt the gentle wind on her face. It was whispering in her ears. She thought of George and looked back at the quarterdeck involuntary, but seeing only two employees in the starboard, she turned and kept looking into the distance, thinking of future possibilities.

At the same time, George appeared on the quarterdeck, his eyes moving to the front of the ship quickly in search of Katherine. He saw her standing looking at the sea. His heart started pounding hard, and he rubbed his eyes to make sure he was not dreaming. "That's the same girl from yesterday. I should go and talk to her before she leaves," he said to himself, heading her way. When he got close he walked slowly and cautiously so as not to scare her. He stood a few feet behind her and stared at her silently, wondering how to talk to her.

Although Katherine had not heard his footsteps, she was thinking of George too.

"Hi," said George. Katherine quickly turned away and saw him smiling at her. She was shocked and did not know what to say.

"Sorry, did I scare you?" said George.

Katherine could not believe her eyes. She shaded her bright eyes with her hand and said excitedly, "Oh, no, I am fine."

"I saw you released some balloons in the air with that little girl yesterday," said George.

"Yeah, she is staying in my cabin with her mother and brother."

"Do you like traveling by ship?" asked George.

"Yeah," answered Katherine.

"This is my first time to go on a trip. I'm having a really good time. It's been really nice seeing a few countries," said George.

Katherine smiled and did not say anything.

"Where are you from?" asked George.

"New York City."

"Really?" said George curiously. "I am from New York City, too. Which part?"

Katherine paused. It was an unexpected question. "We just moved from Boston to New York City a month ago. I can't remember the name of the street. It is close to the central train station."

"Do you like New York City?"

"Yes."

"What about the traffic there?"

Katherine smiled without saying anything.

"Do you like to walk?"

"Yes, of course." Then they walked toward the starboard.

As they were walking, George looked up at the sun, took a deep breath and said, "It is nice weather, isn't it?"

"Yeah, it is. I like it."

"I think we will reach America in one week, if the weather stays like this. I remember it took about ten days from Boston to Liverpool."

"Did you go to England by the same ship?"

"Yes, that is how I know."

"Do you think the weather is going to stay like this until we get there?"

"I don't know. I have a friend who is a sailor in this ship, and he says that it is going to be stormy in a few days, before we reach Boston." George looked up at the sun. "He is my best friend. His name is Daniel. We've known each other for a long time. He is almost always right about the forecast, but I still made a bet with him that we won't see any storms before we reach America."

"What did you bet?" asked Katherine smiling.

"The loser will pay for lunch and dinner and the movies tickets for two days after we get back to New York City."

"I like that bet."

"What do you think?" asked George. "Will we see a storm before we reach America or not?"

Katherine paused for a second and answered, "I don't know."

"Do you agree with me or not?"

Katherine smiled without saying anything.

"All right, let's you and I make that bet too," said George.

Katherine looked at him and smiled. They were almost at the starboard when George suddenly pointed to someone who was coming down from the quarterdeck. "There he is now. Let's go see him." Then he called out to Daniel and they went over to him.

Daniel recognized Katherine even from far. "Hi."

"This is my friend, Angela," George said.

"Good to meet you. My name is Daniel." They shook hands.

"Looks like another sunny day with no sign of storm," said George with a smile. "How are you feeling about the bet we made?"

"Don't forget we have six or seven more days till we get to America," said Daniel.

"I already told Angela about our bet. I think she is willing to make the same bet with one of us." Then he looked at her and continued. "What do you say? Will we see any storms before we reach America?"

Katherine smiled and dropped her head down and said nothing.

"Do you agree with him or me?" asked George.

Katherine looked up at the sky and said, "I think…we won't see any storms on our way."

"Okay, if you lose, you two have to pay for my breakfast, lunch, dinner, and the tickets for the movies for two days," said Daniel.

"And if you lose, you have to pay for all of that for both of us," said George.

"Okay, no problem," Daniel said.

"I am sure you are going to lose this time, so you better start saving your money," said George.

"We will see who is going to lose," said Daniel. Then they laughed together.

"Can you guess where Angela is from?" George asked.

"I was going to ask her that." Daniel said.

"Well, now you get to guess," said George before she said something.

Daniel looked at her thoughtfully for a while and replied, "She is an American."

George said, "Of course she is an American. But which city in America is she from?"

"That is hard to say," said Daniel doubtfully. "But something tells me she is from New York City."

"She lives in New York City, but she moved there from Boston a month ago," George said. Daniel continued. "You know, George, when I saw you two from the quarterdeck, I thought about your drawing that is in the ship's gallery. Did you show it to Angela?"

"No, we didn't go there yet," said George.

"Drawing!" Katherine looked at George. "Are you a painter?"

"I draw sometimes, but I am not a good painter," said George.

"He is being humble," said Daniel. "He is a good painter. I am sure when you see his drawing you are going to like it."

"What is the drawing of?" Katherine asked.

"Why don't you take her to the gallery? It's best if she sees it," said Daniel quickly.

At that time, a member of the ship's staff approached them and said to Daniel, "Excuse me, Mr. Smith. Can we check out the lifeboats now?"

"You can get started. I will join you in a minute," said Daniel, and he turned to George and Katherine. "I've got some work to do, so I will leave you alone. See you two later."

As he was walking away, Katherine asked, "I'd like to see the drawing that he was talking about."

"Do you want to see it right now?"

"Yes, of course."

"Okay, let's go."

In the gallery were fifty drawings by different contemporary artists. As they walked through the carpeted room, Katherine's eyes searched for George's artwork. Finally, George stood before a painting at the end of the room and said, "Here it is."

Katherine got closer to the painting and looked at it without saying anything.

George pointed. "That is a sunset in New York City, this is the Statue of Liberty and the sun setting behind it and a boy and a girl holding hands, running on the shore toward the statue."

Katherine studied the picture carefully, focusing on the boy and girl. Their shadows were long behind them, and the sea was to their right. She got closer, staring at it without blinking, and finally she said, "It is amazing."

"The boy and the girl are running to get back home before dark."

Katherine was fascinated by the painting. It moved her to recall her childhood in New York City. It was the best picture that she had ever seen. She touched the frame gently and said, "It is amazing." Then she looked at George's name and the date at the bottom of the picture. "You drew this two years ago."

George said smiling, "I was in third grade when I drew it for the first time, and I got the best grade in the classroom that day."

"Wow, was it just from your imagination?" asked Katherine.

"It just came."

"It is beautiful. You used very nice colors."

"Thank you."

Katherine's eyes remained glued to the painting. It was the same picture that George had drawn on the seashore of the old shipyard fourteen years ago, when they went to visit his grandmother, but Katherine could not remember that far back. She examined the picture meticulously for a long time. It touched her deeply, reaching down to some of the core moments that she shared with her parents. She began to feel sad, but very soon she realized that George was beside her, and she felt the warmth of a future spent with one who would stay with her in her loneliness. They were together about one hour; then, she went to her cabin.

The moments passed very sweetly for them, and they thought of each other constantly. As they fell in love with each other, they could not wait to see each other as soon as possible.

That night, Katherine received an invitation to dinner from George in the restaurant reserved for the first class passengers. She saw how the various staff members gave him their attention and respect, and she was very curious to know about his position, but she did not want to provoke his curiosity and risk him turning the tables and asking her about her personal life. If that happened, she might have to lie to him again, and she did not want to do that. When dinner was served, the chef came to their table and asked George about the preparation for his birthday. When he left, Katherine asked George immediately, "Is it your birthday?"

George smiled. "Yeah, in two days. I am going to be twenty-five. I have to see who all I am going to invite."

"Can I ask you about your position on this ship?" asked Katherine.

George smiled and said, "I don't hold any position on this ship. I am just here on a vacation, but the owner of the ship is my father. That's why some of the staff knows me."

Katherine looked at him without saying anything. She really liked the way he treated everybody humbly despite the fact he was the boss's son.

George continued. "I came on this trip to see the icebergs."

"Icebergs!"

"Yeah, Daniel has told me about the many icebergs he has seen on his trips."

"Have you seen any of them yourself?"

"Only two small icebergs on the way to England. I hope I see some big ones yet. The captain has informed the staff to notify me immediately when they see an iceberg." Then he looked at his watch. "I forgot to invite the captain to my birthday. I think he is on the bridge now. Let's go see him."

After a short walk, they got to the bridge. The captain, who was seventy years old, had a white beard. He stood at the helm in his uniform and hat, steering the ship. As the door opened, he turned to them and said with a smile, "George."

"Hello, captain, how are you?"

"Good."

"My friend, Angela," George said by way of introduction.

"Hi, I am Steve," said the captain. "It is very good to see you."

"I wanted to invite you to my birthday party. It will be held in two days," George said.

"Thank you for the invitation. I will be there for sure."

"We will be glad to see you there," George said, and then he looked outside. "Have you seen any icebergs since we left England?"

"No, we haven't had any reports of icebergs."

"I have only seen two small icebergs so far on my vacation. I hope to see some big ones before we reach America," George said.

"I am sure we will see some," the captain assured.

George continued. "Daniel told me that he has seen an iceberg as big as mountain, like the one that sank the Titanic."

"It is so awful to think about a ship hitting an iceberg," Katherine said.

"Is it true that the speed of Titanic was what caused that incident?" George asked the captain.

The captain pursed his lips judiciously. "Yes. They had speeded up to finish the trip as quickly as possible and set a new record. It was too late when the watchmen noticed the iceberg, and they couldn't stop the ship in time or even pass to one side of the iceberg." Then he sighed and continued. "Innocent people died for the ambition of somebody who wanted to set a new historical record."

"Icebergs sound very dangerous," said Katherine.

The captain looked at her and smiled. He was very experienced and knew how to talk to worried passengers. He moved to the helm deliberately and said, "Icebergs can be helpful sometimes."

"What do you mean?" asked Katherine.

"Imagine that you are on a ship or a boat that is sinking, and there is nobody around to help you. All you see is an iceberg floating nearby. Now, answer me this: Can that iceberg be as your lifeboat until help arrives?"

Katherine looked at him for several seconds, and then she nodded her head in agreement. "Yes, you are right. It is true."

"You are very experienced, captain," George said, smiling.

The captain smiled without saying anything as he was looking outside. Then they bid the captain goodbye, left the bridge, walked on the quarterdeck, stood by the rails and looked out at the sea. At that time Louis's daughter, Tiffany, arrived at the quarterdeck. It seemed that she was following them and had come there on purpose to bother them. She walked to them and said loudly, "Hi, George."

George turned around quickly and said in wonder, "Tiffany!"

"Yeah, how are you doing?"

George was not happy to see her there, and he glared at her angrily without saying anything.

"I was just taking a walk," said Tiffany. She looked at Katherine and continued. "I saw the two of you in the restaurant a few minutes ago."

"This is my friend, Angela," said George coldly.

"Hi," said Tiffany. Then she put her hand on George's shoulder and continued flirtatiously. "It is a nice night."

George looked at her hand and then turned his face to Katherine.

"I've got to go to my cabin for something. Thank you for the dinner," said Katherine as she took her leave.

Tiffany smiled and asked, "Where is your friend from?"

"She is from New York City. I am sorry. There is someone I need to see," said George, and he hastily departed.

Chapter 21

The next evening, Louis had dinner with George. His son and daughter were with them, too. They were unusually warm to him. Little did he know they planned to kill him that night.

After dinner, as George was leaving the restaurant, Tiffany cornered him. "I want to talk to you about something important."

"Important?" George said. "What is it?"

"I can't tell you here," Tiffany said, looking around furtively.

"What is that you can't tell me here?"

"Come to the stern at twelve o'clock. I will tell you there." Tiffany turned her attention to the table where Louis and Simon sat. "I don't even want my father and brother to know about it. I only want to keep it between you and me."

"Why do you want to tell me there?" George said.

"It is quiet and private. Just be there at twelve o'clock," said Tiffany, and then she returned to Louis and Simon.

Louis asked immediately, "What did he say?"

"Nothing yet, but I told him to meet me at the stern at twelve o'clock."

Louis Looked at his watch and said, "It is 10:30. That gives us plenty of time."

"What should we do now?" asked Simon.

"You two go to your cabin and wait for me there. I will go tell Alex about it. We have to get there thirty minutes before George does, so we can hide."

"What time should I be there?" asked Tiffany.

"Be there twenty minutes before twelve," said Louis. Then he left there.

The stern of the ship was usually darker than the other parts of the deck. It was cold there, and at midnight, it was typically isolated, with only the watchmen in the watchtower looking out for icebergs and other ships and the sound of the engine. It was 11:55, and Tiffany was standing by the rails in the stern, waiting for George. She was the only person around. Louis, Simon, and Alex were hiding behind some large wooden boxes forty feet from where Tiffany was. When Louis saw George, he suddenly said, "He is coming, keep still." Then the three crouched behind the boxes.

George walked past the boxes on his way to the stern.

Simon said impatiently, "It is time, let's kill him now."

"No, wait," said Louis, and he pulled him down. "Let's give them a few minutes."

Tiffany leaned back against the rails, looking at George as he approached. She tried to avoid moving around much so she could keep an eye on where her father and brother were and to make sure George would not see them as they came for him. As George approached, Tiffany said with a smile, "Hi, George."

"What do you want to tell me?" asked George.

Tiffany said, "You know, George, I have had a very good time on this trip, and it was mostly because you were with us." Then she paused.

George had no idea where she was going with this. "What is so important that you had to tell me here?"

Tiffany got closer to him. "It is a beautiful night, isn't it?"

"I have a lot to do, Tiffany, so tell me quick," said George losing his patience.

Tiffany even got closer to him, put her hands on his chest and said, "I don't know how to tell you this so

I'll just come right out with it. I have fallen in love with you, George."

"What?" George backed off quickly and said angrily, "You brought me here at this time of the night to tell me that?"

Tiffany's eyes went to the boxes in search of Louis and Simon and at the same time, she tried to think of something to say. "Let me tell you something."

Louis, Alex and Simon stared at George like hungry hyenas, then Louis stood up and said, "It is time, let's go."

Simon and Alex stood up and pulled socks over their faces, but suddenly from behind them Louis said, "Quick, get down, somebody is coming." They all three got back behind the boxes and listened carefully.

Soon a teenage boy and a girl ran up, laughing. The boy tried to catch the girl. They were from first class, and they were traveling with their parents. As they reached the stern and saw George and Tiffany, they said, "Sorry." They turned around and headed elsewhere.

George looked around and said, "I have to go, I can't stay here anymore." Then he walked away.

Tiffany walked after him and said insistently, "Please, stay here, I want to talk to you."

However, George didn't pay any attention to her and walked away angrily and quickly. As he passed by the boxes, Simon said to Louis, "Where is he going? Will he be back?"

"I don't know," said Louis.

As Tiffany approached them he asked, "Where did he go?"

"I don't know, he just left."

"Will he come back?"

"I don't think so."

"Why did he leave so soon? What did you say to him?"

"As soon as I told him that I loved him, he got mad and left."

Without warning, Louis slapped her hard and she fell to the floor. "I told you tell him about a memory, so you could keep him there longer."

Simon came out of his place and kicked her in the back. "You asked him to marry you?"

Louis stopped him quickly and said, "That is enough."

"I did what you said, but he didn't want to stay there and listen to me," protested Tiffany.

"Shut up and go to your cabin right now," said Louis, and he let her go.

"We will never get another chance to kill him," said Simon. "I told you to attack him as soon as he got to the stern, but you didn't listen."

"Did you want to kill him in public?" Louis turned his head sharply. "Or did you already forget about those damned kids who showed up there?"

"We had enough time to kill him before they showed up."

"Your father is right, we never had a chance to kill him," Alex broke in.

"Bad luck," said Louis as he bit his tongue.

Simon sighed and said plaintively, "We won't get a better chance."

"We have enough time. We will get another chance before we reach America," said Louis.

Alex loosened his belt and tucked in his shirttail and tightened the belt again and opened his switchblade and said, "Don't worry, boy, I won't let him go next time."

"We better leave here now," Louis said. He sent them to their cabins by two different routes, and he left a few minutes after them.

  The next night at about ten o'clock, George was in the entertainment hall with the guests that had come for his birthday party. He was dressed in a black suit and a white shirt and he had on a broad maroon silken bow tie. He was standing by the stairway, talking to Mr. Tomas Foster and his wife, who were from England and who had a business relationship with his father. The captain and Daniel were standing by a table, holding drinks, talking about the weather. Mr. Roger Fulton and his wife from Boston, and Mr. Hamilton and his wife from New York City, stood in the middle of the hall talking. Louis and his son and daughter had been invited too, but they were still in their cabin, discussing their plan. Louis was sure that George would go to the stern with Katherine after the party, so they would wait there for the moment to kill them, with Louis constantly assuring them that they would finish the job successfully this time. But Simon was not convinced. "What if they don't show up there tonight? I think we should kill him in his cabin."

Louis stomped his foot on the floor and his eyes smoldered angrily. "That is nonsense. How can we all three get into his cabin and kill him there? What will we do with the body? That is a stupid idea."

"We will get to America soon, and then we'll be all out of time," said Simon.

"Mark my words. Tonight will be the last night of his life," said Louis. Then they all left to go to the party.

George was still standing by the stairway talking to Mr. Foster and his wife, and he was beginning to wonder where Katherine was. It was ten o'clock, and she had not shown up yet. As he cast another glance at the clock on the wall, he suddenly saw Katherine at the top of the stairs. She had on a long maroon silk dress, the one that Ivano had given her for her twentieth birthday, and she wore the necklace with the rose icon that George's father, Edward Wilson, had given her. She smiled at George and walked elegantly down the stairs. George was fascinated by her beauty. He met her halfway up the stairs and reached out his hand toward her. Katherine put her hand into his and said, "Hi."

George kissed her hand and said, "I am very happy you are here."

"I am sorry that I am late a little."

"Don't worry." They walked down to join the other guests alongside each other.

All eyes were on them. It was the first time for most of the people there to see her. Once downstairs they joined Mr. and Mrs. Foster, and George introduced them.

"I think George's eyes were looking for Ms. Vincent all the while he was talking to us," Mr. Foster said knowingly.

George smiled without saying anything.

"I think you're right. I wondered why he kept looking at the stairs," said Mrs. Foster after her husband.

"You are the most beautiful young couple that I have ever seen in my life," Mr. Fulton said loudly. All the guests nodded their heads in agreement. George and Katherine smiled at each other, they walked over and George introduced her. "Angela Vincent."

"Roger Fulton and my wife, Sarah," said Mr. Fulton.

"Dean Hamilton, my wife, Ana," said Mr. Hamilton.

"I can see this beautiful miss is from America," Mr. Fulton said.

"You have a good eye for women, Mr. Fulton," the captain said as he approached them with Daniel.

"Do you know her?" Mr. Fulton asked.

"I met her when they came to tell me about George's birthday," said the captain.

"Which city do you live in, Miss. Vincent?" Mr. Fulton asked.

Katherine knew it was important that she be consistent, so she told him the same thing that she told George. "I live in New York City. We moved there from Boston a month ago."

"Which part of Boston did you live in?" asked Mr. Fulton.

Katherine paused without saying anything, though Mr. Fulton continued quickly. "The reason I ask is because I lived in Boston all my life and know the city well."

Katherine did not know how to answer. All that came to her mind was a picture of the port of Boston, from when she was kidnapped by Alex fourteen years ago. "We used to live by the port."

"The neighborhood that is in front of the port? You mean Portland?" asked Mr. Fulton.

"Yes."

"I know that neighborhood," Mrs. Fulton said.

At that time, a voice from behind said, "Hi, George."

George and Katherine turned around and saw Louis smiling at them, with Simon and Tiffany standing close behind.

"How are you doing, George?" said Louis.

"This is my uncle, Louis, and my cousins, Simon and Tiffany," George said.

"I am very pleased to meet you, dear guests," said Louis, looking at Katherine and the others. Meanwhile Simon and Tiffany remained behind him and looked at them coldly without saying anything. All the guests introduced themselves.

"All right, everybody is here, let's go and take a seat." Then they all walked over to a big table where dinner had been prepared.

Katherine looked at Louis carefully, her attention drawn to the burn mark on his face and the blood spot in his eyes. Before long, she remembered that one of the people who killed her parents had the same name and the same particulars, and she became worried, but she dismissed the feeling, telling herself, "It is impossible that she would meet the same person, on a ship, much less after all these years. Add to that, he was George's uncle, and there was no way her tragic past could in any way be connected to George." However, she remained slightly worried. George noticed something different about her and asked, "Are you all right?"

"Yeah, I am fine."

As the waiters were serving the dinner, Mr. Foster asked, "George, did you know Miss Vincent before or did you two meet on this trip?"

"I met her on the ship a few days ago," George answered.

"How romantic to become friends while on the ocean," Mr. Foster added.

"Yeah, it really is," said Mr. Fulton.

Daniel spoke up next. "The reason George came on this trip was to see an iceberg, but he was lucky that he met Miss Vincent."

The guests smiled, all except for Louis and his son and daughter.

Daniel continued. "Actually, he didn't even want to come on this trip, but his father insisted." Then he looked at George. "Do you remember that, George?"

George nodded his head with a smile.

"I am sure George has had lots of experiences on this trip," said the captain. "In my opinion, the experience of traveling by sea teaches a person things he can never learn on land."

"I completely agree, captain," Mr. Fulton said.

"Yeah, I agree too," said Louis, trying to bend in. "It was my first trip by sea, and I have experienced many things for the first time in my life. I never thought I would have such a fantastic trip."

Louis was sitting with his ears alert to anything that passed between George and Katherine. His son and daughter, still with cold shoulders and whispering together sometimes, were jealous of her and sought to humiliate her.

"Can I ask Miss Vincent, what are you traveling for? Are you here to experience the icebergs like George?" asked Tiffany.

Katherine looked at her for a few seconds and answered, "I am just traveling."

"We didn't see you in the first class area. Where is your cabin?" asked Tiffany.

"I am in a second class cabin," said Katherine.

Tiffany and Simon looked at each other, and Tiffany continued. "I see. That must be a... different sort of experience."

Katherine became a little embarrassed, hung her head and looked at her plate.

"I am sorry," George said to Katherine tenderly.

Mrs. Fulton said critically to Simon and Tiffany, "It doesn't matter which class someone is in. It has no effect on the experience of being at sea."

Mr. Fulton spoke after his wife. "That's right. I remember when I was young, I traveled all the states by train and saw many cities, and it never once occurred to me that I was travelling in an economy coach." Everybody agreed to that.

Louis was sitting beside Simon, and he whispered slowly into his ear, "You two idiots are going to ruin everything with your foolishness."

Mr. Foster tried to change the subject, so he asked, "Captain, can you tell us when we will reach the port of Boston?"

"We should reach America in five days if the weather is good like today," said the captain.

"Of course, we may have a storm before we get to the port of Boston," Daniel chimed in.

"Storm!" Mrs. Hamilton said with alarm.

"Don't worry, Mrs. Hamilton. It is normal to see storms when you travel by sea," the captain assured everybody. "You all are safe on this ship."

"Captain is right. You don't need to worry as long as you are on this ship," added Daniel.

Mr. Fulton asked Daniel, "How sure are you, young sailor, that we will see a storm?"

"I am positive," said Daniel as he ate daintily. "I have already made a bet with George and Miss Vincent that we will have a storm." Then everyone laughed together, uneasily. After dinner, the waiters brought out the birthday cake. It was a three-layer cake, with twenty-four lit candles. Katherine said slowly into his ear, "Are you ready?"

George smiled and said, "Yeah." Then everybody except for Simon and Tiffany counted to three and sang the birthday song together, and George blew out all the candles. The musicians then struck up some music and the guests began dancing. Daniel brought a harmonica out of his pocket and played along, and George and Katherine held hands and joined the other guests in dance.

Louis, Simon, and Tiffany sat watching everyone closely, and before the party was over, he sent them to their cabin to get ready to go to the deck. Soon thereafter, he said goodbye to George and left as well.

Ten minutes later, as Simon and Tiffany were hiding behind the wooden boxes on the deck, Louis arrived and asked, "Where is Alex?"

"We haven't seen him," Simon answered.

"I told him to wait for us right here. I'll go and get that jackass," Louis said.

"Do you still think that we need him?" Simon asked.

"Yes. Now just wait for me here." Louis headed to the second class. Two minutes later, Alex appeared on the deck. Simon said angrily, "Where the hell have you been, man?"

"I went to the restroom. What is the matter?" Alex said.

"Did you have to go to the restroom now?"

"What? Would you prefer that I take a shit here?"

Simon released his breath, shaking head without saying anything.

"Where is your father?" Alex asked.

"He went to find you, and bring you here," Simon said.

"I'll go after him," Alex said.

"Hush now, and get down. Here comes someone." Tiffany grabbed his jacket, and they quickly crouched behind the boxes.

It was George and Katherine. They were holding hands, walking toward the stern, swinging their hands rhythmically as they walked. They walked past the wooden boxes and got to the stern. They stood there, holding onto the top rail and looking up at the moon. It was in it's last quarter, and there were a few clouds moving slowly across, covering the moon one after another. The night was quiet. It was cold, and nobody was on deck, the only sound was that of the ship's engine. As they were looking at the moon, Katherine said, "This is nice."

"Yes, it is."

They turned to face each other, their eyes locking, their love roaring through their beings. It seemed as if each of them was waiting for the other to say something. George looked at her necklace glinting in the soft moonlight and said, "I love you."

"I love you, too," said Katherine. Then they moved in close for a first, very soft kiss. It was the first time either of them had experienced true love. Then they hugged each other tightly.

Simon, Tiffany, and Alex watched them from behind the boxes, waiting for Louis to attack. Simon said angrily, "Where the hell has he gone? He said he would come right back."

"Perhaps something happened to detain him," Alex said.

"We've got to wait for him. We can't pull this off without him," Tiffany said.

"Oh, shit, now's our chance." Simon looked up at the sky. "That big cloud is about to cover the moon. Let's just do it ourselves."

"No. Did you forget what father said? Please wait," Tiffany insisted.

"We can't wait too long. If we do, we are going to lose this chance, and we may never get another," Simon said.

"Simon is right." Alex touched his nose with his fingers and said, "We can kill them ourselves."

At that time, the big cloud covered the moon and the deck became darker. Simon said hurriedly, "Come on, it is time. Let's do it quick, before the moon comes back out. Tiffany, you stay here and keep a look out." Then they covered their heads with socks and approached them.

George and Katherine were hugging each other, swaying slowly, when suddenly they saw two dark figures moving toward them. "Who is that?" Katherine asked.

"I don't know," George answered. Then they stood apart.

The dark figures stood a few steps away, staring at them without saying anything.

"Who are you?" asked George, but there was no response. Katherine remembered the evening when she was in Louis's house in the old shipyard fourteen years ago. She squeezed George's hand tightly.

"I said who are you?" George asked angrily.

Simon looked up at the moon, which was still covered by the cloud, and he slowly said to Alex, "You go for him, I'll get the girl." Alex pulled his switchblade out of his pocket and they stalked toward them like two wolves converging on their prey.

George noticed the switchblade, so he prepared to defend himself. He pushed Katherine behind him and said, "You better run away."

"No, I can't leave you alone," said Katherine. "I won't go anywhere without you."

Alex lunged at George first and tried to stab his neck, but George caught his wrist in the air. Simon attacked Katherine and grabbed her by the neck to throw her into the sea. Katherine cried out, "George."

Still holding off Alex, George turned around and saw Katherine was in serious danger. He became enraged and he brought his knee up into Alex's stomach with all his might. When Alex doubled over, George delivered a hefty blow to his chin and he fell down on the deck. Then George leaped at Simon, grabbed him from behind and struck him in the face and then several times quickly and in succession. Simon's head jolted and he tumbled to the deck. Then George hugged Katherine and asked, "Are you all right?"

As Katherine was touching her neck, she saw Alex was coming from behind. She turned hastily to George and cried, "Be careful."

At the same time that George turned back, Alex stabbed his right arm with the switchblade. Katherine screamed. The men in the watchtower turned their faces to the scene below, and they reported it immediately.

George's body stiffened and he clenched his fist. His lips were pulled taut against his teeth with anger and determination to fight their attackers. He dodged Alex's next blow and hit him several times hard in the face, and Alex slumped to the ground, his switchblade sliding on the floor. He tried to get up, only to receive another punch in the face that knocked him back down. The blood spurted from his lips and ran down his chin. George took the sock off his head and looked at his face. He cried, "Who are you?" Then he went to Katherine and hugged her and said, "Are you all right?"

"Yeah, I am fine."

Simon was only half-conscious. He stood up, teetered down to the deck again and shook his head to clear it. He heard sounds around him and saw George and Katherine hugging each other by the rails. Alex was unconscious a few feet away, so he staggered to his feet and ran away. Tiffany was still hiding behind the wooden boxes, watching them all times. She left the deck hastily after her brother. At that time, a few staff members ran toward the stern where they arrested Alex. Louis appeared on the deck at the same time and saw the crowd, talking loudly. He thought Simon and Alex were in trouble, and he walked slowly to the wooden boxes to see if Tiffany was there. Finding the hiding spot vacant, he crouched behind the boxes to see the scene better. Alex was handcuffed and on the floor, silent, his head down. One of the staff members was shining a flashlight in Alex's face, looking at him carefully. It was the same Chinese sailor who had seen him with Louis and the foreigners gambling. He finally recognized Alex and said, "I know this man. I saw him and his friends in the storeroom a few nights ago."

"They were two of the people who attacked us. The other one ran away," George exclaimed.

"I saw a young man running like a bullet. That must have been him." The Chinese sailor asked, "Would you recognize him if you saw him again, Mr. Wilson?"

"No, he had his face covered."

"But I can, easily, if I saw him," the Chinese sailor said.

George stepped over to Alex, looking carefully at his face and the bandage on his ears for a few seconds and said, "I have never seen this one before."

Alex was looking at the floor without saying anything, thinking of his cousin, Louis, the only person who could rescue him.

"Where should we look for the other one who escaped?" one of the sailors asked.

"We should search the second class," suggested the Chinese sailor. "We've got to tell the captain about it."

"He is probably asleep. We better tell him tomorrow. It is too late to do anything about it anyway," George said. "You just lock him up, and we will look for the other one tomorrow."

Katherine was standing beside George, gazing full on at Alex. She didn't take her eyes from him, her mind hardening and growing suspicious as she remembered the face of Alex that she had in her mind. She was listening attentively to hear him say something, but he was silent as a stone. She remembered his silver tooth; it was the only thing that indicated he was the same person she was thinking of. As one of the sailors was pinching his mouth and asking for his name forcibly, she saw a tooth gleaming in the light of the flashlight, so she took a closer look. Quickly, her eyes sharpened and she studied him carefully, then she stepped back.

"Do you know him?" George asked quickly.

Katherine quaked inwardly with fear for a moment and answered, "No."

Although she had decided not to tell him at that time, she was sure he was the same person who had kidnapped her fourteen years ago. Very quickly, she remembered George's uncle, Louis, the person who was at his birthday party, and the burn mark on his face and the blood spot in his eyes. As that and Alex's silver tooth were put next to each other like the last pieces of a puzzle, she grew sure he was the same Louis who had killed her parents, and he might even be the one who attacked them with Alex a few minutes ago. At that time, a chill of fear went through her, and all the bitter memories of her early years passed quickly in front of her eyes like a fast motion film reel. "What should I do? For the time being, I will keep quiet and will see what happens," she said to herself.

"All right, take him. We will look for the other one tomorrow," George said.

Louis was still hiding behind the wooden boxes, listening to them. Before they hauled Alex away from the deck, he slid off and went straight to

Tiffany's cabin. He stood by the door and tried to open it, but it was locked. He looked around and called softly, "Hey, it is me, your father. Open the door."

The door opened and he slid inside and Tiffany locked the door after him. Simon was standing by the wall, looking at him guiltily. Louis asked him angrily, "What happened?"

Simon dropped his head down and did not say anything. Tiffany said, "I told them to wait for you, but they didn't listen to me and tried to kill them by themselves."

Louis bit his tongue, ran to Simon, grabbed him by the collar tightly, pushed him against the wall and said angrily, "You ruined everything!"

"We waited for you, but you didn't show up," said Simon meekly.

"Shut up. You think that you made it better? Now everybody is looking for you, and sooner or later they will find you."

"I had my face covered," said Simon.

"Hey, wise guy, one of the staff saw you, when you were running away. They are going to search everywhere tomorrow morning for you."

"What should we do now?" Tiffany asked.

Louis took a deep breath and said, "I will go to second class to see those guys. We need their help."

"Who are you talking about? You mean the foreigners who are in Alex's cabin?" Tiffany asked.

As Louis was staring at the door, he nodded his head. "Yeah, they can be a big help to us."

"What do you want to do?" Simon asked.

Louis's tongue fluttered sharply against his teeth and he bit his lower lip and said, "I will tell you later. You just wait for me here, but you, Tiffany, keep your eyes on George's cabin. We've got to know what is going on." Then he left.

Louis was sure that he would never get another opportunity to kill George by himself, so he could use the foreigners for his plan. It was his best hope. He intended to dull their senses with beer to make them more compliant and less sensitive to the dire ramifications of his plan.

Louis took three packs of beer and went quickly to the storeroom. All the foreigners were there gambling and Louis entered, holding the packs of beer. All the foreigners stood up quickly, and Barnabas ran to him and grabbed the beer from his hands and they all stood around him. Louis knew that he didn't have much time, so he opened the bottles of beer and handed them out, raising a bottle himself and drinking with them. It gurgled down their throats without the preliminary sip. Then Louis opened another bottle for everyone and said, "Enjoy, my friends."

Barnabas kissed the bottle, smelled the beer thirstily, drank it to the last drop, then polished his mouth with his sleeves and said, "I have never seen anyone as generous like Mr. Louis in my life."

Next Louis handed out cigarettes to everyone and said, "I always share my joy with the others, especially with people like you who are really in need. I will be happy to help you whenever I can."

Everybody thanked him. Then he continued. "You know, my friends, I need all of you to work in my factories, but not as a labor. I want you to learn the job and be supervisors in my factories." Then he gave each of them five dollars and smiled. "You may need this before you get to America."

Everybody was surprised, and they thanked him profusely. Adolfo said, "We will be so happy if we can do something for you, Mr. Louis."

"You know, my friends, you are the people who deserve it," Louis said and then he sighed and closed his eyes and opened them again and continued. "But there are some people that when you help them, they betray you instead of thanking you."

The other Hungarian, Zsombor, said, "What sort of rascal would betray somebody who helped him?"

Louis said sadly, "I have someone in my life who betrayed me instead of saying thanks."

"Whoever did that to you deserves to be killed," said Osman angrily.

"I gave him a good job as my assistant, I gave him whatever he needed, but one day, he stole half a million from my safe and ran away."

"What!" everybody said with anger.

"If I were you, I would kill him," Barnabas said as he smoked his cigarette.

The Albanian man, Armend, asked, "What did you do to him, Mr. Louis?"

"Nothing. We couldn't prove he stole the money." Louis sighed. "I am sure that he stole it, because he and I were the only ones who had the keys to that safe. Now, you tell me, my friends, what do you do if somebody betrays you like that?"

"I will kill him," said everybody.

Louis dropped his head down without saying anything.

Barnabas took one step closer and asked, "Where is that bastard now?"

Louis looked at them for a few seconds and said, "You won't believe me if I tell you where he is now."

"Tell us, where is he?" asked Jamal.

"He is on this ship right now."

"What? This ship?" everybody asked in wonder.

"Yeah, he is traveling on this ship, spending my money." Louis sighed.

"I will kill that bastard," Barnabas said.

"You don't know the half of it. He did something else tonight," said Louis.

Everybody asked impatiently, "What did he do?"

"He got our friend Alex in trouble."

"I see that he is not here tonight," Bujar said.

"He wanted to talk to him and help us work things out in a friendly way, but that bastard made trouble for our friend, and told the staff of the ship that he wanted to steal his money. So now, our innocent friend is in jail. It is so sad, and he did it for me. He is so faithful."

Now the anger flamed in all the foreigners who wanted to take his revenge, so that they could show their faithfulness to him. The two Arabs, Osman and his cousin, Jamal, said together, "We will kill him."

"What can we do for you, Mr. Louis? Tell us," Barnabas said.

Louis opened a third round of beer and handed them out and continued. "My friends, you are very kind to me. I will never forget this." Then he passed out more cigarettes.

Armend, the Albanian said, "We are ready to do anything you say. Just tell us what it is."

As Louis dropped his head down thoughtfully, the door opened suddenly and a man stood in the doorway, looking at them. It was the same Chinese sailor who had confronted them there a few nights ago. All eyes went to him. The Chinese sailor yelled, "Hey, are you smoking here again?" Then he walked among them.

Louis recognized him and decided to kill him then and there. It would be a way to get the ball rolling and involve the foreigners in his plan. He looked around at them and said, "This man helped that traitor to put our friend Alex in jail. You, Osman, close the door."

"Yes, sir." Osman ran and closed it. All of them were ready to attack, wanting only to please Louis. The Chinese sailor was in the middle looking at everyone, trying to identify them. "Where is your friend?"

"Who are you talking about?" Louis asked him.

"Don't beat around the bush, you know who I am talking about," the sailor said. "We already arrested your friend. He is in jail now."

Louis did not want the foreigners to hear the truth from the sailor, so he gestured for Barnabas to attack him. Barnabas snuck around behind him and grabbed his neck tightly. His arms were very strong, and the sailor was not able to release himself, all the foreigners brought out their switchblades and stabbed him several times until he was dead. Then they dragged him to the end of the room and hid him behind the big wooden cargo boxes. Louis looked at them and said, "Before we free our friend from jail, I will go to first class to see what is going on."

"Do you want me to come with you, Mr. Louis?" Barnabas asked.

"No, thanks. You all better stay here and wait for me. I will be right back." Then he left there to go and see Simon and Tiffany.

Louis was happy to have the Chinese sailor out of the way--the only witness who had seen Simon. With the foreigners on his side, he began to feel that everything was under his control again.

He went to Tiffany's cabin and knocked on the door and called, "Open up. It is your father."

Simon was hidden inside. At the sound of his voice, he immediately opened the door and Louis scampered inside and asked, "Where is Tiffany?"

"She didn't come back yet," Simon said. "Tell me, what did you do down there?"

"We killed the guy who saw you running away."

"You killed him?" Simon said in disbelief.

"Yeah, the foreigners helped me do it. The guy came to the storage room to find you, so we killed him and hid him behind some cargo boxes."

"What will you do with his body?"

"We will throw him overboard when the time is right."

"What should I do? Should I stay here?"

"Yeah, you just stay here and wait for me. I am going to go see Tiffany. We need to know what is going on in George's cabin. I will be right back." Then he walked out.

He walked along the corridor cautiously, seeing nobody along the short distance between. His cabin was at the end of the corridor, and there was a little den on each side of the door. As he got closer, he heard a weak whistle. He saw Tiffany was gesturing for him from the den that was on the left side of the door, but before he could get to her, he heard some voices coming from behind. He stopped and turned around and saw George and Katherine coming toward him. Immediately he walked toward them and said loudly, "Hey, George." As he approached them, he held George's arm and asked worriedly, "What has happened?"

"We were attacked by two men in the stern. They tried to kill us," George said as he held his arm with his other hand.

"I heard it from one of the staff members, and I wanted to see how you were doing. Who were these men? Did you know them?" Louis said.

"No, but one of them is in jail now. The other one ran away," George answered.

"What did he say? What is his name?"

"He didn't say anything."

"I don't understand why they attacked you. You don't have a problem with anybody," Louis said and then he put his hand on his arm gently and continued. "How are you feeling now? Are you in pain?"

"A little. It will be all right."

"Do you need me to bring you anything?"

"No, thanks."

Louis turned to Katherine and said with a smile, "I am sure she will take good care of you."

Katherine stared at the burn mark on his face and the blood spot in his eye for a long time, and she became afraid.

"Are you sure you don't need anything?" Louis asked.

"I'm sure," George said.

Then Louis said goodnight and walked away."

Katherine felt danger all around, with Louis and Alex's faces in front of her eyes at all times, and she couldn't hide her worry from George, so she decided to tell him about it. As they walked toward his cabin, she looked back at Louis, who was looking at them as he was walking away. She stopped and turned back and gazed at him.

"Why did you stop? Is something wrong?" George asked.

Katherine kept her eyes on Louis until he turned the corner, then she turned to George and remained silent for a long time. George could see she was perplexed and worried, and he demanded, "Are you all right?"

Katherine looked into his eyes without saying anything. So many questions were passing through her mind she had no idea where to start. It was like she had been fighting a battle in her mind by herself for her entire life, and now she had to find some way to share it with another person. She also knew that George was the only one who could help her in that situation, so she began with what she knew about Louis. "I am sorry to ask you this question, but you told me that man is your uncle, right?"

George looked at her in wonder and said, "Do you mean Louis, the one who was here a minute ago?"

"Yes."

George looked at her and answered, "Actually, he is my half-uncle."

"Do you know him well? Does he live in New York City?"

"I don't know him well, because we didn't associate with them for many years. They didn't even talk to my parents throughout all those years until two weeks ago, before I came on this trip. He came to my father and asked him for forgiveness for his past." Then he added, "Why did you ask about him? Do you know him?"

Katherine breathed deeply, dropped her head down and said nothing. Her face grew mournful, and she picked her head up and looked at George, her eyes tearful.

"What is the matter?" George asked. "Is something bothering you? Tell me, please."

Katherine burst into tears. "I have to tell you something. My name is not Angela; my real name is Katherine, Katherine Vincent. I was kidnapped from America and taken to Italy fourteen years ago."

George's eyes filled with astonishment. He remembered the news of the disappearance of the

Vincent family. "What? You are that Katherine? I am George Wilson. My father, Edward Wilson, was your father's best friend. Don't you remember?"

Katherine looked at him carefully for a while and seemed to recall a few memories of her childhood with his family, and she was filled with warmth and said, "George." Then they hugged each other tightly.

Katherine continued. "They killed my parents and kidnapped me."

George was following her words with breathless astonishment, his senses dulled by his emotions. He held her by her shoulders. "Who did that to you?"

"Their names were Louis and Alex. Louis had the same burn mark on his face and the blood spot in his eye as your uncle, and the other one, Alex, had a silver tooth, like the man who had attacked us tonight."

George was in shock. "What?" Then his eyes searched around for a moment carefully, and he took her into his cabin quickly and locked the door.

Tiffany was hiding behind an artificial tree in the den, listening to their conversations, the coast was clear she moved back quickly to her cabin. Louis and Simon were waiting for her inside. They

306

opened the door for her and she slid inside. Louis locked the door and asked, "Tell me, what is going on? Where are they now?"

Tiffany looked him in the eye for a few seconds and said with scorn, "Do you know who that girl is?"

"Who are you talking about?" Louis asked.

"I am talking about the girl who is with George."

"I don't care who she is, tell me where are they now?"

"Don't you care about her? She is Katherine, the little girl who was kidnapped by you and your stupid cousin, Alex, fourteen years ago."

Alarm went off in Louis. "Who?" Katherine?" His mouth opened with terror, his inside collapsed and he felt empty.

Tiffany continued. "I heard it from her before they went to his cabin. She recognized you."

Louis looked at Simon for a moment, took a few steps and sat heavily on a chair, staring directly at the door without blinking. He was thinking of the gang who cut off Alex's ears and he said to himself, "They might be on the ship, and if they are they will cut off my ears, too." He quickly decided to do something before they got to him or, before he got thrown in jail like Alex. So he decided to get help from the foreigners, who were waiting for him in the storage room. It was his only chance.

"What the hell is going on here?" Simon said.

Tiffany walked closer to Louis and asked, "Do you remember her?"

"Everything is over," Simon said disparagingly.

"Everything is not over yet. We have one more chance," Louis said.

"What are you going to do?" Simon demanded.

"There are six people who can help us, and all of them are ready to do whatever it takes," Louis said.

"You are talking about those losers in the storeroom," Simon interrupted him and grinned. "Do you really think you can count on them?"

"Yes. They killed that sailor who could have identified you, and we can use them to kill George and the others who are with him. We've got to hurry before we lose the element of surprise. Come on, let's go." He stepped out cautiously holding a pack of beer that he had brought from his cabin, and Simon and Tiffany followed him.

When they reached the storage room his eyes searched around carefully, and then he entered with Simon and Tiffany. All the foreigners came up to them.

Louis said quickly, "My son, Simon, and my daughter, Tiffany." Then he handed the beer to Barnabas and shook his head as if with great concern. "I have a bad news for you, my friends. The staff members are looking for the sailor we killed. They are going to search all parts of the ship for him tomorrow morning. All this my daughter overheard. Then he turned to Tiffany. "Right?"

"Yes, I heard it from them," Tiffany replied.

"They will search everywhere in the next few hours, and eventually they will find him, I am sure," Louis said.

"But nobody knows that we killed him, right, Mr. Louis?" Barnabas said.

Louis looked sharply into their eyes to emphasize his point. "No. But this damn sailor told some of his colleagues about us before he came here, and they all know where your cabin is. I am sure this will be the first place to be searched. When they find him, they will arrest all of us." Then he took a deep breath and sighed. "We will be thrown in a dungeon for the rest of our lives. You have no idea how horrible the dungeons are in America." Then he dropped his head down.

A look of terror came into the foreigner's faces as they looked at one another. The enormity of situation burst upon them, and they did not know what to do. Finally, their eyes turned to Louis, and Barnabas asked, "What should we do, Mr. Louis?"

Louis said, "I know how to solve this problem."

Moods began to pick up, and they asked together, "What do you want to do, sir?"

Louis opened the beer and handed them out. "You drink up, and I will tell you what we have to do. We need to release our friend Alex from jail first; then, we need to kill that bastard who betrayed me and all of those who want to arrest us. We don't have much time. We've got to act quickly, before it is too late." They all were listening to him carefully, their lips following his words as they nodded in agreement. Jamal interposed sternly, "Yeah, Mr. Louis is right. We've got to kill them before they kill us."

"I know we have the guts to do it," Louis encouraged, trying to form solidarity.

Barnabas said, "We all are with you, Mr. Louis."

Then everybody said after him, "Yes, we all are with you."

"You are so faithful. I knew I could count on you. I already told my family about you, and they agreed with me that you deserve the best," Louis said to them admiringly. Then he turned to Simon and Tiffany and said, "We are going to go free Alex from jail now. You two wait for us here. We will be back in a few minutes."

"What should we do if they come to search here?" asked Simon.

"Don't worry. They won't search the ship before dawn. That's what they said," said Louis. Then he walked out and the foreigners followed him.

The place where Alex was being held was a room at the end of a corridor on the same level. An armed guard was inside, watching him. Louis and the others approached slowly, and Louis said, "Hello, would you open the door?"

"Who is calling?" asked the guard.

"I am Louis Wilson, the brother of Edward Wilson, the owner of this ship. I want to see the bastard who tried to kill my nephew," Louis said.

Alex was very happy when he heard his voice. He was sitting on the floor, looking at the door.

"Yes, sir." The guard opened the door immediately. Louis and the foreigners attacked him, stabbed him in the stomach until he was dead and released Alex from his handcuffs. Then they all returned to the place where Simon and Tiffany were. Before they got there, Louis talked to Alex privately about everything was going on, and his plan for solving any problems that might arise.

When they got inside, Louis opened the last bottle of beer, handed it to Alex, put his hand on his shoulder and said, "We are so happy that you are here with us."

"Thank you all. Thank you very much," said Alex before taking a drink.

Louis raised the pistol that he had taken from the guard and said, "We need more guns. Each of us needs two. They keep them in the armory, and it is somewhere in first class. We've got to get them before those bastards get there. We are going to win this fight."

Everybody approved the idea and laughed gleefully. Louis turned his head to the hatchet that was mounted on the wall and said to Barnabas, "Take that hatchet, my friend. We are going to need it."

"Yes, sir," said Barnabas, and he took the hatchet from its place and then Louis led the way to first class.

He was in front of them as the leader the entire way, telling them to kill anyone who tried to restrain them, for he knew George already knew about him and Alex through Katherine, and he would be arrested very soon. There was nowhere to run in that part of the ocean, so he made a decision to sink the ship with all the passengers on board, although he did not talk about it to his men, not even to his son and daughter, for he thought they might be scared and give up. He needed them to stick with him for the duration of his plan, and after that, they would have no other choice but to follow him.

They encountered no one on their way to the armory room. As they reached it, Louis told Barnabas to break the small iron box that was installed on the wall, and Louis got the key and opened the door and they went inside. His eyes searched the pistols on the shelves, and then he looked down at the boxes of dynamite. He smiled, having found the thing that he needed to sink the ship. He went over and took one of the pistols for himself, and then he handed the others to his men. They all felt more powerful and confident, now that they were armed.

Louis looked at them and said, "Listen to me very carefully. You've got to hide your guns in your clothes and use your switch blades to kill anyone."

"Yes sir."

"Now, we've got to go to the radio room. I don't want them to send any messages to other ships about us."

"You are very smart, Mr. Louis. You predict everything and prevent things before they happen," Jamal said.

Louis smiled. "I have to. Otherwise, we are not going to win."

Then they all followed him toward the radio room.

When they got there, Louis kicked in the door. Two men were inside, sending and receiving coded messages over the radio. They stopped working and asked, "Who are you? What are you doing here?"

"Shut up," said Louis, and he put guns to their heads and took them to the corner of the room. "Listen to what I tell you. You two just stay here and don't send any messages."

"What is going on here?" asked one of the staff members in terror.

"I said, shut up," said Louis, and he turned to Simon and Tiffany. "You two stay here and watch them until we come back. If they make any foolish movement, you don't wait for me. Kill them."

"When will you be back?" asked Simon.

"In a few minutes. We've to get to George before he tells any of the other passengers about it."

As they walked out they encountered a staff member who was coming to the radio room. He looked at them suspiciously as they were passing by, but before he opened the door of the radio room, the Moroccan, Jamal, stood in front of him, pulled the gun out of his clothes and shot him down. Louis ran to him quickly and said, "What are you doing, man? Why did you kill him?"

"He would have seen your son and daughter in there. That's why I killed him," said Jamal.

Louis bent over the staff member, touched his neck and said, "He is dead. Take him in."

Jamal and his cousin and Barnabas dragged him inside the radio room.

Simon asked Louis, "Who is that?"

"He was going to cause us trouble. That's all you need to know. We will be right back." Then he left with all his men and went directly to George's cabin, where they found the door unlocked. Louis opened the door and called familiarly, "Hey, George, I want to tell you something." However, there was no response. He quickly searched the cabin and said angrily, "Damn it, they are gone."

"Where do you think he is?" Alex said.

Louis thought for a second and said, "I think he went to see his black friend. Let's go. We've got to stop them as soon as possible." They all walked to Daniel's cabin.

As they were walking in the corridor toward the cabin, Daniel came out with George and Katherine, and confronted them. They were only a few feet away, and there was no friendliness in their faces. They seemed an organized group, and Louis was leading them. He pulled out his gun, took aim at them and said, "Don't move."

At that time, a passenger in first class appeared at the end of the corridor behind Katherine. Upon seeing Louis with his gun drawn, he froze in position. Louis quickly spotted him, but before he could fire, the man jumped back and ran away. As Armend ran toward him, Louis cried, "Stop, let him go. It's best if you stay here."

"He will tell the other people if we don't kill him," said Armend.

"Don't worry, I have a better idea." Louis looked at the foreigners and said, "You just stay on both sides of the corridor and keep a watch. If anyone comes, you can shoot." Then he and Alex walked up to George. They stood in front of him, and Louis looked at the foreigners who filled the end of the corridor. They were far enough away that they would not hear their conversation. He turned to George with a ferocious smile of revenge, and his eyes practically gloating as he spoke. "I know she told you about us, but it is too late. You have nowhere to run."

"What do you think? You can escape here?" said George angrily.

"You had better give yourselves up right now, before you make things worse for yourselves." Daniel said.

Louis looked at Daniel contemptibly. "Hey, you, black boy, you better worry about yourself, not your friends."

Daniel was looking at him with anger, thinking that they could be the murderer of his father. He looked at the guns in their hands without saying anything. Louis looked at Katherine, clicked his tongue and said, "You are very smart to be able to recognize us after fourteen years."

Katherine looked into his eyes, her senses burning. She remembered her parents and all the problems she went through, and the tension that had been simmering in her boiled up to the surface, her eyes and voice were hard and cold and brooding hate grew in her. "Murderer, you killed my parents," she cried as she attacked him.

George was standing beside her, and he immediately held her shoulders tightly and stopped her advance. Louis put the gun to her head and said, "Hey, do you want me to send you to the place where your parents are?"

As Katherine was looking at him, she relapsed into silence. Louis turned to Alex and said, "She is the one who caused you to lose your ears."

Alex was looking at Katherine, his face suffused with anger, and he put on his toughest look and rushed over to her as he cried, "I will kill you."

Louis stopped him immediately and grinned with pride."No, no, no, I have a better idea." Then he called his men and took them to the armory room, where he locked them inside before heading to the radio room with all his men.

All his men worried that the man who had run away from them saw them, and they knew that they would be identified very soon, so they wanted to know what Louis was going to do to resolve that problem. Louis could see the worry in their faces, and he was happy that they felt they had no other choice but to follow him. Before they got to the radio room, he stopped and addressed them very seriously. "My friends, listen to me. We only have one chance to get out of this situation. We've got to leave this ship as soon as possible. We can take the lifeboats, but first we need to sink the ship." Then he held their gaze with his.

All the men looked at one another with uncertainty without saying anything. They did not want to say anything against him.

Louis continued. "I am sure the man who saw us has already told many people, and very soon, they will rush to kill us."

The foreigners were very frightened, and they just wanted to get out of there as soon as possible. Jamal slowly raised his hand.

"What is it, my man?" Louis said seriously.

"How far can we get in the lifeboats? I mean can we reach America?" Jamal asked hesitatingly.

"Don't worry about anything. I will send a message to some of the other ships to help us. There are many ships in the area, and they will find us by dawn." Then he looked around and smiled. "Everything is under control, and everything is going to be fine." From there he led the way to the radio room. Louis entered the room first, and he saw one of the radiomen lying on the ground, dead. "What is going on here?" he asked Simon.

"He was trying to run away," Simon said smugly.

"Good job," said Louis. Then he turned to the other staff member. "Tell me how far away the nearest ship is. Send a message that we are sinking and need help."

The man looked up at him with fear and said nothing.

"Why are you staring at me?" Louis said angrily. "This ship is going to sink very soon for real. Come on, man, send the message."

"The nearest ship to us is about six or seven hours away," said the man.

"Good. You just tell them that our ship is sinking and give them our correct position. Be careful what you say, send only the message that I told you." Then he stood over him and put the gun to his head until the message was sent, then he shot him down and he destroyed all the equipments in the room, so nobody could contact any other ships. Everybody stood quietly, watching the scene. Louis looked at the foreigners and said, "My friends, please stay outside. I want to talk to my son and daughter for a minute in private."

Everybody left the room and closed the door. Simon said angrily, "Tell me what the hell is going on over here? Do we have to kill everybody on this ship? Why did you send that message to the other ship?"

"Tell us, what are you going to do?" Tiffany said after her brother.

Louis sighed and said, "Listen to me. Some people saw us when we were taking George and that girl to the armory room. We tried to kill them, but they ran away and we couldn't find them."

"Oh, shit. What should we do now?" said Simon.

"Don't worry, we have one more chance. It is the only chance," Louis said.

"What is it?" Tiffany asked.

"We've got to blow up the ship with all the passengers on board," Louis said.

"What? Are you crazy?" Simon said.

"There is no other choice, boy. We are going to be arrested very soon, so we've got to sink this damn ship before that can happen. We can use the lifeboats to get away."

"Just how far do you think we can go with those little boats?" Simon grinned. "All the way to America?"

"The other ships already got our message and will be here in a few hours to help us. We've got to blow up the ship soon."

"How do you want to do that?" Simon asked.

"There is some dynamite in the armory room, enough to send this damn ship down. Now, we all go there together, but after that, you and Alex and three of those men take the dynamite to the boiler room."

"What are you talking about? Why would I go with them to do that?" Simon stated.

"Listen to me. I don't trust those jackasses. You've got to be there to lead them." Louis held his shoulder tightly. "You are the only one that I can trust, my son. Tiffany and I and the other three men will get the lifeboats ready and will wait for you on the deck."

Simon hung his head and said nothing, reluctantly giving his consent. Louis continued. "Get to the deck quickly after you set off the dynamite. We won't have time." Then they hastened toward the armory room with Alex and the foreigners.

George, Katherine, and Daniel were in the armory room when they heard rushing clatter of footsteps and the sound of the lock. The door opened and Louis entered. Simon, Tiffany, Alex, and Barnabas stood behind him, and the others waited out on the deck, looking around. Louis's eyes diverted to the floor to the boxes of dynamite. He kicked one of the boxes and said, "Take them out."

George was standing between Katherine and Daniel, watching as they moved the boxes of dynamite. He stepped forward angrily. "What are you going to do with that?"

Louis put his gun to his chest. "You are a pigheaded fool, and I'll kill you if you try to restrain us."

Simon approached him and punched him in the face without warning, and said, "Shut up. I am sick and tired of you. Want to know what that punch was for? That was for the punch you gave me on the deck."

George staggered for a moment, but he recovered quickly and brought his hand to his face, his tongue working against the bite until blood oozed from the corner of his mouth. Katherine and Daniel ran over to him and held him up by his arms. It was all Daniel could do to remain silent. His eyes flared with anger, and rage swelled within him. Louis put the gun to his head and said bitterly, "Hey, you, black boy, want to say something?"

Daniel glared at him angrily.

"Soon it will be too late. Let's go," Louis said. They took the boxes of dynamite out, and Louis locked the door and put the key in his pocket. Alex, Zsombor, Jamal, and Bujar hauled the dynamites downstairs to the boiler room, the group being led by Simon while Louis went to the bridge with Tiffany and the three others. At one point Louis told them to wait for him, and he returned to the armory room and stood by the door and called Daniel from outside, "Hey, black boy, I just remembered something I wanted to tell you before you all go down with the ship. Want to guess what it is? Never mind, I'll tell you straight out. It was Alex and I who killed your father that night fourteen years ago." Then he walked away laughing.

Daniel was shocked as memories flooded his mind, led by the moment he found his father with a bloodied head outside the house. He ran to the door, smashed the iron door with his fist and cried fiercely, "Bastard...I will kill you."

George ran to him and held his shoulders, trying to calm him down, but Daniel kept striking the door as if to break it down and wreak his vengeance on

Louis. Despite his wild efforts, the door did not budge.

The news was reported to the captain. His plan was to stop the violence before more people lost their lives, and the situation required the help of the entire staff. First, the captain went to the bridge to make sure that his staff was safely engaged in their duties. Upon arriving there, he found himself face to face with Louis and his men. Louis raised the gun at him and the three who were accompanying him and said, "Hey, captain, go inside the bridge and tell them to stop the ship right now."

The captain and his staff walked inside the bridge, and Louis, Tiffany and his men followed them. The man steering the ship said nervously, "Hi, captain."

The captain asked Louis angrily, "Why are you doing this? Why did you kill those people? What do you want, man?"

Louis put the gun to his head and said, "Did you hear what I told you? Tell them to stop the ship right now."

The captain looked at him for a second, and he walked to the man at the helm, picked up the receiver and told the men in the boiler room to turn off the engines.

Louis walked to him and continued. "Now, tell your men to get two lifeboats ready."

The captain looked at the gun and then he walked outside with his staff. As they were walking toward the lifeboats, Louis looked up at the sky. It was growing dark. Clouds were everywhere, and the moon had disappeared in the clouds. There was a change in the air, along with the wind and rain. Louis had realized it, but it was too late, there was no other way but to get out of the ship as soon as possible. As they reached the lifeboats and the sailor was getting them ready, Louis told Barnabas to break the other boats with the hatchet, so nobody could use them. When the captain heard this, he grabbed Louis's collar and cried, "No, you can't do it, you can't."

Louis put the gun on his chest and fired and he tumbled backward to the floor. Louis addressed the sailors menacingly. "If any of you wants to join him, I will be glad to send him to the same hell."

Suddenly the sound of an explosion was heard from the lower levels, and the ship shook slightly. Louis pointed the gun at the sailors and cried, "Did you get the boats ready?"

"This one is ready," said one of the sailors.

Louis turned to Osman and Armend. "Me, Barnabas and my daughter will go in this boat now. You, my son and your other friends come in the other boat. They will be here in a minute."

"Shouldn't we wait for Simon?" Tiffany asked.

"No, don't worry about him; he will come with the other boat." Then he got in and held Tiffany's hand and helped her in. Barnabas jumped in after them, and the sailors rolled the boat down to the sea. As the boat touched the water, Simon, Alex, and the other foreigners rushed up to the railing by the lifeboats. Simon asked Armend and Osman, "Where is my father?"

"They just left the ship."

Simon looked up at the sky. It was dark and the wind was picking up, and it made him start to worry. Still, they had no other choice but to leave the ship as soon as possible with the only boat that was still intact. He looked at the sailors that were getting the boat ready, and he knew he had to get off the ship before he got mobbed by angry passengers, so he put his gun to the head of one of the sailors and cried, "Did you get it ready?"

Yes, sir," the sailors answered together.

At that time, two sailors came running up and asked, "What is going on here?"

"Shut up," Simon said, and he shot them down. The sailors who were standing by the lifeboat stood frozen there, looking terrified. They had no desire to do anything to make them angry. Simon, Alex, and the foreigners rushed to get in the boat, and Simon said to the sailors, "Send the boat down carefully, and do not try anything stupid. Otherwise you are going to wind up dead like the others."

The sailors nodded their heads gently without saying anything. Then the boat moved slowly down toward the water. The wind picked up and howled around the ship, and the lifeboat moved and knocked against the ship. It was a nervous wind that brought with it rain, and the sea looked very scary in the darkness. Simon, Alex, and the others grew worried, wishing they hadn't left the ship. However, it was too late, and all their bridges had been burned. As the boat was going downward, it suddenly stopped and was left hanging in the air between the deck and the water. The sailors had turned off the winch. Simon cried, "What the hell is going on up there? Send the boat down." He heard no reply. He cried again, "Bastards, I will kill you. Send the boat down." He turned his face toward the other lifeboat and shouted, "Dad, come back, we need your help." Then they all cried together for help and kept looking after the lifeboat, but they could see no sign that they heard them and the lifeboat disappeared into the distance. There was nowhere to run. Down was the cold, killing water, and up were the angry, vengeful passengers, ready to kill them. There was no hope left for them. The wind blew fierce and strong, it rained hard, and the boat was getting heavy with the rain, so Simon decided to throw the others into the sea, hoping that would buy him enough time to figure out a way to survive. He talked to Alex secretly, and they pulled their guns, killed the others quickly and threw them into the sea. At that time, the wind howled around and knocked the lifeboat against the ship again, and this time it developed a large crack. Simon went to the front, Alex went to the rear and they gripped the ropes that were holding the boat suspended. They knew the boat would not last long in that strong wind and it would be broken to pieces, so they preferred to take their chances up on the ship. Intending to beg the forgiveness of George and some of the others in the ship, they both began calling for help.

There was nobody on the deck. All the sailors had gone to the lower levels to see the damage that had been wrought by the explosion. George, Katherine, and Daniel were still locked in the armory room. As they were shouting for help, a sailor who was passing by heard them, and he quickly broke down the door. As they left the room, Daniel asked, "Did they blow up the ship?"

"I just heard it. I am going down there to see what it looks like."

"Where is the captain?"

"They killed him."

"What?" Daniel closed his eyes.

"Oh, my goodness," George said.

"Where are those bastards now?" asked Daniel.

"Some of them left in one of the lifeboats, and the others are stuck overboard. They can't go anywhere."

"We better go down to see what is going on," George said. Then they all walked downstairs hurriedly.

The ship was scuttled in the last boiler room by the explosion, and water was entering through a large gap. All the watertight doors were open, and water spilled into the next boiler rooms. Very soon, it would enter the other compartments as well.

Daniel was in front of them when they got to the boiler room, but water already filled most parts of that level, and it was heading toward the higher levels. He saw two dead stockers floating in the water in front of him. He turned back and cried, "Water is coming up. We've got to send all passengers to first class as quickly as possible."

The people were terrified, and panicked movements and voices were heard everywhere as people cried out and left their cabins empty-handed. Children cried out in terror, holding their parents' hands and running with them toward the highest level. Daniel, George, and Katherine along with the crew helped out as many as they could. When they were sure that nobody was left, they went to the main deck to check out the situation.

The wind and rain were still blowing hard, and nobody was seen on the deck. They went directly to the bridge. Daniel walked inside first and saw the captain on the floor, his chest covered with blood. Two other sailors were dead next to him. He quickly walked over, knelt down beside the captain, held his hand tightly and cried softly, his teeth clenched and his fingers curled into a fist. He punched the floor and cried, "I will kill you." Then he walked with determination out toward the lifeboats, and George, Katherine, and three sailors followed him.

Simon and Alex were still in the lifeboat, holding onto the ropes, which were being moved by the wind, crying for help. Daniel looked down at them, listening to them for a few seconds. He wrinkled his brow and said to the sailors, "Bring them up."

"But they have guns," one of the sailors said.

"Don't worry, bring them up," Daniel said.

The sailors obeyed and turned on the winch and pulled up the lifeboat. As it was coming up, Daniel told the two in the lifeboat to throw the guns into the sea. Alex quickly complied, but Simon hid one gun under his belt and covered it with his shirt, then he cried, "We don't have any more guns. Now please help us."

Daniel kept looking at them, and he recognized them in the lightning, as they got closer to the deck. He remembered the scene of his father dead on the ground outside the house fourteen years ago, and the captain with a bloody chest dead on the floor inside the bridge. His lips drew taut against his teeth and his eyes lit up with hatred. His chin stuck out, and his whole body weaved ready to strike. As the boat came even with the deck, Alex jumped in the ship first. Daniel punched him in the face with all his might, knocking him down to the floor, and he grabbed his head and slammed it on the floor repeatedly as hard as he could, and he cried furiously, "I will kill you, I will kill you." Then he turned to Simon. The look in his eyes was cold and deadly. He seemed ready to destroy everything and nobody would dare to stop him.

Simon was very scared, but his brain came to the rescue. He cringed on the floor in front of George and cried, "Don't kill me, please. That was all my father's fault. He cheated us. It was all his plan. Don't kill me."

Daniel attacked him and kicked him in the face as he cried, "Bastard." He bent over him and pushed his neck against the floor, trying to strangle him. Simon got a big cut on his face, and the blood oozed down. He could barely breathe under Daniel's strong hands. He reached his hands toward George and begged him for help, for he knew that he was the only one who might feel pity. George was very impressed by the scene, and he quickly ran to Daniel, held his shoulders and tried to calm him down. Nevertheless, Daniel would not relent. Finally, George calmed him down a little and got him to release his hold on Simon. Simon lay crumpled on the floor, touching his neck and crying. The sailors who were standing over Alex said, "Mr. Smith. He is dead."

Daniel turned his face to Alex for a moment and said, "He deserved it."

Two sailors came running up and asked frantically, "What should we do, Mr. Smith? The people are very scared."

"Where are they?" Daniel asked.

"All of them are in the entertainment hall."

Daniel looked at them thoughtfully for a few seconds. George said, "We can't use the lifeboats, they destroyed them all."

"We should talk to them. We need to give them hope. Tell them that a ship is on the way to help us."

George said, "That is a good idea. Let's go talk to them."

The entertainment hall was full of passengers, talking nervously. The children were huddled around their parents asking them questions about the horrible situation they were stuck in. Everybody was waiting to hear word from the captain. Some of them stopped talking when Daniel entered with George, Katherine, and the sailors. They stood in the middle of the hall, and Daniel cried huskily, "Quiet."

The people told one another to remain silent, and soon everybody listened attentively, staring at them quietly with frightened eyes. Daniel said, "The ship has been blown up."

"Who did it? Where are those bastards? I am going to kill them," said a passenger from second class.

"They are not in the ship now. They left in a lifeboat," Daniel answered.

"Why did they do it?" another man asked.

"I don't know," Daniel said attempting to understate the gravity of the situation. "We already sent a message to the other ship and they will be here in the next few hours."

"How can they find us in this storm? And with the ship sinking?" a man said fearfully.

"It is going to be too late. We will all be dead by the time they get here," another man said.

"We checked the damage in the boiler room. The ship has at least six hours before it sinks, and they will be here before that. You all just stay here in this room," Daniel said. Then he walked down to the lower levels with George and Katherine, and the sailors followed them.

Thirty minutes later, they walked to the deck. It was dark, and the clouds still covered the moon. The storm had stopped, as had the wind, and all was quiet. They looked around, searching for a ship in the distance, but not a single light was seen. The sailors shot off distress rockets in order to be seen by any ship that might be passing by.

Chapter 22

Louis's wife, Emily, and his older son, Dennis, had planned to kill Edward Wilson the same night that the Destiny was to sink. They stayed in Edward's house after dinner, and for an excuse to do so, Emily acted like she was feeling faint, so that they could sleep in their house that night. They were sure that their plan would work. However, Bernard, the servant at Edward's house, realized their scheme. He heard them from the window of the room where they were. It was about 11:00 p.m. that he went outside to look for the dog and had heard their laughter. The window was cracked open, and they were smoking cigarettes next to it. He got closer, leaned against the wall and listened carefully. Dennis said as he was laughing, "You performed your role very well--those pigheaded people really believed you."

"We've got to get his belongings. Otherwise, we are going to be miserable for our whole life."

"I hope Dad already got his mission done," said Dennis.

"Your dad is good at this kind of thing. I am sure that he killed him by now," Emily said.

It was then Bernard realized why Louis had gone on that trip. He was pushing his back against the wall hard and breathing fast. He did not move an inch so as not to be seen by them.

Dennis exhaled the smoke through the open window and they both threw their cigarette butts outside and said, "When we kill this old man tonight, we are going to possess all his belongings."

"That's right," said Emily with confidence.

Bernard knew he should not waste time, and he had to tell Edward what was going on as soon as possible, so when they closed the window, he slid back and got away.

He told Edward all that he had heard. His face was red with anger, Edward said, "I thought they changed." Then a deep worry came into his eyes and he said, "I hope George is fine." He took a few steps and said, "I need to send him a telegram and let him know to beware of Louis."

"What are you going to do with this woman and her son?" Bernard asked.

Edward took a deep breath and said, "I'll let them stay here tonight. I will tell you what I want to do later. First, I better send that telegram. You just act normal."

Emily and Dennis were confident the others had believed them, and they would bide their time until the moment came to kill Edward. With him and George out of the way, they would soon be rich. They stayed awake, keeping awareness of everything that was going on outside that room. Dennis went out a few times to make sure that everything was all right. It was one o'clock in the morning when he went to the living room for the last time to make sure everybody was asleep. He sat on the couch, looking around. It was quiet. Only the big clock on the wall made a sound. There was a glimmering candle in the cupboard. His eyes searched around carefully, and when he was satisfied all was well, he stood up and walked to Bernard's room, which was next to the kitchen. He remained behind the door for a few seconds, listening carefully. No sounds came from inside, and he was sure that he was asleep. Then he returned to Emily.

"What is going on?" Emily asked, jumping out of the bed.

"Everything is all right. Let's go, it is time."

"Are they asleep?"

"Yeah."

"Wait, let me go first." Emily walked, and Dennis followed a little way behind her.

They walked very slowly, their eyes searching in the light of the candle. They went directly to Edward's room, where they stayed behind the door for a few minutes to make sure everything was all right. Dennis brought out a piece of rope from under his shirt and held it, looking at Emily. Emily said softly, "We are not going to need that--put it away." Then she put her fingers on the doorknob, turned it very slowly, opened it and went inside, and Dennis went in after her and closed the door behind him.

It was pitch black. Their eyes went to the bed, and they could see a sleeping figure in the darkness covered with a white blanket. They were very scared, but they had to finish their job. They approached him carefully and stood by the bed, looking down at him. Edward was lying on his back, and they could hear his breathing. They looked at each other one last time and then they attacked. Dennis's hands went to his neck to strangle him, but at that time Edward jumped out of the bed and grabbed his hands, and from behind the curtains came some others. It was the marshal and his two men. Bernard came in the room, holding two big candles in his hands. The marshal and his men subdued them in no time and arrested them. Edward approached them, looked at them angrily and said, "Shame on you, I thought you had changed."

Emily and Dennis had dropped their heads down remorsefully and did not say anything. The marshal and his men were standing behind them quietly, waiting for Edward to finish. The door of the room was open, and everybody was looking at Edward. Edward turned to the marshal and said, "Take them away, Marshal. I don't want to see their faces anymore."

"Yes, sir," the marshal said. Before he handcuffed them, Dennis pushed the men who were standing behind him and got away. The marshal shouted, "Catch him."

Dennis ran to the room where they were and jumped out through the window and ran away. The men ran after him, but he was running faster and they lost him in the dark. After fifteen minutes, they came back without him. The marshal said angrily, "You lost him."

"He disappeared in the dark," one of the men answered.

The marshal looked at Edward and said, "Mr. Wilson, don't worry, I will arrest him very soon."

Edward nodded his head without saying anything. Then the marshal told his men to take Emily in the car. Bernard was still holding the candles in his hands standing beside Edward all the time. He said, "Did you talk to the marshal about George?"

"Yeah," Edward said as he nodded his head.

The marshal took two steps toward them and said, "I was sure Louis would try something when he gambled everything away in his saloon that night."

"I didn't know anything about it," Edward said, and he took a deep breath and dropped his head. Everybody could see a deep worry and sadness in him. He continued ruefully, "My son didn't want to go on that trip, but I sent him. Now he is in danger. It is all my fault."

As time went by, the sense of worry grew intolerable, and he became suffused with pain and sorrow. Bernard said devoutly, "We need to pray for George."

His concern was making Edward much less sure of himself than he had been, but upon hearing it from Bernard, he remembered that God's grace was always on him, despite his failures, so he kept on praying and vowed never to abandon hope.

Chapter 23

It was almost 6:00 a.m., and the people in the entertainment hall were still waiting for a rescue ship. A silence had fallen in the room. The water had reached underneath first class, and it seemed that it would not take long to penetrate into the hall. The people there were whispering to one another to go out on the deck.

Outside was quiet, with only the sound of a few seagulls to be heard. The sky had cleared to a hard, thin blue, the sea was calm, and the ship was moving very slowly with the current. George and Katherine were inside the bridge, looking around, when they suddenly saw an iceberg emerge from obscurity. Katherine said, "Look at that!"

"I see it," George said with wonder. They stared at it silently.

It was a big iceberg, and it was about one hundred feet away. It seemed to be moving toward them, in line with the ship's heading, and it was moving a little faster than the ship because it was drawn along by deep currents. At that time, Daniel entered the bridge and said, "The water has reached the level below first class. I told the people to come to the deck."

"Look," George exclaimed, pointing.

Daniel looked steadily at the iceberg for a few seconds. "It is huge. I think it is getting close to us. I hope it is not going to hit our ship."

"It is moving very slowly," Katherine said.

"The ship is going to sink very soon," Daniel said.

"What should we do?" George asked.

"I don't know," said Daniel as his eyes searched the distance for a ship. Then their eyes went to the people rushing onto the deck, trying to reach the highest place.

Katherine was looking at the iceberg the whole time. As it got closer, she noticed through a rupture in the ice a flat part on the iceberg, and it quickly impressed her as a safe place to be. She remembered what the captain had said about using an iceberg as a lifeboat. So she cried, "I have an idea. We can get on that iceberg. Look at the flat part. We can all fit there."

George and Daniel studied the iceberg, their brows furrowed, and they grew serious, saying together, "Yeah, you are right; we can use it as a lifeboat."

George asked, "But how can we get there?"

"We've got to get very close to it," Daniel said. "We must attach the ship to the iceberg, so the people can get on. I think I know what to do."

"Look, it is getting closer," Katherine said.

"We've got to get everything ready," said Daniel, and he walked out and called all of the sailors to prepare whatever they would need to secure the ship to the iceberg.

The people were running in fear on the deck. Many of them ran to the lifeboats, only to find them hopelessly ripped apart. Their eyes searched everywhere for a ship, but they saw nothing, only a big iceberg close to them, and it seemed to be getting closer, and this made them even more afraid.

The sailors got all of the gear ready in the port, and waited for the moment the iceberg was close enough.

The iceberg was moving slowly toward that side of the ship where the sailors were. Finally, after fifteen minutes the part of the iceberg that was under the water struck the ship very gently, shaking it a little. Now, there was a short distance between the cap of the iceberg and the place where the sailors stood-- about fifteen feet. They all were looking at the flat part of the iceberg. Daniel cried, "We've got to get on there." Then he tied the rope to a grapnel and

345

threw it to the iceberg through the rupture with all his might, and the grapnel stuck in the ice on the left side of the rupture. George hugged him tightly and cried happily, "You did it, you did it!"

"We still need to hook a few more grapnels, so that we can make a bridge to the other side."

"Yeah, you are right," said George. They quickly tied ropes to the other grapnels and threw them to the iceberg, but only one of them caught and held while the rest of them just bounced off and dropped into the water. They kept trying for a few minutes, but they could not put any more grapnels on the iceberg. George said, "You know what? I am going to take some rope over to the iceberg, so when you throw the grapnels, I can fix them in place."

"Good idea, but let me do it," Daniel said.

"No," George objected.

Katherine held George's arm tightly and said, "George, it is too dangerous."

George answered, "Don't worry; I know what I'm doing."

Daniel said, "Let's flip a coin."

"Okay, go ahead."

"We don't have much time," Daniel said, and he quickly reached into the pocket of his shirt and took out a coin. There was a picture of a ship on one side, and on the other side there were depicted some flying petrels. It was the same coin Katherine had found fourteen years earlier when she was playing in a broken fishing boat on the beach in the old shipyard with George and Daniel, to whom she had given it. Daniel always carried it with him on his trips.

Daniel asked, "The birds or the ship?"

George said smiling, "I am sure you'd like to choose the ship as always, but this time I choose the ship." Daniel nodded and flipped the coin in the air. It landed shipside up. "All right, I go and you stay here."

Katherine held his arm and said, "George, please be careful."

"Don't worry, I will," said George, and they looked at each other for a few seconds. They needed no words to express what was in their hearts, for it was the same thing. Katherine smiled with him. "I am sure you can do it."

George crossed over to the other side of the rail and studied the distance between the ship and the ice. He held the top rail with one hand and in the other the rope, tugging on it to make sure the grapnel was stuck well in the ice, then he took hold of the rope with both hands and moved to the iceberg swiftly and skillfully.

All eyes were on him. Most of the people did not know what he was doing, and they asked one another what was going to happen. Daniel and the sailors were standing by the rails, watching him, ready to help him in case something went wrong. Katherine was holding the top rail tightly, her eyes closed, praying, when suddenly Daniel cried, "He did it." Katherine opened her eyes and saw George was on the iceberg, looking at her. She waved at him, and then she looked up at the sky and said, "Thank God."

Daniel and the sailors threw a few levers and a hammer to the iceberg, and George secured them deeply in the ice. They quickly made a bridge using the ropes and the boards. Now that people began to realize what was taking place, they began to hasten to the port, where they waited to hear something from the sailors. Daniel quieted them and said firmly, "Listen to me. The ship is sinking. We've got to get over to the iceberg. We have no other choice."

One man who was a passenger in second class said angrily, "Where is the ship that was on the way to help us?"

"The storm has changed our position and they can't find us," said Daniel.

"You lied to us," the man said, some of the other second-class passengers appearing to take his side.

George took a few steps toward the people and exclaimed, "It is not the time to argue. The wise thing to do is get to the iceberg right now."

Katherine was standing by George, and she added, "He is right. That iceberg is the only safe place for us. We've got to get there as quickly as possible."

The man said, "You expect us to leave the ship and get on that piece of ice? You've lost your mind. We will stay here and wait for the rescue ship."

Another man said, "If we get on the iceberg, what then! Who is going to find us there? How long we can stay there without any food? No, better to stay here and, if necessary to die here." Then he walked away with some others toward the top deck.

Katherine cried, "For God's sake, get on the iceberg. The ship is going to sink very soon." But they paid no attention to her and kept walking away. Many of the passengers were torn and did not know what to do. At that time, the Jewish man who had helped Katherine in Liverpool get to the Destiny walked up to Katherine with his family, his hands on his children's shoulders and his wife behind him.

"I had a dream last night, our ship was sinking, but before it sank, a rainbow appeared and we all went over it and got to land and finally we were saved. I believe God sent this iceberg to us. I am going to go there with my family." He and his family walked over the bridge toward the iceberg without hesitation. Mr. Fulton and his wife got closer to Katherine and said with smile, "You are right, young fellows. This iceberg is the only safe place for us now."

Mr. Foster walked forward and said, "I agree. My wife and I are coming, too." Then they walked to the iceberg, both couples holding hands.

The Jewish man cried, "Come on, people. There is plenty of room over here."

By now, many people were encouraged to get on the iceberg, and they began to rush toward the bridge. Daniel cried, "The bridge cannot hold all of you at once." Then he stood in front of the bridge with the crew to control the flow of people. George and Katherine stood by to help in any way they could.

Katherine saw Tina's mother, Margaret, standing about twenty feet away, looking at the iceberg. She seemed undecided about whether or not to stay on the ship. Katherine quickly walked through the crowd, reached her and asked, "Why are you standing here? Come on, you've got to get on the iceberg."

Tina asked, "Angela, do you really think that is a good idea?"

"No, it is not," said Margaret dispiritedly as she held onto her children tightly.

Katherine saw fear and irresolution in her eyes, and she said hurriedly, "There is no other choice. Come on; do not waste any time. The ship is sinking." Then she helped them get to the bridge.

Time was short and the ship was getting lower and lower in the water. It would not be long now. Some of the crewmembers looked around for mothers and their children among the people and sent them to the iceberg before the men. After fifteen minutes, nearly a thousand people were on the iceberg, just as the ship's deck began to slant downwards a little, causing the ropes of the bridge to tighten. Noticing this, Daniel turned to George and Katherine and said, "You two better get to the iceberg right now."

"There are still many people on the ship," said George.

"I will be here with the crew to help send them over," Daniel said.

George looked at Katherine, held her hands and said, "You go. I will join you in a few minutes."

Katherine said, "No, I don't want to go without you."

Daniel insisted, "Listen to me. The bridge is not going to last very much longer. You've got to get on the iceberg right now."

"What about you?" George asked.

"Don't worry about me. I will join you there in time," Daniel said, and he pushed them onto the bridge and they walked quickly over to the iceberg.

Many people had noticed the increasing tension in the ropes supporting the bridge, and they tried to rescue themselves, rushing suddenly to get to the iceberg, but Daniel and the crew would not let them all go at once. The people who refused to leave the ship were still on the top deck, shaking their heads and looking down at those who were crossing over to the iceberg. Daniel and the crew were trying to send as many people over as quickly as possible, for they knew the bridge was beginning to falter. As they were helping the people, Daniel noticed Simon was among those trying to get to the bridge. He had dropped his head down hoping he wouldn't be recognized. Daniel turned stiffly to him with wide eyes, his brain brimming with anger. He grabbed his collar and cried, "You are not going anywhere." Then he struck him in the face with all his might and blood spurted from his mouth and he continued to strike him again and again. Simon fell to the floor. Then Daniel ran to help an old man who had fallen on the bridge while trying to get to the iceberg. Simon dragged himself to his feet and looked at Daniel knowing he would never get to the iceberg as long as Daniel was there. So he walked in the crowd and got closer to the bridge and pulled out the pistol from under his shirt and shot Daniel in the chest. Then he dropped the pistol on the floor and stepped back a few feet to blend in among the other people. Daniel cried out, gripped his chest, for it seemed the bullet had touched his heart, then he fell on the bridge rolled over and into the water between the ship and the iceberg. The coin that he had kept with him since childhood falling out of his pocket and flashing a few times before disappearing with him into the water forever. Everybody was quiet for a few moments, their eyes searching for the one who shot him down. George cried, "No!" Then he walked toward the bridge, but Katherine held him back, for she knew that nobody could do anything for Daniel. The people ran to the bridge together, the crew unable to stop them, when suddenly the ship jerked down and the grapnels and levers came out of the iceberg and hit those who were on the bridge, which collapsed, sending them into the water as the ship moved away from the iceberg. The people knew they could not get to the iceberg, and as the water reached the main deck they began running and screaming, trying to get to the highest place on the ship. As the ship lurched beneath them, the rear of the ship began to slide down into the water and the bow rose up high and stood upright in the ocean for a minute. Then the Destiny plunged into the icy ocean and a huge wave washed the people overboard. The cold water penetrated their skin like razor blades, and into the ocean, they plunged down, down, down. They struggled back to the surface, some of them swimming as hard as they could to get away from the ship, grabbing onto wooden boxes and any objects floating on the water, others were trapped in the water and went down with the ship.

The people on the iceberg were standing shoulder to shoulder, witnessing the awful incident and helpless to do anything about it. Many of them turned away, unable to bear the scene of people screaming and drowning, but some of them watched those who were still alive in their life jackets and on the floating objects, crying out for help, until their voices grew weaker and weaker and muffled in the freezing cold ocean. Within an hour all, the flotsam had drifted away and disappeared into the distance.

All the people gathered in the middle of the iceberg, but George and Katherine remained staring at the sea. Katherine turned her face to George, knowing he was thinking of his best friend, Daniel, now lost to him forever. She stayed next to him, so he would not be alone in his sorrow. That was the only thing she could do for him at that time. They stayed there for a while before joining the others.

The people were so disappointed, wondering if they would ever be rescued from the iceberg, moving through the ocean aimlessly. They feared the cold and starvation, and hope was in short supply. George and Katherine walked among them, returning to their place at the edge of the iceberg. They took off their life jackets, sat on them and looked into the distance, searching for any sign of a ship certain they would be saved. Both were silent for about twenty minutes, then George started talking about Daniel, crying at times. He talked of the day he was with Daniel and Katherine at the beach in the old shipyard; Daniel had drawn a picture of a ship and it was washed away by a wave. Katherine tried to remember, but it was all a blur in her mind. They stayed there on watch until 3:00

p.m., and then George walked to the middle of the iceberg to check on the others while Katherine stayed behind. As she was looking at the sea, she suddenly saw a ship in the distance, about ten miles away. It was a passenger ship bound for England. Katherine turned back and cried, "A ship! A ship!"

The people heard her and thought that a rescue ship found them, so everybody ran to see, with George in the lead. Katherine said, pointing, "Look!"

George waved at the ship and cried, "We are here!" Then he told everybody to do the same thing, so everybody waved and cried for help. At first, they thought the ship had seen them and was responding, but soon it became clear that it was going in the other direction. All eyes stared silently at the ship as it seemed to grow smaller and smaller. One of the women said, "It is getting away."

"It is not coming," one of the men said.

George cried, "We've got to keep waving. They may see us."

But the ship didn't change course and disappeared in distance. The people on the iceberg were devastated, feeling as if they had lost their last chance at being rescued. Some of them cried, "We all are going to die here."

George turned to them and said, "Don't say that. We should be happy that we are in a shipping lane. It means that eventually one will find us. We must stand watch at all the times so we don't miss a single opportunity."

Mr. Fulton and some of the others said, "Yes, he is right. We can't miss a single opportunity."

The people were encouraged now, so many of them stayed there with George and Katherine, looking into the distance for any sign of a ship.

They stood watch until dark, but no other ships were spotted. They returned to the middle of the iceberg in disappointment, with only a few men staying to stand watch.

When darkness fell, it was pitch black in the cleft where the people were. The sky was brushed clean, and the moon was like a cradle, shining on the iceberg. Everything seemed cold, even the stars. A few seagulls sat on the peaks of the iceberg and called out at times. The people sat on their lifejackets, cold and hungry, some of them whispering prayers. Now, all the passengers, first and second-class, were equal. Many of them thought back on their lives and asked God for forgiveness. Mothers told their children to pray, hoping that prayers made by the innocent would reach the ears of God. After a little while, George and Katherine came and walked among them until they reached the little girl, Tina, and her mother and brother. As soon as Tina recognized them, she said, "Angela, it is me, Tina."

Katherine bent over her and touched her face with her cold fingers and said, "How are you doing, Tina?"

"Can you stay here with us?" Tina asked.

"Sure," Katherine said, and then she looked at George and they both squatted down beside her.

"How will a rescue ship see us in the dark?" Tina asked.

"Don't worry, we have some stuff to make a fire," George answered. "There are some people over there watching, and as soon as they see a ship, they will call us."

"When will a ship come to rescue us?" Tina asked.

"They are going to find us soon, my dear," Katherine said as she touched the girl's head.

Tina smiled and brought some crackers out from her jacket and said, "Let's eat them." Then she handed some to Katherine.

Katherine took the crackers, but upon seeing a little girl about the same age as Tina, sitting with her mother next to George, she stretched out her hand to her and said, "Would you like some crackers?"

The girl looked at the crackers, turning to her mother for permission. Her mother thanked Katherine and told her daughter to take them. As they started to eat, they heard the cries of other children asking their parents for food. Katherine said, "Poor things--they are hungry."

Tina's mother, Margaret, brought a little plastic bag that held some cookies out of her bag and said, "We need to share these with the other children." Then she handed the bag to Katherine, who grabbed the bag and walked quickly to the children with George and handed out the cookies. Even after that, some of the children were so hungry they kept on crying. As Katherine and George were walking among the people, the Jewish man approached carrying a long cotton bag, and said, "I have some bread and cheese. Perhaps the children will like them."

"Thank you, sir," Katherine said. Then they shared the food among the children. The parents were so happy and grateful their spirits were rejuvenated and they felt they could tolerate being there for a while longer, until help arrived.

Everybody was sitting looking and listening for any sign of a ship in the silent night. George and Katherine went back to the edge of the iceberg and joined those who were standing watch.

The first night after storm was very cold, and everything was frosty. Many people were underdressed, and a few of them lacked a lifejacket, so they had to sit directly on the ice. George and Katherine remained on watch until dawn, but no other ships were seen. As the sun came out, they suddenly heard the cry from the middle of the iceberg, a rising, hysterical cry. George and Katherine ran to see what was wrong. They found everybody looking toward the end of the iceberg. George and Katherine passed through and saw an old man on the ground. He was dead. They knelt beside him, and George held his hand. It was as cold as a piece of metal. A woman nearby was whimpering, saying, "We all are going to freeze like him."

George turned to her and said, "This man was sick. I saw that yesterday. He lay on the ice all night long for sure because he did not have a lifejacket, and that's why he died."

"How long do you think we can stay on this piece of ice and wait for help?" a man said loudly and angrily. "Look around. We are surrounded by these peaks. Nobody can find us."

Another man, one of the second-class passengers, said, "This iceberg will be our graveyard."

A woman cried, "I wish I would have died with the others on the ship. At least I wouldn't be suffering like this."

Katherine stood up and said seriously, "Don't be disappointed. Don't let the fear win. The next ship that passes by here will find us, I am sure of it. We just need to keep hope alive."

The crowd looked at her quietly. The Jewish man approached her and said, "I choose to believe that we will be rescued soon, that God sent this iceberg before the ship sank, and that he is going to save us from here, too."

Some people were reminded of the miracles of God and they turned that into renewed hope, but many others shrugged their shoulders hopelessly and walked away. George was still kneeling beside the dead man, looking up at the surrounding icy peaks, his brain sifting through the possibilities. Finally, he stood up and said firmly, "I have an idea."

"What is it?" Katherine asked.

George continued pointing to the highest peak. "We have to mark the peaks surrounding us, to improve our chance of being seen."

Katherine looked up at the peaks and said, "But how?"

"I can do it," George answered.

'How can you get up there without any supplies?" Katherine asked.

"I will show you," George said. He ran to the edge of the iceberg and picked up a lever that had been left from the bridge, and ran back to the others and said, "We can put this up there, but I need something to tie on it."

Katherine quickly untied a maroon scarf that was on her shoulders and said, "Here, use this."

"That's perfect." George said. Then he tied it onto the lever and looked up at the highest peak. Katherine hugged him. "Be careful."George smiled at her; then, he started climbing the iceberg.

The crowd was silent and watchful, fearing to miss any part of this, what may prove to be their salvation. Even the seagulls on the peaks were looking down silently at him. George's spread fingers gripped the iceberg as he held the lever with the other hand, his feet finding support through contact, his chest pressed against the ice so that he wouldn't slip. However, the sharp slope of the iceberg worked against him, and after ascending a few feet, he fell back down and got up quickly. Katherine ran to him and put her hands on his shoulders and said, "Are you all right?"

"Yeah, I am fine," George said as he looked up at the peak. "I will get there this time."

"The sides are too steep," Katherine said.

"Don't worry, I know how to do it," George said. Then he untied the scarf from the lever and asked Katherine to put it on his back and he tied it with the scarf, so both hands were free to grip the iceberg, and then he started up again.

He was climbing up like a real mountain climber, and in five minutes, he put a little distance between the people below and his position on the iceberg. All eyes looked up at him; the seagulls sensed danger and flew away when he approached. George struggled up the steep slope wearily, and after fifteen minutes, he topped the peak. He looked down at Katherine and cried, "I made it."

"Yes!" Katherine cried happily.

George looked around into the distance for a few seconds, but saw nothing. He tied the scarf to one side of the lever and sank the other sharp side into the ice with several hard blows until it was secure, and then he slowly climbed down.

He was looking for the same path he had used to climb up, but it was very difficult, and after a few minutes, he had advanced only a few feet. There was still fifteen feet left when suddenly he lost his hold and began sliding down, stopping only when he had reached the bottom.

Katherine cried, "George!" Then she and Mr. Fulton took hold of his arms and helped him up. George's arms had been scratched from the sharp ice and were bleeding.

"Your arms," Katherine said.

George rolled up his sleeves and said, "Don't worry, it is not too deep. I'll be all right. Look up there. Now a rescue team will be able to see that for miles."

Mr. Fulton put his hand on his shoulder and said, "You did your best. I am proud of you. You've got to sleep now; you both were awake all night long."

"We are all right," said Katherine.

Fulton took off his and his wife's lifejackets, handed them over and said, "Listen to me. Go get some rest now. These people are going to need you tonight. Don't worry, I will be on watch." Then he walked toward the edge of the iceberg with his wife. George and Katherine went to a corner, put the lifejackets on the ice and lay down next to each other. In no time, they were deeply asleep.

Many people were encouraged when they saw the sign on the top of the iceberg. They tried to spend most of their time at the cleft with the others looking out for ships, but some were still despondent and they had no hope to be rescued, and some even had begun to believe the iceberg would melt and fall apart. Mr. Fulton and the Jewish man walked among them, speaking encouragement, talking to them about the friends and relatives who were worried about them, and they got many to pray and in this way spread solidarity. At twelve o'clock, Mr. Fulton asked the violinist, the only member of the band who had brought his instrument with him, to play something. He played some happy music, and Mr. Fulton and his wife and a few others danced.

George and Katherine awakened to the noise, and for a moment, they thought they had been rescued. George said, "What is going on?"

"I don't know," Katherine said. Then they walked over to the crowd.

Mr. Fulton and his wife were still dancing when he saw George and Katherine. He walked over to them and took hold of their hands and said satirically, as always, "You, young couple, come on, dance with us."

"What is going on here?" George asked

"Nothing. We are just dancing."

George and Katherine looked at each other smiling and they began dancing. It would encourage the others, and they knew it.

After that, they went to those who were standing watch. They stayed with them all day long, their eyes searching into the distance, but they did not see anything.

When the sun went down and evening approached, a new wave of fear and hopelessness poured over the iceberg. The Jewish man shared the last loaf of bread among the children. The people were so cold and weak; they did not think they would last till dawn. Nearly all of them were at their wits' end, convinced that only an act of God could save them. Some looked up at the heavens, hoping for something miraculous, some of the women sat with their fingers crossed in the holy sign, their eyes closed and praying, some of the people recalled secret sins and blamed themselves. They remembered the old man who had died the previous night and became even more afraid. They began to view the iceberg as a grand leech, sucking what little warmth remained in their bodies. The night seemed more fearful now, and even the sounds of the seagulls struck fear, as they seemed like vultures hovering above them, waiting for them to die. A dense mist clung to the iceberg, and for most of the people, it seemed a mist of creeping death. That and the vultures hovering overhead and the bitter cold coalesced about and within them. Everything around them seemed drenched in sadness, even the gentle wind sighed sadly. The moon was quarter high, its silver edge slipping above the top of the iceberg. It looked like an old and ragged moon, throwing the cleft into shadow. Everything around the people was impersonal and aloof, even their shadows were heavy. George and Katherine walked among them silently, wading through the sound of murmured complaints. They felt on their shoulders the gravity of the situation and the weight of responsibility to the people, and they tried everything to keep their hope alive. Katherine looked at the children and said, "Poor kids. What must they be thinking at this time?"

George took a deep breath and walked over to where Tina was, sitting on her mother's legs and shivering from cold. Katherine stood over them and looked at them. As Tina recognized her she said, "I am freezing."

Katherine knelt beside them, kissed her on the cheek and said, "Everything is going to be all right, my dear."

She turned to Tina's brother, crouching against his mother's side, and she put her hand on his shoulder. "We are going to be saved."

"Yeah, we are all right," Margaret said as she hugged her kids tighter.

"We will check back with you soon," Katherine said. They returned to the guards as silently as they had come.

As the guards recognized them, one of them said, "I think we have drifted out of the shipping lane."

Another man said disappointedly, "Yeah, he is right."

Katherine took two steps, and as she was looking into the distance, she said, "But we shouldn't give up. We've got to keep on looking."

"I am sure we will be saved by tomorrow," George said. "You all can go and get some rest. We are going to be here."

The men stood up and walked away to the middle of the iceberg. At that time Mr. Fulton and his wife came up to them, and Mr. Fulton said, smiling, "Tell us, my heroes, did you see any ships?"

"No," George answered tiredly.

"I am sure something will come along soon," said Mr. Fulton, and he brought a pocket whisky out from his jacket and reached it out toward George. "Come on, it will help warm you up a little."

George grabbed it and stretched his hand out to Katherine. She said, "No, I am fine."

George drank a little and handed it back to Mr. Fulton. "Thanks."

Mr. Fulton's eyes looked up at the peaks, and he said, "Thank you, George, for putting up that sign. I'm sure it is going to help."

"I hope so, because these people can't tolerate much more," Katherine said.

"They are going to be all right by tomorrow," Mr. Fulton continued. Then they resumed their search for ships.

It was freezing cold. The people placed their fingers under their armpits to keep them warm. All were heavy lidded, dozing at times until the chill awakened them. Nobody could stay awake. Even Mr. Fulton and his wife went to the middle of the iceberg, and in an hour they all finally fell asleep.

George and Katherine continued their sentinel, their eyes searching the darkness carefully.

At two o'clock Katherine walked to the middle of the iceberg to check on the others, while George remained in his position. The night was silent, the waning moon was going down, and the iceberg was still, even the sound of seagulls was no longer to be heard. Katherine approached, seeing no movement among the seated figures, which were aglow with gray frost. For a moment, she remembered the old man who had died last night, and she was scared that they all would freeze like him. She called, "Hello.", but she did not see any movement at all. She ran back to George and said with fear, "Come on. They are not moving at all. We've got to wake them up or else they are going to freeze like that man."

As they approached the others and looked at them for a few seconds, and George cried loudly, "Hello."

He waited a few seconds and then said, "Everyone, wake up, wake up."

A few people opened their eyes and sluggishly turned their faces toward the voice and closed them again, assuming they were dreaming, while most of them remained asleep and unresponsive. George and Katherine zigzagged among them, stirring them with their feet and calling for them to wake up. "You've got to stay awake and move around. Otherwise you are going to freeze."

Katherine cried, "We have to fight the cold. We will be saved in a few hours."

She stayed near the children and continued. "Hey, you, parents, do it for your kids." Then she knelt beside Tina, who was sitting on her mom's legs, and put her hand on her shoulder and stirred her and said, "Hey."

"We are awake," Margaret said.

"Is a rescue ship here?" Tina said, shivering.

"No, but they will be very soon."

Now all of the people were awake, and the children started crying as they woke up. A few people began to complain all over again.

George cried, "Lean against each other, so you can keep warm, and move around as you are sitting there."

Mr. Foster walked over and said, "George is right. We cannot give up. We've got to fight the cold."

Mr. Fulton said loudly, "They are right. Come on, get closer, folks." Then he and his wife moved their lifejackets closer to the people beside them. Soon all the others moved in and huddled close to one another. George and Katherine stayed with the children for a few minutes before returning to keep watchful eyes on the distant shipping lane.

An hour later, the moon was down and all on the iceberg were silent again; all of the people were asleep now. George and Katherine were still awake, exhausted after their long vigil. They were cold, and their muscles cramped from prolonged exposure to cold. As they were leaning against each other and looking into the distance, George put his head on her cheek and closed his eyes. Katherine could feel his warm breath against her skin, her hands crept out from her armpit and went around his shoulders, and then her eyes closed slowly. She was the last person on the iceberg to fall asleep.

When the sun rose, it shone clearly on the iceberg, and the sign on top of could be seen for miles. The sky was clear and a few seagulls hovered overhead. Everybody was asleep, practically piled on top of one another. George and Katherine were asleep in the same place, a thin layer of ice having covered them all over like a chrysalis. A ship appeared from afar, a passenger ship that was heading to America. There were two men in the watchtower, and one of them spotted the sign on the iceberg, saying to his colleague, "Look at the size of that iceberg."

The other one looked at the iceberg with the spotting scope and said, "You're right, and I see something on top. It looks like a flag."

The first one said, "We've got to report it to the captain."

"Are you sure it's important enough to report?"

"We have to report everything we see, that's what the captain said." They went to report their finding, and the captain commanded that the ship slow down and head toward the iceberg.

On the iceberg, everybody was asleep, and George and Katherine were still at the edge of the iceberg. The watchmen cried, "There are two people on the iceberg," and when they got closer, they cried loudly, "Hello, do you hear us?" They saw no signs of any movement. One of the watchmen looked down at the captain. "I think… they are dead."

"I see many people in the middle of the iceberg," the other watchman cried out.

"They should be from the Destiny. Let's get them on the ship," the captain said.

As the ship neared the iceberg, Katherine opened her eyes a little and closed them again, fighting against the cold. She could barely move her face. She seemed to be frozen, the sound of the ice shell crumbling accompanied her movements, and she thought she must be dreaming, but she heard voices, so she blinked hard and looked at George leaning on her. She picked up her head slightly and saw a big ship in front of her. At first, she did not believe it was real. She rubbed her eyes, blinked hard and looked again. The watchmen cried, "I see movement! They are alive!"

Katherine listened to the voices carefully and realized that what she was seeing was real. She put her hand on George's face and said weakly, "George, wake up. We are saved."

George's eyes were closed, and he did not move at all. Fearing the worst, Katherine shook his shoulders and cried out in her weak voice, "Please, open your eyes, George!"

George opened his eyes, moved a little and said, "What happened?"

"Look. It's a ship."

George rubbed his eyes and heard the voices coming from the ship. "Is it real? Am I dreaming?" he asked.

"It is real. Let's go tell the others." They went to the middle of the iceberg.

Everyone was asleep, leaning against one another. George and Katherine walked among them, stirring them awake and telling them about the rescue ship. As the people heard the news, God formed a lighthouse in front of them and they raised their hands to the sky and thanked Him. Then they all walked to the edge of the iceberg to see the ship. It was the happiest moment of their lives. The ship docked at the iceberg, and they all were taken aboard.

Now, all the survivors of the Destiny were talking about George and Katherine, the ones who gave them hope in the end, whose courage and tolerance had saved them, calling them heroes.

After three days, they reached the port of Boston. Many people were waiting there to greet them. Edward Wilson was among them, restlessly waiting to see his son, a light of worship in his eyes. He looked at George with tearful eyes and thanked God. Many friends and city officials were standing next to him. When George got off the ship, he went directly to him and they hugged each other tightly for a long time as they cried. Katherine was standing behind George. She tried to recall memories from her childhood as she looked at Edward's face. Pictures of her homeland and the entire contents of her mind were different than the land she had come back to after so many years. George looked at Katherine and said to Edward, smiling, "I want to introduce you to someone."

Edward said with a smile, "Hi."

"Hi," Katherine said.

George quickly interrupted them. "I believe you two have already met."

As Edward was looking at her, he tried hard to remember. After a few seconds he said, "I don't know, it's been so long…"

George smiled and said, "Yes, it has been a long time, and she has changed a lot. This is Katherine, Katherine Vincent, the little girl. You looked for her for years."

Edward squinted and looked into her eyes and face carefully; then his eyes went to her necklace. It was the same one he had given to her before she was kidnapped, and his eyes filled with tears; it was the best moment of his life. He could barely believe his eyes, his son had come back home safely, and

Katherine, the one who he was looking for her for years, was in front of him, as he said, "My dear Katherine." Then he hugged her and thanked God for her return. It appeared he would have that chance to make up for his past, and he intended to make the most of it. After three weeks, George and Katherine were married, and they lived happily ever after.

Throughout all the years of hardship Katherine experienced, she maintained the belief, despite all the odds being against her, that a bright future awaited her, and a voice that whispered in her ear that everything would be all right. Fueled by her small belief, she found the hope to go forward, even in the most horrible of situations, and in Rosa's house saw a little light in distance that cut through the darkness. This hope gave her the strength to fight against those who meant her harm, allowing her the few moments that added up to a chance to be rescued by Ivano. It gave her the strength to reach her homeland and urged her onto the iceberg to save those she could. She drew strength from dire circumstances and learned how to deal with the unknowns in her life. For years she fought to remain on wings that carried her far from her home to many different places and finally brought her back again, to the place where she belonged and to a family like

George's who truly loved her. The wings called Destiny.

Printed in Great Britain
by Amazon